PENGUIN BOOKS

The Outcry

Henry James was born in 1843 in New York City, of Scottish and Irish ancestry. His father was a prominent theologian and philosopher, and his elder brother, William, is also famous as a philosopher. He attended schools in New York and later in London, Paris and Geneva, entering the Law School at Harvard in 1862. In 1865 he began to contribute reviews and short stories to American journals. In 1875, after two prior visits to Europe, he settled for a year in Paris, where he met Flaubert, Turgenev and other literary figures. However, the next year he moved to London, where he became so popular in society that in the winter of 1878-9 he confessed to accepting 107 invitations. In 1898 he left London and went to live at Lamb House, Rye, Sussex. Henry James became a British citizen in 1915, was awarded the Order of Merit, and died in 1916.

Henry James wrote some twenty novels, the first published being *Roderick Hudson* (1875). Other titles include *The Europeans*, *Washington Square*, *The Portrait of a Lady*, *The Bostonians*, *The Princess Casamassima*, *The Tragic Muse*, *The Spoils of Poynton*, *The Awkward Age*, *The Ambassadors* and *The Golden Bowl*.

Toby Litt was born in 1968. He is the author of *Adventures in Capitalism*, *Beatniks*, *Corpsing*, *deadkidsongs* and *Exhibitionism*.

HENRY JAMES

The Outcry

With an Introduction and Notes by Toby Litt

PENGUIN BOOKS

PENGUIN BOOKS

Published by the Penguin Group
Penguin Books Ltd, 80 Strand, London WC2R 0RL, England
Penguin Putnam Inc., 375 Hudson Street, New York, New York 10014, USA
Penguin Books Australia Ltd, 250 Camberwell Road, Camberwell, Victoria 3124, Australia
Penguin Books Canada Ltd, 10 Alcorn Avenue, Toronto, Ontario, Canada M4V 3B2
Penguin Books India (P) Ltd, 11 Community Centre, Panchsheel Park, New Delhi – 110 017, India
Penguin Books (NZ) Ltd, Cnr Rosedale and Airborne Roads, Albany, Auckland, New Zealand
Penguin Books (South Africa) (Pty) Ltd, 24 Sturdee Avenue, Rosebank 2196, South Africa

Penguin Books Ltd, Registered Offices: 80 Strand, London WC2R 0RL, England

www.penguin.com

First published in the USA by Charles Scribner's Sons 1911
Published with a new Introduction in Penguin Classics 2001
3

Copyright 1911 by Charles Scribner's Sons
Introduction and notes copyright © Toby Litt 2001

Set in 11/13.6 pt Postscript ITC Berkeley Oldstyle
Typeset by Rowland Phototypesetting Ltd, Bury St Edmunds, Suffolk
Printed in England by Clays Ltd, St Ives plc

Contents

Introduction

The Outcry was written in two different forms by two different Henry Jameses – one, the James of 1909, in reasonable health, and optimistic about his chances of finally writing a successful play; another, the James of 1911, ill, recently bereaved, and feeling almost certainly that in converting his unproduced play into a novel he was merely making the best of a bad situation. The play version of *The Outcry* was written, with amazing speed, whilst James was comfortably resident in the Reform Club; the novel, during the desolate months after returning home to Boston with his dying brother, William. The finished work – as one might expect – is an odd and fascinating hybrid: a novel, the rapidity and lightness of which place it alongside James's novels of the 1890s, but whose moral complexity and formal revisedness render it equally comparable to the novels of the New York Edition.

With republication of *The Outcry*, the common image of James, the Master, in his latest years – tangled up in convolutions, obsessed with a dead world which may only ever have existed in his imagination – is likely to receive something of a knock. Here, we have an author reacting almost instantaneously to a contemporary scandal, and producing, within six months, a highly topical comedy. The novel itself, despite the delays of composition and publication, made its appearance just two and a half years after the Norfolk Holbein (of which more later) was put up for sale.

A further stereotypical image of the Late James, that of a man who had written himself beyond all but the most loyal of his readers, is also likely to be overturned: *The Outcry* was a great success.

Its story, identical in play and novel form, is deftly constructed and frivolously treated. Whilst recognizably embedded within the tradition of the Edwardian drawing-room comedy, complete with plot-twists, passionate infatuations and witty curtain lines, *The Outcry*, at moments, seems to anticipate the work of later writers. The Yankee 'money-monster' Breckenridge Bender wouldn't be out of place at one of Jay Gatsby's parties (or in almost any one of Fitzgerald's novels); and when Lord Theign is described as 'giving good advice, at the top of his lungs, to four hundred and fifty children' he could almost be a P. G. Wodehouse character.

The world of *The Outcry* is a very Modern one, complete with fast cars, electricity, telegrams, sensational newspapers, advertisements, publicity machines and 'people who come up to the city on the Tube'. The action is centred around two disobedient daughters – one, a gambler, the other, an idealist; one offstage, one on. There is a very definite gap between the older generation (the patrician Lord Theign, the elegant Lady Sandgate) and the younger (Hugh Crimble, 'one of the quite new connoisseurs', and Theign's daughters, Lady Imber and Lady Grace). There are also clear divisions between the Old World and the New, the old and the new money, and perhaps most startlingly the old and new values.

The satire of *The Outcry* is far broader than that of James's other late works. Character names, for example, are closer to caricature: the rival connoisseurs, Bardi and Pappendick; the alliterative Lady Lappington, who culpably flogs her Longhi; the comically lugubrious butler, Gotch (who might almost be the ancestor of Lurch, the comically lugubrious butler of *The Addams Family*); Lord Theign himself, the rich representative of England, a 'thane' who holds land given him by the King (and artworks belonging properly to the nation); Breckenridge Bender, whose surname is nineteenth-century slang for a sixpence, represents a richer, wilder America where 'the eagle screams like a thousand steam-whistles and the newspapers flap like the leaves of the forest'; Lord John, the plainest of plain men; Lady Sandgate, whose resistance *will* inevitably crumble; Hugh Crimble, another crumbler, whose name, in East Country dialect, means 'to creep slyly'[1]; Lady Grace, who brings just that; Lady Imber, who embarrasses her family and who is – in the French – 'imberbe', beardless, but still behaves like a prodigal son.

In a letter to Harley Granville-Barker, James wrote explaining why he thought a production of *The Outcry* in Moscow would be pointless: 'It's essentially of this, our own, air and of these conditions – an Anglo-American *opportune* comedy or *pièce d'occasion* of which the very subject and basis of interest and irony relate but to England and her art-wealth and the US and their art-grab and their grab-resources.'[2]

At the heart of the story is a question of attribution: Lord Theign owns a painting which has for generations been known as a Moretto,[3] but which may in fact turn out to have all along been a Mantovano;[4] and whereas a Moretto, costing a mere

1 Even more vividly pertinent is the phrase 'to crimble i'th'poke', meaning 'to fly from an agreement, to act cowardly'.

2 *Henry James: Letters*, edited by Leon Edel, vol. IV, pp. 704–5.

3 Moretto da Brescia, 1498–1554. The *Macmillan Dictionary of Art* describes Moretto as: 'One of the most distinguished painters of Brescia of the 16th century.' He painted 'direct, solemn and often moving depictions of religious subjects. He was also an innovative portrait painter'.

4 Mantovano was, Henry James thought, entirely his own fictional creation. However, see letter from James on p. xxvi.

£10,000, holds no interest whatsoever for the acquisitive Mr Bender, a Mantovano – at £100,000 – most definitely does. That £100,000, that Mantovano, would, in its cash form, allow Lord Theign to pay off his first daughter's gambling debts (Lady Imber loses heavily at bridge) with plenty over to help maintain the estate; in its pictorial form, it would allow his second daughter, Lady Grace, to marry the thus-established art expert, Hugh Crimble, whose low origins require something of a boost. Standing in the middle of all this, middle-aged and middlebrow, is Lord John, to whose mother Lady Imber has contracted her debt. He loves, or says he loves, Lady Grace, and will do anything he can to secure her hand. If Lord Theign's selling the Mantovano will assist him towards this, he will persuade him to sell; if Theign's retaining it helps more, Lord John will dissuade, or prevent. Mr Breckenridge Bender doesn't care at all for the painting's provenance or its aesthetic qualities, merely for its cash value. He wants, Lord John explains, 'an *ideally* expensive thing'.

As the action progresses, the question of the painting's attribution (Mantovano or Moretto?) becomes increasingly irrelevant: Bender is no longer interested in buying it from Lord Theign, whichever it is, if Theign insists upon selling it cheap. Hugh Crimble, though he works towards a tenfold increase in the painting's value, is – alongside his beloved Lady Grace – the most passionate voice against its being sold. In the end, the painting – whatever it turns out to be – has acquired an immense new value: notoriety. The battle to gain or retain possession of the Mantovano/Moretto is fought out in the newspapers and magazines. To put it in completely contemporary terms, *The Outcry* is about spin and counter-spin. In typically Jamesian fashion, these vulgarities are kept offstage – but they are what determines the ultimate destination of the painting, and of two sets of hearts.

Henry VIII, Mister Hanns and Christina of Denmark

At one o'clock in the afternoon of 12 March, 1538, in the Royal Court of Brussels, Mister Hanns, the painter, and Philip Hoby, Henry VIII's special emissary, were admitted into the presence of Christina of Milan, youngest daughter of Christian II of Denmark and Isabella of Hungary, niece to the Emperor Charles V. Holbein was there to 'take her physiognomy'; Hoby to 'well note her answers, her gestures and countenance . . . that he may at his return declare the same to the King's Majesty'.

Ever since the death of Jane Seymour, Henry's ambassadorial spies had been interrogating the courts of Europe for a replacement Queen. Reports of Christina had, up to this point, been very favourable: 'She is not soo pewre whyt, as was the late Qweyn, whois soal God pardon; but she hathe a syngular good countenaunce, and when she chancesithe to smyl, ther aperithe two pittes in her cheikes, and won in hir chyne, the which becommythe hyr right excellently well.'[5]

As widow to the Duke of Milan, Christina wore mourning in the Italian style. Holbein completed his sketch in three hours, and he and Hoby set out on the return journey to London that evening.

There is a report of how they, and the likeness, were received:

On the very same day, the 18th [of March, 1538], the painter sent by this King to Flanders came back with the Duchess' likeness, which, I am told, has singularly pleased the King, so much so, that since he

5 References in this section are to Arthur B. Chamberlain, *Hans Holbein the Younger*, Chapter XX, 'The Duchess of Milan'.

saw it he has been in much better humor than he ever was, making musicians play on their instruments all day long. Two days after he went to dine at a splendid house of his, where he had collected all his musicians, and, after giving orders for the erection of certain sumptuous buildings therein, returned home by water, surrounded by musicians, and went straight to visit the duchess of Suffocq, the mother-in-law of the duke of Norfolk, and the wife of his brother, and ever since cannot be one single moment without masks, which is a sign he proposes to marry again, unless he does all that by way of dissimulation whilst the bishope of Tarbes is here still.

Henry VIII seems not to have been dissimulating. He commissioned from Holbein a full-length portrait of Christina. Soon after delivering his completed painting, Holbein was rewarded with a royal licence to export 600 tuns of beer. The King was obviously delighted with his work. However, the marriage did not take place. There is an apocryphal remark, attributed to Christina, 'That she had but one head, if she had two one of them should be at his majesty's service.' More reliably reported is a conversation with Thomas Wriothesley, Henry's Ambassador to the Low Countries. '"Asfor myn inclination," quod she, "what shuld I saye? You know that I am at thEperrurs commaundement",' and again, '"You knowe I am thEmperours poore servaunt, and must followe his pleasour."'

Holbein was soon being sent to take the likeness of Anne of Cleves.

The Selling of the 'Norfolk Holbein'

By 1908, Holbein's painting of 'Christina of Denmark, Duchess of Milan' had been on display in the National Gallery for over twenty-five years – a loan from the Duke of Norfolk. It had been widely assumed that this well-loved picture would, one day, be donated to the nation. However, in 1908, the Duke of Norfolk 'informed the National Gallery that he was receiving large offers for the picture; and that he might at any moment receive an offer which, in view of the anxious financial future for all landowners, he might feel obliged to accept for the reduction of his liabilities'.[6]

In May 1909, an offer *was* accepted – with certain provisos. The most important of these was that the Trustees of the National Gallery were to be given the 'option' of one month's grace during which they could attempt to match the offer. (Not quite exactly – for the picture dealers handling the sale, Colnaghi's, pledged £2,000 towards the purchase price of £72,000, were the picture to stay in the country.)

As the National Gallery had no money to spend on acquisitions, the matter was passed over to the National Art-Collections Fund.[7] 'The pathetic appeal made by Sir Charles Holroyd[8] at the annual meeting of the fund will never be forgotten by those who were privileged to be present . . .'[9]

Letters were sent out, and appeared in the *Morning Post*, the *Daily Telegraph* and *The Times*:

Sir – The committee of the National Art-Collections Fund feel it their duty to make a strong appeal to all lovers of art in favour of the preservation of this celebrated picture for this country . . . The sum is large; the moment is not the most favourable; but the committee

---

6 *The Times*, 5 May 1909.
7 This was not an isolated case. 'Before 1912, 52 Rembrandts, 21 Rubens, 11 Holbeins, 5 Velasquez and 7 Vermeers had been lost abroad . . .' *Saved for the Nation: The Achievement of the National Art-Collections Fund*, London, 1973, p.5.
8 The Director of the National Gallery.
9 *The Connoisseur*, 24, May–Aug. 1909, pp. 183–4.

nevertheless hopes that, although the time is short, contributions will be forthcoming, from men of wealth and from others according to their means, sufficient to save the country from the great loss that is threatened.

There was an outcry.

Within a short time, the Treasury had been cajoled into donating £10,000. The National Art-Collections Fund was left with a shortfall of £60,000. Pledges of money began to arrive, but neither fast nor large enough. The most accurate account of the appeal was written fifteen years later by Isodore Spielmann, one of the Honorary Secretaries of the Fund.[10] The denouement reads a little like the climax of a Sherlock Holmes story:

. . . we were becoming increasingly despondent and unhappy, and felt that only a miracle could save us. Moreover a fresh anxiety was that the Whitsuntide holidays would commence in the last week of our option, and our last chance would go by Whit Monday.

I had intended to go to the country for a much-needed rest over the holidays, but the honorary officers and most members of the Committee had already left town, and I decided to remain on the faint chance of something turning up. I went to my office daily during Whit week, and on Tuesday morning, June 1, something did turn up.

Among the letters was one written on Sunday, May 30 (Whit Sunday), from a lady at a health resort in Germany addressed to the National Art-Collections Fund, 47, Victoria Street, London, which ran: 'X . . . begs a wire be sent her stating the amount so far collected for Holbein's Duchess of Milan and whether cheques must be sent or whether a reference to her bank would be sufficient to be valid. X . . . relies upon the National Art-Collections Fund keeping her

10 *The Nineteenth Century and After*, Oct. 1924.

name completely private, whether any result comes from this letter or not.'

I read the letter again and again and wondered if we were being hoaxed or if the lady was mentally sound . . .

They were not; she was.

The identity of the anonymous female donor has never officially been revealed. However, in his account of the purchase, Isodore Spielmann – whether deliberately or not – drops several hints. The most important of these is the mention of the letter having come from 'a lady at a health resort in Germany'. This can be dated to 30 May 1909. He also, in passing, says that she – along with the other principals – had passed away by the date of his article, October 1924. A further clue is added by the Earl of Crawford and Balcarres, in his introduction to *Art Treasures for the Nation: Fifty Years of the National Art-Collections Fund*. The anonymous donor's cheque, he writes, 'constituted a third part of her whole estate'.

1909 *The Painting and the Play*

'The Holbein Duchess has been saved – by a veiled lady who has bought her off for £40,000. Can you lift the veil?'

So wrote James on 4 June 1909, to his good friend Edmund Gosse. The purchase of the painting had been reported in that morning's *Times*. It is likely, though, that James had been following the drama from the outset. However, it is unclear at what stage he decided that here was an apt subject for a play. The idea may first have come to life when an attempt was made to coax James back into writing for the theatre. The best account of this comes from Leon Edel:

Early in 1909 Charles Frohman, the American producer, began to lay plans for a repertory season in London at the Duke of York's Theatre. The moving spirit behind the repertory plan was J. M. Barrie. He enlisted the aid of those men who had contributed to the success of the repertory movement in England which, even before the turn of the century, had begun to breathe new life into the British stage. Harley Granville-Barker . . . joined their ranks. They engaged the discriminating services of Allan Wade . . . who at the moment was in charge of the Abbey Theatre's season in London. [George Bernard] Shaw, John Galsworthy, Granville-Barker, Somerset Maugham, John Masefield and Henry James were invited to write plays. Shaw wrote *Misalliance*, Galsworthy *Justice*, Granville-Barker *The Madras House* and Henry James *The Outcry*. Barrie contributed *The Twelve-Pound Look* and *Old Friends*, two one-act plays, and arranged George Meredith's unfinished comedy *The Sentimentalists* for the stage.[11]

James's experience of writing the stage version of *The Outcry* seems to have been one of almost complete satisfaction. Living in London, at the Reform Club, he began drafting the play in the early autumn of 1909. On 16 October, he wrote to Granville-Barker, 'I feel myself really to be getting on with *The Outcry* (if you'll kindly not mention the title!).' By 17 December, the first draft was completed – and an energized James was writing in his notebook, 'The process of the *Outcry* has been of enormous benefit and interest to me . . . – it has cast so rich and large and vivid a light upon my path: the august light, I mean, of the whole matter of method.'

The Master had *learnt* something – something he meant to put to use in future works.

As with almost all James's previous attempts to write for the

11 *The Complete Plays of Henry James*, edited by Leon Edel, p. 761.

stage, this one ended in failure – though not, it should be said, through any fault of the play's.

On 6 May 1910, King Edward VII died. During the period of the funeral and national mourning, all theatres were closed. The repertory season planned by Frohman and Barrie was cancelled. James was paid £200 and recovered his rights to the play.

1911 The Play and the Novel

'Unutterable, unforgettable hour – with those that followed . . . all unspeakable.' So wrote James shortly after attending the burial of his brother William. He stayed on in America, moving into Irving Street, Boston, with his brother's family, and working steadily at novelizing *The Outcry*. 'He walked a great deal. Maugham quoted him as saying, "I wander about the great empty streets of Boston and I never see a living creature. I could not be more alone in the Sahara."'[12] A few years later, he wrote to a friend: 'That autumn, winter and spring (1910–11) which I spent in Cambridge and New York – well, I shall go down to my grave without having breathed to another ear what I went through with then.'[13]

When James recast *The Outcry* as a novel, he made almost no changes to the story as such. Some scenes and passages which had been cut from earlier drafts of the play were reinstated. There were minor changes to the wording of individual lines of dialogue. More commonly, James supplied a brief description of how he imagined a line being delivered. This is one of the delights of reading the novel. It is

12 Leon Edel, *Henry James: A Life*, New York, 1985, p. 669.
13 ibid., p. 691.

as if the reader were present at a dress-rehearsal, with James directing.

Lord Theign remained a moment, and the heat of his resentment remained. He looked with a divided discretion, the pain of his indecision, from his daughter's suitor and his approved candidate to that contumacious young woman and back again; then choosing his course in silence he had a gesture of almost desperate indifference and passed quickly out by the door to the terrace.

The gently probing, confident yet diffident tone of this will be familiar to any reader of James's other late novels.

James has often been accused of writing dialogue too literary ever to succeed in a real theatre. George Bernard Shaw, whilst being generally supportive of James's theatrical efforts, made this observation some years after attending a 1917 production of *The Outcry:* 'I experimented on my friends between the acts by repeating some of the most exquisite sentences from the dialogue. I spoke fairly and distinctly, but not one of my victims could understand me or even identify the words I was uttering.'[14]

There is therefore a sense in which the dialogue of the novelized *Outcry* is returning home rather than being transported abroad.

(It should perhaps be added that *The Outcry*, stymied by the death of Edward VII, did not – during James's lifetime – get a chance either to fail or succeed in the theatre. The popularity of the novel may suggest it stood a better chance than James's previous dramas.)

Dialogue in *The Outcry* is far less oblique than in the final short stories ('Crapy Cornelia' and 'The Bench of Desolation')

14 *The Complete Plays of Henry James*, edited by Leon Edel, p. 765.

James was writing around the same time. There are far fewer of his trademark elisions, hesitations and misunderstandings. In fact, some of the dialogue is – for James – startlingly direct. Lord Theign is exasperated so far as to say 'damme', and the free-spoken Breckenridge Bender blasphemes 'What the h—'. (Not, it should be added, in the stage version.)

This was not the first time that James's fiction had been influenced by his drama. In the novels he wrote during the late 1890s, James employed what he called his 'scenic method'. This required, in *The Awkward Age*, an unprecedented reliance upon dialogue and, in *What Maisie Knew*, a rapidly evolving series of very brief episodes. Here, James was taking heed of the lessons he had learnt whilst writing, and cutting, and re-cutting, *Guy Domville* and his other plays. Yet even in his later novels, *The Ambassadors*, *The Wings of the Dove* and *The Golden Bowl*, the reader often gets a sense of the proscenium arch, of stage left and right.

Whilst reading *The Outcry*, it is interesting to speculate how much, for James, the 'scenic method' was a theatre of the mind – where the point of view was, in one sense, fixed: the dress-circle.

In turning his unproduced play into a publishable novel, James had to make numerous necessary transformations: stage directions, for example, become descriptions of rooms – sometimes with an almost comic awkwardness.

This, in the play:

The front drawing room at LADY SANDGATE'S house in Bruton Street, with an entrance right, straight from staircase and upper landing and lobby, and a communication a good deal left of centre with the back drawingroom, by the disposition and glimpse of which latter the impression of another entrance and exit within it, from and to the rest of the house, is given. LADY SANDGATE comes in right, meeting GOTCH, her Butler, who comes out of the back drawingroom; surprised at not immediately finding the visitor to whom she has been called.

Becomes, in the novel:

Lady Sandgate, on a morning late in May, entered her drawing-room by the door that opened at the right of that charming retreat as a person coming in faced Bruton Street; and she met there at this moment Mr Gotch, her butler, who had just appeared in the much wider doorway forming opposite the Bruton Street windows an apartment not less ample, lighted from the back of the house and having its independent connection with the upper floors and the lower. She showed surprise at not immediately finding the visitor to whom she had been called.

The longest completely new passages James introduced are the six full-length portraits of the major characters: Lady Sandgate (p. 4), Lord John (pp. 8–9), Mr Breckenridge Bender (p. 19), Lady Grace (p. 22), Hugh Crimble (pp. 31–2) and Lord Theign (pp. 49–50). These contain the finest, and funniest, writing in the book.

Lady Sandgate is beautifully summarized: 'She might have consented, or even attained, to being but gracefully stupid, but she would presumably have confessed, if put on her trial for restlessness or for intelligence, that she *was*, after all, almost clever enough to be vulgar.' Lord John is even more devastatingly sketched: 'Active yet insubstantial, he was slight and short and a trifle too punctually, though not yet quite lamentably, bald.' And Breckenridge Bender, whose character note in the play is a scant 'fifty-six', expands to the fantastic bathos of:

Fortune, felicity, nature, the perverse or interfering old fairy at his cradle-side – whatever the ministering power might have been – had simply overlooked and neglected his vast wholly-shaven face, which thus showed not so much for perfunctorily scamped as for not treated, as for neither formed nor fondled nor finished, at all. Nothing seemed to have been done for it but what the razor and the sponge, the tooth-brush and the looking-glass could officiously do; it had in short resisted any possibly finer attrition at the hands of fifty years of offered experience. It had developed on the lines, if lines they could be called, of the mere scoured and polished and initialled 'mug' rather than to any effect of a composed physiognomy; though we must at the same time add that its wearer carried this featureless disk as with the warranted confidence that might have attended a warning headlight or a glaring motor-lamp. The object, however one named it, showed you at least where he was, and most often that he was straight upon you.

James has a certain amount of fun describing people as if they were paintings ('Lady Sandgate neither affirmed nor denied; she only turned on him her thick lustre.') and paintings people ('And don't meanwhile, just *don't*, those splendid eyes of the fellow seem consciously to plead? The women, bless them, adore him . . .').

Henry James on 'The Outcry'

'"The Outcry" deals with a question sharply brought home of late to the conscience of English Society – that of the degree in which the fortunate owners of precious and hitherto transmitted works of art hold them in trust, as it were, for the nation, and may themselves, as lax guardians, be held to account by public opinion. Mr Henry James's study of the larger morality of the matter, if we may so call it, and which is the case of a lax rather than a jealous guardian, becomes conspicuous and acute. Hence springs the drama, almost a national as well as a personal crisis – a rapid, precipitated action, moving through difficulties to a happy issue.'[15]

This, the original dust-jacket text, is the closest James came to writing a Preface to *The Outcry*. His attitude towards what turned out to be his final completed novel (though, of course, *he* wasn't to know it) was ambivalent. As the author of *The Golden Bowl*, James couldn't help but view *The Outcry* as a lesser work. Writing to Edith Wharton, shortly after publication, James compared the two:

You speak at your ease, *chère Madame*, of the interminable and formidable job of producing, *à mon âge* another *Golden Bowl* – the most arduous and thankless task I ever set myself. However, on all that *il y aurait bien des choses à dire*; and meanwhile, I blush to say, the *Outcry* is on its way to a fifth Edition (in these few weeks) whereas it has taken the poor old G. B. eight or nine years to get even into a third.[16] And I should have to go back and live for two continuous years at Lamb House to write it (living on dried herbs and cold water – for 'staying power' – meanwhile); and that would be very bad for me, would probably indeed put an end to me altogether. My own sense is that I don't want, and oughtn't to try, to attack ever again anything *longer* (save for about seventy or eighty pages more) than *The Outcry*. That is *déjà assez difficile* – the 'artistic economy' of that

---

15 Leon Edel and Dan H. Laurence, *A Bibliography of Henry James*, London, 1961, p. 148.

16 'Nevertheless, the three impressions of *The Golden Bowl* exceeded the four impressions (a fifth never eventuated) of *The Outcry* by 1000 copies; it was exceeded in turn only by *Hawthorne* as the largest seller of any of James's English editions.' ibid., p. 128.

inferior little product being a much more calculated and ciphered, much more cunning and (to use your sweet expression) crafty one than that of five G. B. s. The vague verbosity of the Oxus-flood (*beau nom!*) terrifies me – *sates* me; whereas the steel structure of the other form makes every *parcelle* a weighed and related value. Moreover nobody is really doing (or, *ce me semble*, as I look about, can do) *Outcries*, while all the world is doing G. B. s – and *vous même*, *chère Madame, tout le premier:* – which gives you really the cat out of the bag![17]

James's disparaging tone is explained later. He says that about *The Outcry* 'hangs the inferiority, the comparative triviality, of its primal origin'. An origin he refers to elsewhere as 'the unutterable Theatre!'

In an earlier letter to Wharton, James dismissed *The Outcry* almost entirely: 'It is of course nothing but my Barrie-and-Frohman comedy, *The Outcry* of two years ago (just that now), then never acted through general collapse, simply printed, a little misleadingly – with such a running comment as merely represents decent interpretation and expression.'[18]

This is slightly disingenuous. James's letters to fellow writers (and particularly to Wharton) were always a strange mixture of self-disparagement and self-aggrandizement.

In 1911, James was still smarting from the lack of success (in terms of sales) of the New York Edition of his novels and tales. He had been looking to them to support him in his old age, but they weren't going to. *The Outcry*, by contrast, was a late and unexpected bonus – for which James was far from ungrateful.

His cash accounts for 'Income 1911' record: 'Oct. 18: From

17 *Henry James: Letters*, edited by Leon Edel, vol. IV, p. 591.
18 ibid., p. 587.

J. B. Pinker, as Methuen's royalty on *Outcry*, less diminution, £262.18.11'.[19] To put this in perspective, James had, on 16 July, roughly £932 in the bank. His 1911 royalties for the entire twenty-four volume New York Edition were £52.8.8.

The Real and the Invented

Although far from being a *roman-à-clef*, *The Outcry* contains a number of characters based upon real-life models.

Lord Theign approximates to Lord Norfolk, most particularly in his desire to sell a painting that is a National Treasure; Mr Breckenridge Bender is similar to art-acquisitive Americans such as Mr Frick and J. Pierpont Morgan.

The closest similarity, however, is that of Hugh Crimble and James's friend Hugh Walpole.

Walpole recognized this. Writing to his mother shortly after the book came out, he said, 'I had some delightful days with Henry James last week. I am supposed, everyone tells me, to be the hero of his new novel, and certainly the physical description is something like – the rest not at all.'[20]

There are a number of nice exchanges going on here. Firstly, James himself was being fictionalized by Walpole at the same time as he was writing *The Outcry*.

In his novel, *Fortitude*, Walpole found it 'agreeable to be able to present some aspects of his adored Henry James under the guise of the famous old novelist Henry Galleon. Indeed the scene in which the old warrior discusses the young writer's beginning and shows him the road he should follow was very closely based

19 *The Complete Notebooks of Henry James*, edited by Leon Edel and Lyall H. Powers, p. 605. J. B. Pinker was James's literary agent.
20 *Hugh Walpole: A Biography*, Rupert Hart-Davis, London, 1985, p. 86.

on the Master's spoken and written injunctions to Hugh.'[21]

In describing Crimble as Walpole, James was deftly – if entirely unconsciously – returning the compliment.

When *The Outcry* was published, Walpole (unsurprisingly) reviewed it very positively in the *Evening Standard and St James's Gazette*:

It is rather late in the day to quarrel with the Henry James mannerisms . . . He is great enough to afford himself the luxury of making the heavy father of his story use the same astonishing locutions as the journalist *jeune premier* . . . It is on an original topic, and one of singular burning interest to many . . . The book is one to be doubly valued for its ulterior motive and intrinsic beauties.[22]

James wrote flirtatiously to thank him for the review:

Darling, darling little Hugh! . . . I have just been reading the *Standard* at breakfast, and I am touched, I am melted, by the charming gallantry and magnanimity of it – my notices of *your* compositions having been so comparatively tepid. Tit *not* for Tat! Well, D. D. L. H. (it looks like 'd—d' little H., – but isn't meant for that), you do the thing handsomely when you do do it – and I seem to myself to swim in a blaze of glory – I shall wear my thrifty old hat when I go out like a wreath of the bay imitated in fine gold. Had I known you meant to crown me I should have liked to say a thing or two for your guidance – however incorrect such proceeding would have been as from author to reviewer. It wouldn't have been – between *us* – however from Author to Reviewer but from Friend (putting it mildly) to Friend and *Maître* to *Élève*. Never mind – you will sell the edition for me and no edition of mine has ever sold yet![23]

21 ibid., p. 81.
22 *Evening Standard and St James's Gazette*, 11 October 1911, p. 6.
23 *Henry James: Letters*, edited by Leon Edel, vol. IV, p. 585.

James thought fondly enough of Walpole to bequeath him £100 in his will.

After James died, Walpole dedicated two books – *The Apple Trees* and *The Killer and the Slain* – to his memory.

Another fictionalization in the novel rebounded upon James in an unexpected way. A month after the novel's début, James found himself replying to a letter from Robert C. Witt:[24]

Dear Sir,

I am almost shocked to learn, through your appreciative note, that in imaginatively projecting, for use in *The Outcry*, such a painter as the Mantovano, I unhappily coincided with an existing name, an artistic identity, a real one, with visible examples, in the annals of art. I had never heard (in I am afraid my disgraceful ignorance) of the painter the two specimens of whom in the National Gallery you cite; and fondly flattered myself that I had simply excogitated, for its part in my drama, a name at once plausible, that is of good Italian type, and effective, as it were, for dramatic bandying-about. It was important, you see, that with the great claim that the story makes for my artist I should have a suppositious one – with no awkward existing data to cast a possibly invidious or measurable light. So *my* Mantovano was a creature of mere (convincing) fancy – and this revelation of my not having been as inventive as I supposed rather puts me out! But I owe it to you none the less that I shall be able – after I have recovered from this humiliation – to go and have a look at our N.G. interloper. I thank you for this and am faithfully yours,

Henry James

24 As Honorary Secretary (along with Isodore Spielmann) of the National Art-Collections Fund, Mr Witt had been intimately involved with the purchase of the Holbein. Which, no doubt, was one reason for his particular interest in James's latest book. *Henry James: Letters*, edited by Leon Edel, vol. iv, pp. 640–41.

There are, in fact, two Mantovanos listed in the *Macmillan Dictionary of Art*: Rinaldo Mantovano (*fl.* Mantua *c.* 1527–39) and Marcello Venusti [Marcello Mantovano] (*b.* Como, ?1512–1515; *d.* Rome, 14 Oct. 1579). Of the two, it is Marcello Mantovano who has a single painting, NG1194 – *After Michelangelo, The Purification of the Temple* – listed in *The National Gallery Complete Illustrated Catalogue*. And even this is a questionable attribution.

A great number of non-fictional painters are mentioned in the text: Sir Joshua Reynolds, Pietro Longhi, Sir Thomas Lawrence, Albert Cuyp, Claude Lorraine, Thomas Gainsborough, George Romney, John Singer Sargent, J. M. W. Turner, John Constable, John Crome, Hercules Brabazon, Vandermeer – better known as Jan Vermeer – Moretto da Brescia, Peter Paul Rubens and Michelangelo.

Holbein himself is not mentioned, although James had employed him previously: his famous painting in the National Gallery supplied James with the title for *The Ambassadors*;[25] he also provided a key to the short story 'The Beldonald Holbein'.

In her article 'Henry James's *The Outcry* and the Art Drain of 1908-9', Adeline R. Tinter identifies real-life models for a couple of James's invented paintings:[26] 'One is the portrait by Sir Joshua Reynolds of Lord Theign's grandmother, the beautiful Duchess of Waterbridge, and the other is Lady Sandgate's great-grandmother by Sir Thomas Lawrence.' The latter, she says, is 'reminiscent of a portrait that did wind up in America, that of Miss Farren who became the Countess of Derby'. This was bought by J. Pierpont Morgan in 1904, but

---

25 'Holbein's *The Ambassadors*: A Pictorial Source for *The Ambassadors*', *Henry James and the Lust of the Eyes: Thirteen Artists in His Work*, Adeline R. Tinter, London, 1993, pp. 87–94.

26 *Apollo*, 113. (Feb. 1981), pp. 110–12.

remained in England until 1913. The 'Beautiful Duchess of Waterbridge' has two models, one for its appearance, which 'seems to suggest the portrait of *Anne, Duchess of Cumberland*, owned by Lady Waterford and hanging on the walls of Ford Castle where James was a weekend guest. Waterbridge and Waterford are names close enough to warrant implied similarity.'; and one for its ambiguous status: '[J. Pierpont] Morgan's purchase of the stolen *The Duchess of Devonshire* by Gainsborough which took place as soon as the picture was restored to Agnew's in 1901 seems to be the model behind the fictive "Duchess of Waterbridge" . . . which Bender wants so badly. Cass Canfield's biography of Morgan reports him as having said, "I must have the Duchess", words suggesting Bender's similar statements . . .'

In 1913, on the occasion of his seventieth birthday, James himself became the subject of a painted portrait by one of the non-fictional artists listed above, John Singer Sargent. It is owned today by the National Portrait Gallery.

Sargent himself is listed in *The Times* of 14 June 1909 as having subscribed £40 towards the fund to purchase the Norfolk Holbein; also mentioned are Edmund Gosse, Robert C. Witt and George Bernard Shaw. Henry James, however, does not appear to have been a contributor.

BOOK FIRST

I

'No, my lord,' Banks had replied, 'no stranger has yet arrived. But I'll see if any one has come in – or who has.' As he spoke, however, he observed Lady Sandgate's approach to the hall by the entrance giving upon the great terrace, and addressed her on her passing the threshold. 'Lord John, my lady.' With which, his duty majestically performed, he retired to the quarter – that of the main access to the spacious centre of the house – from which he had ushered the visitor.

This personage, facing Lady Sandgate as she paused there a moment framed by the large doorway to the outer expanses, the small pinkish paper of a folded telegram in her hand, had partly before him, as an immediate effect, the high wide interior, still breathing the quiet air and the fair pannelled security of the couple of hushed and stored centuries, in which certain of the reputed treasures of Dedborough Place beautifully disposed themselves; and then, through ample apertures and beyond the stately stone outworks of the great seated and supported house – uplifting terrace, balanced, balustraded steps and containing basins where splash and spray were at rest – all the rich composed extension of garden and lawn and park. An ancient, an assured elegance seemed to reign; pictures and preserved 'pieces,' cabinets and tapestries, spoke, each for itself, of fine selection and high distinction; while the originals of the old portraits, in more or less deserved

3

salience, hung over the happy scene as the sworn members of a great guild might have sat, on the beautiful April day, at one of their annual feasts.

Such was the setting confirmed by generous time, but the handsome woman of considerably more than forty whose entrance had all but coincided with that of Lord John either belonged, for the eye, to no such complacent company or enjoyed a relation to it in which the odd twists and turns of history must have been more frequent than any dull avenue or easy sequence. Lady Sandgate was shiningly modern, and perhaps at no point more so than by the effect of her express repudiation of a mundane future certain to be more and more offensive to women of real quality and of formed taste. Clearly, at any rate, in her hands, the clue to the antique confidence had lost itself, and repose, however founded, had given way to curiosity – that is to speculation – however disguised. She might have consented, or even attained, to being but gracefully stupid, but she would presumably have confessed, if put on her trial for restlessness or for intelligence, that she *was*, after all, almost clever enough to be vulgar. Unmistakably, moreover, she had still, with her fine stature, her disciplined figure, her cherished complexion, her bright important hair, her kind bold eyes and her large constant smile, the degree of beauty that might pretend to put every other question by.

Lord John addressed her as with a significant manner that he might have had – that of a lack of need, or even of interest, for any explanation about herself: it would have been clear that he was apt to discriminate with sharpness among possible claims on his attention. 'I luckily find *you* at least, Lady Sandgate – they tell me Theign's off somewhere.'

She replied as with the general habit, on her side, of bland reassurance; it mostly had easier consequences – for herself – than the perhaps more showy creation of alarm. 'Only off in the park – open to-day for a school-feast from Dedborough, as you may have made out from the avenue; giving good advice, at the top of his lungs, to four hundred and fifty children.'

It was such a scene, and such an aspect of the personage so accounted for, as Lord John could easily take in, and his recognition familiarly smiled. 'Oh he's so great on such occasions that I'm sorry to be missing it.'

'I've *had* to miss it,' Lady Sandgate sighed – 'that is to miss the peroration. I've just left them, but he had even then been going on for twenty minutes, and I dare say that if you care to take a look you'll find him, poor dear victim of duty, still *at* it.'

'I'll warrant – for, as I often tell him, he makes the idea of one's duty an awful thing to his friends by the extravagance with which he always overdoes it.' And the image itself appeared in some degree to prompt this particular edified friend to look at his watch and consider. 'I should like to come in for the grand *finale*, but I rattled over in a great measure to meet a party, as he calls himself – and calls, if you please, even me! – who's motoring down by appointment and whom I think I should be here to receive; as well as a little, I confess, in the hope of a glimpse of Lady Grace: if you can perhaps imagine *that!*'

'I can imagine it perfectly,' said Lady Sandgate, whom evidently no perceptions of that general order ever cost a strain. 'It quite sticks out of you, and every one moreover has for some time past been waiting to see. But you haven't then,' she added, 'come from town?'

'No, I'm for three days at Chanter with my mother; whom, as she kindly lent me her car, I should have rather liked to bring.'

Lady Sandgate left the unsaid, in this connection, languish

no longer than was decent. 'But whom you doubtless had to leave, by her preference, just settling down to bridge.'

'Oh, to sit down would imply that my mother at some moment of the day gets up —!'

'Which the Duchess never does?' – Lady Sandgate only asked to be allowed to show how she saw it. 'She fights to the last, invincible; gathering in the spoils and only routing her friends?' She abounded genially in her privileged vision. 'Ah yes – we know something of that!'

Lord John, who was a young man of a rambling but not of an idle eye, fixed her an instant with a surprise that was yet not steeped in compassion. 'You too then?'

She wouldn't, however, too meanly narrow it down. 'Well, in this house generally; where I'm so often made welcome, you see, and where —'

'Where,' he broke in at once, 'your jolly good footing quite sticks out of *you*, perhaps you'll let me say!'

She clearly didn't mind his seeing her ask herself how she should deal with so much rather juvenile intelligence; and indeed she could only decide to deal quite simply. 'You can't say more than I feel – and am proud to feel! – at being of comfort when they're worried.'

This but fed the light flame of his easy perception – which lighted for him, if she would, all the facts equally. 'And they're worried now, you imply, because my terrible mother is capable of heavy gains and of making a great noise if she isn't paid? I ought to mind speaking of that truth,' he went on as with a practised glance in the direction of delicacy; 'but I think I should like you to know that I myself am not a bit ignorant of why it has made such an impression here.'

Lady Sandgate forestalled his knowledge. 'Because poor Kitty Imber – who should either never touch a card or else learn to suffer in silence, as I've had to, goodness knows! – has thrown herself, with her impossible big debt, upon her father? whom she thinks herself entitled to "look to" even more as a lovely young widow with a good jointure than she formerly did as the mere most beautiful daughter at home.'

She had put the picture a shade interrogatively, but this was as nothing to the note of free inquiry in Lord John's reply. 'You mean that our lovely young widows – to say nothing of lovely young wives – ought by this time to have made out, in predicaments, how to turn round?'

His temporary hostess, even with his eyes on her, appeared to decide after a moment not wholly to disown his thought. But she smiled for it. 'Well, in that set —!'

'My mother's set?' However, if she could smile he could laugh. 'I'm much obliged!'

'Oh,' she qualified, 'I don't criticize her Grace; but the ways and traditions and tone of this house —'

'Make it' – he took her sense straight from her – 'the house in England where one feels most the false note of a dishevelled and bankrupt elder daughter breaking in with a list of her gaming debts – to say nothing of others! – and wishing to have at least those wiped out in the interest of her reputation? Exactly so,' he went on before she could meet it with a diplomatic ambiguity; 'and just that, I assure you, is a large part of the reason I like to come here – since I personally don't come with any such associations.'

'Not the association of bankruptcy – no; as you represent the payee!'

The young man appeared to regard this imputation for a moment almost as a liberty taken. 'How do you know so well, Lady Sandgate, what I represent?'

She bethought herself – but briefly and bravely. 'Well, don't you represent, by your own admission, certain fond aspirations? Don't you represent the belief – very natural, I grant – that more than *one* perverse and extravagant flower will be unlikely on such a fine healthy old stem; and, consistently with that, the hope of arranging with our admirable host here that he shall lend a helpful hand to your commending yourself to dear Grace?'

Lord John might, in the light of these words, have felt any latent infirmity in such a pretension exposed; but as he stood there facing his chances he would have struck a spectator as resting firmly enough on some felt residuum of advantage: whether this were cleverness or luck, the strength of his backing or that of his sincerity. Even with the young woman to whom our friends' reference thus broadened still a vague quantity for us, you would have taken his sincerity as quite possible – and this despite an odd element in him that you might have described as a certain delicacy of brutality. This younger son of a noble matron recognized even by himself as terrible enjoyed in no immediate or aggressive manner any imputable private heritage or privilege of arrogance. He would on the contrary have irradiated fineness if his lustre hadn't been a little prematurely dimmed. Active yet insubstantial, he was slight and short and a trifle too punctually, though not yet quite lamentably, bald. Delicacy was in the arch of his eyebrow, the finish of his facial line, the economy of 'treatment' by which his negative nose had been enabled to look important and his meagre mouth to smile its spareness away. He had pleasant but hard little eyes – they glittered, handsomely, without promise – and a neatness, a coolness and an ease, a clear instinct for making point take, on his behalf, the place of weight and immunity that of capacity, which represented somehow the art of living at a high pitch and yet at a low cost. There was that in his satisfied air which still suggested sharp wants – and this was withal the ambiguity; for the temper of these appetites or views was certainly, you would have concluded, not such as always to sacrifice to form. If he really, for instance, wanted Lady Grace, the passion or the sense of his interest in it would scarce have been considerably irritable.

'May I ask what you mean,' he inquired of Lady Sandgate, 'by the question of my "arranging"?'

'I mean that you're the very clever son of a very clever mother.'

'Oh, I'm less clever than you think,' he replied – 'if you really think it of me at all; and mamma's a good sight cleverer!'

'Than I think?' Lady Sandgate echoed. 'Why, she's the person in all our world I would gladly most resemble – for her general ability to put what she wants through.' But she at once added: 'That is if –!' pausing on it with a smile.

'If what then?'

'Well, if I could be absolutely certain to have all her kinds of cleverness without exception – and to have them,' said Lady Sandgate, 'to the very end.'

He definitely, he almost contemptuously declined to follow her. 'The very end of what?'

She took her choice as amid all the wonderful directions there might be, and then seemed both to risk and to reserve something. 'Say of her so wonderfully successful *general* career.'

It doubtless, however, warranted him in appearing to cut insinuations short. 'When you're as clever as she you'll be as good.' To which he subjoined: 'You don't begin to have the opportunity of knowing how good she is.' This pronouncement, to whatever comparative obscurity it might appear to relegate her, his interlocutress had to take – he was so prompt with a more explicit challenge. 'What is it exactly that you suppose yourself to know?'

Lady Sandgate had after a moment, in her supreme good humour, decided to take everything. 'I always proceed on the assumption that I know everything, because that makes people tell me.'

'It wouldn't make *me*,' he quite rang out, 'if I didn't want to! But as it happens,' he allowed, 'there's a question it would be convenient to me to put to you. You must be, with your charming unconventional relation with him, extremely in Theign's confidence.'

She waited a little as for more. 'Is that your question – *whether* I am?'

'No, but if you are you'll the better answer it.'

She had no objection then to answering it beautifully. 'We're the best friends in the world; he has been really my providence, as a lone woman with almost nobody and nothing of her own, and I feel my footing here, as so frequent and yet so discreet a visitor, simply perfect. But I'm happy to say that – for my pleasure when I'm really curious – this doesn't close to me the sweet resource of occasionally guessing things.'

'Then I hope you've ground for believing that if I go the right way about it he's likely to listen to me.'

Lady Sandgate measured her ground – which scarce seemed extensive. 'The person he most listens to just now – and in fact at any time, as you must have seen for yourself – is that arch-tormentor, or at least beautiful wheedler, his elder daughter.'

'Lady Imber's *here*?' Lord John alertly asked.

'She arrived last night and – as we've other visitors – seems to have set up a side-show in the garden.'

'Then she'll "draw" of course immensely, as she always does. But her sister won't be in that case with her,' the young man supposed.

'Because Grace feels herself naturally an independent show? So she well may,' said Lady Sandgate, 'but I must tell you that when I last noticed them there Kitty was in the very act of leading her away.'

Lord John figured it a moment. 'Lady Imber' – he ironically enlarged the figure – '*can* lead people away.'

'Oh, dear Grace,' his companion returned, 'happens fortunately to be firm!'

This seemed to strike him for a moment as equivocal. 'Not against *me*, however – you don't mean? You don't think she has a beastly prejudice —?'

'Surely you can judge about it; as knowing best what may – or what mayn't – have happened between you.'

'Well, I try to judge' – and such candour as was possible to Lord John seemed to sit for a moment on his brow. 'But I'm in fear of seeing her too much as I want to see her.'

There was an appeal in it that Lady Sandgate might have been moved to meet. 'Are you absolutely in earnest about her?'

'Of course I am – why shouldn't I be? But,' he said with impatience, 'I want help.'

'Very well then, that's what Lady Imber's giving you.' And as it appeared to take him time to read into these words their full sense, she produced others, and so far did help him – though the effort was in a degree that of her exhibiting with some complacency her own unassisted control of stray signs and shy lights. 'By telling her, by bringing it home to her, that if she'll make up her mind to accept you the Duchess will do the handsome thing. Handsome, I mean, by Kitty.'

Lord John, appropriating for his convenience the truth in this, yet regarded it as open to a becoming, an improving touch from himself. 'Well, and by *me*.' To which he added with more of a challenge in it: 'But you really know what my mother will do?'

'By my system,' Lady Sandgate smiled, 'you see I've guessed. What your mother will do is what brought you over!'

'Well, it's that,' he allowed – 'and something else.'

'Something else?' she derisively echoed. 'I should think "that," for an ardent lover, would have been enough.'

'Ah, but it's all one job! I mean it's one idea,' he hastened to explain – 'if you think Lady Imber's really acting on her.'

'Mightn't you go and see?'

'I would in a moment if I hadn't to look out for another matter too.' And he renewed his attention to his watch. 'I mean getting straight at my American, the party I just mentioned—'

But she had already taken him up. 'You too have an American and a "party," and yours also motors down —?'

'Mr Breckenridge Bender.' Lord John named him with a shade of elation.

She gaped at the fuller light. 'You *know* my Breckenridge? – who I hoped was coming for me!'

Lord John as freely, but more gaily, wondered. 'Had he told you so?'

She held out, opened, the telegram she had kept folded in her hand since her entrance. 'He has sent me that – which, delivered to me ten minutes ago out there, has brought me in to receive him.'

The young man read out this missive. '"Failing to find you in Bruton Street, start in pursuit and hope to overtake you about four."' It did involve an ambiguity. 'Why, he has been engaged these three days to coincide with myself, and not to fail of him has been part of my business.'

Lady Sandgate, in her demonstrative way, appealed to the general rich scene. 'Then why does he say it's me he's pursuing?'

He seemed to recognize promptly enough in her the sense of a menaced monopoly. 'My dear lady, he's pursuing expensive works of art.'

'By which you imply that I'm one?' She might have been wound up by her disappointment to almost any irony.

'I imply – or rather I affirm – that every handsome woman is! But what he arranged with me about,' Lord John explained, 'was that he should see the Dedborough pictures in general and the great Sir Joshua in particular – of which he had heard so much and to which I've been thus glad to assist him.'

This news, however, with its lively interest, but deepened the listener's mystification. 'Then why – this whole week that I've been in the house – hasn't our good friend here mentioned to me his coming?'

'Because our good friend here has had no reason' – Lord John could treat it now as simple enough. 'Good as he is in all ways, he's so best of all about showing the house and its contents that I haven't even thought necessary to write him that I'm introducing Breckenridge.'

'I should have been happy to introduce him,' Lady Sandgate just quavered – 'if I had at all known he wanted it.'

Her companion weighed the difference between them and appeared to pronounce it a trifle he didn't care a fig for. 'I surrender you that privilege then – of presenting him to his host – if I've seemed to you to snatch it from you.' To which Lord John added, as with liberality unrestricted, 'But I've been taking him about to see what's worth while – as only last week to Lady Lappington's Longhi.'

This revelation, though so casual in its form, fairly drew from Lady Sandgate, as she took it in, an interrogative wail. 'Her Longhi?'

'Why, don't you know her great Venetian family group, the What-do-you-call-'ems? – seven full-length figures, each one a gem, for which he paid her her price before he left the house.'

She could but make it more richly resound – almost stricken, lost in her wistful thought: 'Seven full-length figures? Her price?'

'Eight thousand – slap down. Bender knows,' said Lord John, 'what he wants.'

'And does he want only' – her wonder grew and grew – '"What-do-you-call-'ems"?'

'He most usually wants what he can't have.' Lord John made scarce more of it than that. 'But, awfully hard up as I fancy her, Lady Lappington went *at* him.'

It determined in his friend a boldly critical attitude. 'How horrible – at the rate things are leaving us!' But this was far from the end of her interest. 'And is that the way he pays?'

'Before he leaves the house?' Lord John lived it amusedly over. 'Well, *she* took care of that.'

'How incredibly vulgar!' It all had, however, for Lady Sandgate, still other connections – which might have attenuated Lady Lappington's case, though she didn't glance at this. 'He makes the most scandalous eyes – the ruffian! – at my great-grandmother.' And then as richly to enlighten any blankness: 'My tremendous Lawrence, don't you know? – in her wedding-dress, down to her knees; with such extraordinarily speaking eyes, such lovely arms and hands, such wonderful flesh-tints: universally considered the masterpiece of the artist.'

Lord John seemed to look a moment not so much at the image evoked, in which he wasn't interested, as at certain possibilities lurking behind it. 'And are you going to *sell* the masterpiece of the artist?'

She held her head high. 'I've indignantly refused – for all his pressing me so hard.'

'Yet that's what he nevertheless pursues you to-day to keep up?'

The question had a little the ring of those of which the occupant of a witness-box is mostly the subject, but Lady

Sandgate was so far as this went an imperturbable witness. 'I need hardly fear it perhaps if – in the light of what you tell me of your arrangement with him – his pursuit becomes, where I am concerned, a figure of speech.'

'Oh,' Lord John returned, 'he kills two birds with one stone – he sees both Sir Joshua and you.'

This version of the case had its effect, for the moment, on his fair associate. 'Does he want to buy *their* pride and glory?'

The young man, however, struck on his own side, became at first but the bright reflector of her thought. 'Is that wonder for sale?'

She closed her eyes as with the shudder of hearing such words. 'Not, surely, by *any* monstrous chance! Fancy dear, proud Theign —!'

'I can't fancy him – no!' And Lord John appeared to renounce the effort. 'But a cat may look at a king and a sharp funny Yankee at anything.'

These things might be, Lady Sandgate's face and gesture apparently signified; but another question diverted her. 'You're clearly a wonderful showman, but do you mind my asking you whether you're on such an occasion a – well, a closely interested one?'

'"Interested"?' he echoed; though it wasn't to gain time, he showed, for he would in that case have taken more. 'To the extent, you mean, of my little percentage?' And then as in silence she but kept a slightly grim smile on him: 'Why do you ask if – with your high delicacy about your great-grandmother – you've nothing to place?'

It took her a minute to say, while her fine eye only rolled; but when she spoke that organ boldly rested and the truth vividly appeared. 'I ask because people like you, Lord John, strike me as dangerous to the – how shall I name it? – the common weal; and because of my general strong feeling that we don't want any more of our national treasures (for I regard my great-grandmother as national) to be scattered about the world.'

'There's much in this country and age,' he replied in an off-hand manner, 'to be said about *that*.' The present, however, was not the time to say it all; so he said something else instead, accompanying it with a smile that signified sufficiency. 'To my friends, I need scarcely remark to you, I'm all the friend.'

She had meanwhile seen the butler reappear by the door that opened to the terrace, and though the high, bleak, impersonal approach of this functionary was ever, and more and more at every step, a process to defy interpretation, long practice evidently now enabled her to suggest, as she turned again to her fellow-visitor, a reading of it. 'It's the friend then clearly who's wanted in the park.'

She might, by the way Banks looked at her, have snatched from his hand a missive addressed to another; though while he addressed himself to her companion he allowed for her indecorum sufficiently to take it up where she had left it. 'By her ladyship, my lord, who sends to hope you'll join them below the terrace.'

'Ah, Grace hopes,' said Lady Sandgate for the young man's encouragement. 'There you are!'

Lord John took up the motor-cap he had lain down on coming in. 'I rush to Lady Grace, but don't demoralize Bender!' And he went forth to the terrace and the gardens.

Banks looked about as for some further exercise of his high function. 'Will you have tea, my lady?'

This appeared to strike her as premature. 'Oh, thanks – when they all come in.'

'They'll scarcely *all*, my lady' – he indicated respectfully that he knew what he was talking about. 'There's tea in her ladyship's tent; but,' he qualified, 'it has also been ordered for the saloon.'

'Ah then,' she said cheerfully, 'Mr Bender will be glad –!' And she became, with this, aware of the approach of another visitor. Banks considered, up and down, the gentleman ushered in, at the left, by the footman who had received him at the main entrance to the house. 'Here he must be, my lady.' With which he retired to the spacious opposite quarter, where he vanished, while the footman, his own office performed, retreated as he had come, and Lady Sandgate, all hospitality, received the many-sided author of her specious telegram, of Lord John's irritating confidence and of Lady Lappington's massive cheque.

II

Having greeted him with an explicitly gracious welcome and both hands out, she had at once gone on: 'You'll of course have tea? – in the saloon.'

But his mechanism seemed of the type that has to expand and revolve before sounding. 'Why; the very first thing?'

She only desired, as her laugh showed, to accommodate. 'Ah, have it the last if you like!'

'You see your English teas –!' he pleaded as he looked about him, so immediately and frankly interested in the place and its contents that his friend could only have taken this for the very glance with which he must have swept Lady Lappington's inferior scene.

'They're too much for you?'

'Well, they're too many. I think I've had two or three on the road – at any rate my man did. I like to do business before –' But his sequence dropped as his eye caught some object across the wealth of space.

She divertedly picked it up. 'Before tea, Mr Bender?'

'Before everything, Lady Sandgate.' He was immensely genial, but a queer, quaint, rough-edged distinctness somehow kept it safe – for himself.

'Then you've *come* to do business?' Her appeal and her emphasis melted as into a caress – which, however, spent itself on his large high person as he consented, with less of demonstration but more of attention, to look down upon her. She could therefore but reinforce it by an intenser note. 'To tell me you *will* treat?'

Mr Bender had six feet of stature and an air as of having received benefits at the hands of fortune. Substantial, powerful, easy, he shone as with a glorious cleanness, a supplied and equipped and appointed sanity and security; aids to action that might have figured a pair of very ample wings – wide pinions for the present conveniently folded, but that he would certainly on occasion agitate for great efforts and spread for great flights. These things would have made him quite an admirable, even a worshipful, image of full-blown life and character, had not the affirmation and the emphasis halted in one important particular. Fortune, felicity, nature, the perverse or interfering old fairy at his cradle-side – whatever the minis- tering power might have been – had simply overlooked and neglected his vast wholly-shaven face, which thus showed not so much for perfunctorily scamped as for not treated, as for neither formed nor fondled nor finished, at all. Nothing seemed to have been done for it but what the razor and the sponge, the tooth-brush and the looking-glass could offici- ously do; it had in short resisted any possibly finer attrition at the hands of fifty years of offered experience. It had developed on the lines, if lines they could be called, of the mere scoured and polished and initialled 'mug' rather than to any effect of a composed physiognomy; though we must at the same time add that its wearer carried this featureless disk as with the warranted confidence that might have attended a warning headlight or a glaring motor-lamp. The object, however one named it, showed you at least where he was, and most often that he was straight upon you. It was fearlessly and resistingly across the path of his advance that Lady Sandgate had thrown herself, and indeed with such success that he soon connected

her demonstration with a particular motive. 'For your grandmother, Lady Sandgate?' he then returned.

'For my grandmother's *mother*, Mr Bender – the most beautiful woman of her time and the greatest of all Lawrences, no
matter whose; as you quite acknowledged, you know, in our
talk in Bruton Street.'

Mr Bender bethought himself further – yet drawing it out;
as if the familiar fact of his being 'made up to' had never had
such special softness and warmth of pressure. 'Do you want
very, *very* much —?'

She had already caught him up. '"Very, very much" for her?
Well, Mr Bender,' she smilingly replied, 'I think I should like
her full value.'

'I mean' – he kindly discriminated – 'do you want so badly
to work her off?'

'It would be an intense convenience to me – so much so
that your telegram made me at once fondly hope you'd be
arriving to conclude.'

Such measure of response as he had good-naturedly given
her was the mere frayed edge of a mastering detachment,
the copious, impatient range elsewhere of his true attention.
Somehow, however, he still seemed kind even while, turning
his back upon her, he moved off to look at one of the several,
the famous Dedborough pictures – stray specimens, by every
presumption, lost a little in the whole bright bigness. '"Conclude"?' he echoed as he approached a significantly small
canvas. 'You ladies want to get there before the road's so much
as laid or the country's safe! Do you know what this *here* is?'
he at once went on.

'Oh, you can't have *that!*' she cried as with full authority –
'and you must really understand that you can't have everything.
You mustn't expect to ravage Dedborough.'

He had his nose meanwhile close to the picture. 'I guess it's a bogus Cuyp – but I know Lord Theign *has* things. He won't do business?'

'He's not in the least, and can never be, in my tight place,' Lady Sandgate replied; 'but he's as proud as he's kind, dear man, and as solid as he's proud; so that if you came down under a different impression – !' Well, she could only exhale the folly of his error with an unction that represented, whatever he might think of it, all her competence to answer for their host.

He scarce thought of it enough, on any side, however, to be diverted from prior dispositions. 'I came on an understanding that I should find my friend Lord John, and that Lord Theign would, on his introduction, kindly let me look round. But being before lunch in Bruton Street I knocked at your door —'

'For another look,' she quickly interposed, 'at my Lawrence?'

'For another look at *you*, Lady Sandgate – your great-grandmother wasn't required. Informed you were here, and struck with the coincidence of my being myself presently due,' he went on, 'I despatched you my wire, on coming away, just to keep up your spirits.'

'You *don't* keep them up, you depress them to anguish,' she almost passionately protested, 'when you don't tell me you'll treat!'

He paused in his preoccupation, his perambulation, conscious evidently of no reluctance that was worth a scene with so charming and so hungry a woman. 'Well, if it's a question of your otherwise suffering torments, may I have another interview with the old lady?'

'Dear Mr Bender, she's in the flower of her youth; she only yearns for interviews, and you may have,' Lady Sandgate earnestly declared, 'as many as you like.'

'Oh, you must be there to protect me!'

'Then as soon as I return —!'

'Well,' – it clearly cost him little to say – 'I'll come right round.'

She joyously registered the vow. 'Only meanwhile then, please, never a word!'

'Never a word, certainly. But where all this time,' Mr Bender asked, 'is Lord John?'

Lady Sandgate, as he spoke, found her eyes meeting those of a young woman who, presenting herself from without, stood framed in the doorway to the terrace; a slight fair grave young woman, of middle stature and simply dressed, whose brow showed clear even under the heavy shade of a large hat surmounted with big black bows and feathers. Her eyes had vaguely questioned those of her elder, who at once replied to the gentleman forming the subject of their inquiry: 'Lady Grace must know.' At this the young woman came forward, and Lady Sandgate introduced the visitor. 'My dear Grace, this is Mr Breckenridge Bender.'

The younger daughter of the house might have arrived in preoccupation, but she had urbanity to spare. 'Of whom Lord John has told me,' she returned, 'and whom I'm glad to see. Lord John,' she explained to his waiting friend, 'is detained a moment in the park, open to-day to a big Temperance school-feast, where our party is mostly gathered; so that if you care to go out –!' She gave him in fine his choice.

But this was clearly a thing that, in the conditions, Mr Bender wasn't the man to take precipitately; though his big useful smile disguised his prudence. 'Are there any pictures in the park?'

Lady Grace's facial response represented less humour perhaps, but more play. 'We find our park itself rather a picture.'

Mr Bender's own levity at any rate persisted. 'With a big Temperance school-feast?'

'Mr Bender's a great judge of pictures,' Lady Sandgate said as to forestall any impression of excessive freedom.

'Will there be more tea?' he pursued, almost presuming on this.

It showed Lady Grace for comparatively candid and literal. 'Oh, there'll be plenty of tea.'

This appeared to determine Mr Bender. 'Well, Lady Grace, I'm after pictures, but I take them "neat." May I go right round here?'

'Perhaps, love,' Lady Sandgate at once said, 'you'll let me show him.'

'A moment, dear' – Lady Grace gently demurred. 'Do go round,' she conformably added to Mr Bender; 'take your ease and your time. Everything's open and visible, and, with our whole company dispersed, you'll have the place to yourself.'

He rose, in his genial mass, to the opportunity. 'I'll be in clover – sure!' But present to him was the richest corner of the pasture, which he could fluently enough name. 'And I'll find "The Beautiful Duchess of Waterbridge"?'

She indicated, off to the right, where a stately perspective opened, the quarter of the saloon to which we have seen Mr Banks retire. 'At the very end of *those* rooms.'

He had wide eyes for the vista. 'About thirty in a row, hey?' And he was already off. 'I'll work right through!'

III

Left with her friend, Lady Grace had a prompt question. 'Lord John warned me he was "funny" – but you already know him?'

There might have been a sense of embarrassment in the way in which, as to gain time, Lady Sandgate pointed, instead of answering, to the small picture pronounced upon by Mr Bender. 'He thinks your little Cuyp a fraud.'

'That one?' Lady Grace could but stare. 'The wretch!' However, she made, without alarm, no more of it; she returned to her previous question. 'You've met him before?'

'Just a little – in town. Being "after pictures," ' Lady Sandgate explained, 'he has been after my great-grandmother.'

'She,' said Lady Grace with amusement, 'must have found him funny! But he can clearly take care of himself, while Kitty takes care of Lord John, and while you, if you'll be so good, go back to support father – in the hour of his triumph: which he wants you so much to witness that he complains of your desertion and goes so far as to speak of you as sneaking away.'

Lady Sandgate, with a slight flush, turned it over. 'I delight in his triumph, and whatever I do is at least above board; but if it's a question of support, aren't you yourself failing him quite as much?'

This had, however, no effect on the girl's confidence. 'Ah, my dear, I'm not at all the same thing, and as I'm the person in the world he least misses –' Well, such a fact spoke for itself.

'You've been free to return and wait for Lord John?' – that was the sense in which the elder woman appeared to prefer to understand it as speaking.

The tone of it, none the less, led her companion immediately, though very quietly, to correct her. 'I've not come back to wait for Lord John.'

'Then he hasn't told you – if you've talked – with what idea he has come?'

Lady Grace had for a further correction the same shade of detachment. 'Kitty has told me – what it suits her to pretend to suppose.'

'And Kitty's pretensions and suppositions always go with what happens – at the moment, among all her wonderful happenings – to suit her?'

Lady Grace let that question answer itself – she took the case up further on. 'What I can't make out is why this *should* so suit her!'

'And what *I* can't!' said Lady Sandgate without gross honesty and turning away after having watched the girl a moment. She nevertheless presently faced her again to follow this speculation up. 'Do you like him enough to risk the chance of Kitty's being for once right?'

Lady Grace gave it a thought – with which she moved away. 'I don't know how much I like him!'

'Nor how little!' cried her friend, who evidently found amusement in the tone of it. 'And you're not disposed to take the time to find out? He's at least better than the others.'

'The "others"?' – Lady Grace was blank for them.

'The others of his set.'

'Oh, his set! That wouldn't be difficult – by what I imagine of some of them. But he means well enough,' the girl added; 'he's very charming and does me great honour.'

It determined in her companion, about to leave her, another brief arrest. 'Then may I tell your father?'

This in turn brought about in Lady Grace an immediate drop of the subject. 'Tell my father, please, that I'm expecting Mr Crimble; of whom I've spoken to him even if he doesn't remember, and who bicycles this afternoon ten miles over from where he's staying – with some people we don't know – to look at the pictures, about which he's awfully keen.'

Lady Sandgate took it in. 'Ah, like Mr Bender?'

'No, not at all, I think, like Mr Bender.'

This appeared to move in the elder woman some deeper thought. 'May I ask then – if one's to meet him – who he is?'

'Oh, father knows – or ought to – that I sat next him, in London, a month ago, at dinner, and that he then told me he was working, tooth and nail, at what he called the wonderful modern science of Connoisseurship – which is upsetting, as perhaps you're not aware, all the old-fashioned canons of art-criticism, everything we've stupidly thought right and held dear; that he was to spend Easter in these parts, and that he should like greatly to be allowed some day to come over and make acquaintance with our things. I told him,' Lady Grace wound up, 'that nothing would be easier; a note from him arrived before dinner —'

Lady Sandgate jumped the rest. 'And it's for *him* you've come in.'

'It's for him I've come in,' the girl assented with serenity.

'Very good – though he sounds most detrimental! But will you first just tell me *this* – whether when you sent in ten minutes ago for Lord John to come out to you it was wholly of your own movement?' And she followed it up as her young friend appeared to hesitate. 'Was it because you knew why he had arrived?'

The young friend hesitated still. '"Why"?'

'So particularly to speak to you.'

'Since he was expected and mightn't know where I was,' Lady Grace said after an instant, 'I wanted naturally to be civil to him.'

'And had he time there to tell you,' Lady Sandgate asked, 'how very civil he wants to be to you?'

'No, only to tell me that his friend – who's off there – was coming; for Kitty at once appropriated him and was still in possession when I came away.' Then, as deciding at last on perfect frankness, Lady Grace went on: 'If you want to know, I sent for news of him because Kitty insisted on my doing so; saying, so very oddly and quite in her own way, that she herself didn't wish to "appear in it." She had done nothing but say to me for an hour, rather worryingly, what you've just said – that it's me he's what, like Mr Bender, she calls "after"; but as soon as he appeared she pounced on him, and I left him – I assure you quite resignedly – in her hands.'

'She wants' – it was easy for Lady Sandgate to remark – 'to talk of you to him.'

'I don't know *what* she wants,' the girl replied as with rather a tired patience; 'Kitty wants so many things at once. She always wants money, in quantities, to begin with – and all to throw so horribly away; so that whenever I see her "in" so very deep with any one I always imagine her appealing for some new tip as to how it's to be come by.'

'Kitty's an abyss, I grant you, and with my disinterested devotion to your father – in requital of all his kindness to me since Lord Sandgate's death and since your mother's – I can never be too grateful to you, my dear, for your being so different a creature. But what is she going to gain financially,'

Lady Sandgate pursued with a strong emphasis on her adverb, 'by working up our friend's confidence in your listening to him – if you *are* to listen?'

'I haven't in the least engaged to listen,' said Lady Grace – 'it will depend on the music he makes!' But she added with light cynicism: 'Perhaps she's to gain a commission!'

'On his fairly getting you?' And then as the girl assented by silence: 'Is he in a position to pay her one?' Lady Sandgate asked.

'I dare say the Duchess is!'

'But do you see the Duchess *producing* money – with all that Kitty, as we're not ignorant, owes her? Hundreds and hundreds and hundreds!' – Lady Sandgate piled them up.

Her young friend's gesture checked it. 'Ah, don't tell me how many – it's too sad and too ugly and too wrong!' To which, however, Lady Grace added: 'But perhaps that will be just her way!' And then as her companion seemed for the moment not quite to follow: 'By letting Kitty off her debt.'

'You mean that Kitty goes free if Lord John wins your promise?'

'Kitty goes free.'

'She has her creditor's release?'

'For every shilling.'

'And if he only fails?'

'Why then of course,' said now quite lucid Lady Grace, 'she throws herself more than ever on poor father.'

'Poor father indeed!' – Lady Sandgate richly sighed it.

It appeared even to create in the younger woman a sense of excess. 'Yes – but he after all and in spite of everything adores her.'

'To the point, you mean' – for Lady Sandgate could clearly but wonder – 'of really sacrificing you?'

The weight of Lady Grace's charming deep eyes on her face

made her pause while, at some length, she gave back this look and the interchange determined in the girl a grave appeal. 'You think I *should* be sacrificed if I married him?'

Lady Sandgate replied, though with an equal emphasis, indirectly. '*Could* you marry him?'

Lady Grace waited a moment. 'Do you mean for Kitty?'

'For himself even – if they should convince you, among them, that he cares for you.'

Lady Grace had another delay. 'Well, he's his awful mother's son.'

'Yes – but you wouldn't marry his mother.'

'No – but I should only be the more uncomfortably and intimately conscious of her.'

'Even when,' Lady Sandgate optimistically put it, 'she so markedly likes you?'

This determined in the girl a fine impatience. 'She doesn't "like" me, she only *wants* me – which is a very different thing; wants me for my father's so particularly beautiful position, and my mother's so supremely great people, and for everything we have been and have done, and still are and still have: except of course poor not-at-all-model Kitty.'

To this luminous account of the matter Lady Sandgate turned as to a genial sun-burst. 'I see indeed – for the general immaculate connection.'

The words had no note of irony, but Lady Grace, in her great seriousness, glanced with deprecation at the possibility. 'Well, we *haven't* had false notes. We've scarcely even had bad moments.'

'Yes, you've been beatific!' – Lady Sandgate enviously, quite ruefully, felt it. But any further treatment of the question was checked by the re-entrance of the footman – a demonstration explained by the concomitant appearance of a young man in eye-glasses and with the ends of his trousers clipped together as for cycling. 'This must be your friend,' she had only time to say to the daughter of the house; with which, alert and reminded of how she was awaited elsewhere, she retreated before her companion's visitor, who had come in with his guide from the vestibule. She passed away to the terrace and the gardens, Mr Hugh Crimble's announced name ringing in her ears – to some effect that we are as yet not qualified to discern.

IV

Lady Grace had turned to meet Mr Hugh Crimble, whose pleasure in at once finding her lighted his keen countenance and broke into easy words. 'So awfully kind of you – in the midst of the great doings I noticed – to have found a beautiful minute for me.'

'I left the great doings, which are almost over, to every one's relief, I think,' the girl returned, 'so that your precious time shouldn't be taken to hunt for me.'

It was clearly for him, on this bright answer, as if her white hand were holding out the perfect flower of felicity. 'You came in from your revels on purpose – with the same charity you showed me from that first moment?' They stood smiling at each other as in an exchange of sympathy already confessed – and even as if finding that their relation had grown during the lapse of contact; she recognizing the effect of what they had originally felt as bravely as he might name it. What the fine, slightly long oval of her essentially quiet face – quiet in spite of certain vague depths of reference to forces of the strong high order, forces involved and implanted, yet also rather spent in the process – kept in range from under her redundant black hat was the strength of expression, the directness of communication, that her guest appeared to borrow from the unframed and unattached nippers unceasingly perched, by their mere ground-glass rims, as she remembered, on the bony bridge of his indescribably authoritative (since it was at the same time decidedly inquisitive) young nose. She must, however, also have embraced in this contemplation, she must more or less again have interpreted, his main physiognomic mark, the degree to which his clean jaw was underhung and his lower lip protruded; a lapse of regularity made evident by a suppression of beard and moustache as complete as that practised by Mr Bender – though without the appearance consequent in the latter's case, that of the flagrantly vain appeal in the countenance for some other exhibition of a history, of a process of production, than this so superficial one. With the interested and interesting girl sufficiently under our attention while we thus try to evoke her, we may even make out some wonder in her as to why the so perceptibly protrusive lower lip of this acquaintance of an hour or two should positively have contributed to his being handsome instead of much more logically interfering with it. We might in fact in such a case even have followed her into another and no less refined a speculation – the question of whether the surest seat of his good looks mightn't after all be his high, fair, if somewhat narrow, forehead, crowned with short crisp brown hair and which, after a fashion of its own, predominated without overhanging. He spoke after they had stood just face to face almost long enough for awkwardness. 'I haven't forgotten one item of your kindness to me on that rather bleak occasion.'

'Bleak do you call it?' she laughed. 'Why I found it, rather, tropical – "lush." My neighbour on the other side wanted to talk to me of the White City.'

'Then you made it doubtless bleak for *him*, let us say. *I* couldn't let you alone, I remember, about *this* – it was like a shipwrecked signal to a sail on the horizon.' 'This' obviously meant for the young man exactly what surrounded him; he had begun, like Mr Bender, to be conscious of a thick solicitation of the eye – and much more than he, doubtless, of a tug at the imagination; and he broke – characteristically, you would have been sure – into a great free gaiety of recognition.

'Oh, we've nothing particular in the hall,' Lady Grace amiably objected.

'Nothing, I see, but Claudes and Cuyps! I'm an ogre,' he said – 'before a new and rare feast!'

She happily took up his figure. 'Then won't you begin – as a first course – with tea after your ride? If the other, that is – for there has been an ogre before you – has left any.'

'Some tea, with pleasure' – he looked all his longing; 'though when you talk of *a* fellow-feaster I should have supposed that, on such a day as this especially, you'd find yourselves running a continuous *table d'hôte*.'[1]

'Ah, we can't work sports in our gallery and saloon – the banging or whacking and shoving amusements that are all most people care for; unless, perhaps,' Lady Grace went on, 'your own peculiar one, as I understand you, of playing football with the old benighted traditions and attributions you everywhere meet: in fact I think you said the old idiotic superstitions.'

Hugh Crimble went more than half-way to meet this description of his fondest activity; he indeed even beckoned it on. 'The names and stories and styles – the so often vain legend, not to be too invidious – of author or subject or school?' But he had a drop, no less, as from the sense of a cause sometimes lost. 'Ah, that's a game at which we *all* can play!'

'Though scarcely,' Lady Grace suggested, 'at which we all can score.'

The words appeared indeed to take meaning from his growing impression of the place and its charm – of the number of objects, treasures of art, that pressed for appreciation of their importance. 'Certainly,' he said, 'no one can ever have scored much on sacred spots of *this* order – which express so the grand impunity of their pride, their claims, their assurance!'

'We've had great luck,' she granted – 'as I've just been reminded; but ever since those terrible things you told me in town – about the tremendous tricks of the whirligig of time and the aesthetic fools' paradise in which so many of us live – I've gone about with my heart in my mouth. Who knows that while I talk Mr Bender mayn't be pulling us to pieces?'

Hugh Crimble had a shudder of remembrance. 'Mr Bender?'

'The rich American who's going round.'

It gave him a sharper shock. 'The wretch who bagged Lady Lappington's Longhi?'

Lady Grace showed surprise. 'Is he a wretch?'

Her visitor but asked to be extravagant. 'Rather – the scoundrel. He offered his infernal eight thousand down.'

'Oh, I thought you meant he had played some trick!'

'I wish he had – he could then have been collared.'

'Well,' Lady Grace peacefully smiled, 'it's no use his offering *us* eight thousand – or eighteen or even eighty!'

Hugh Crimble stared as at the odd superfluity of this reassurance, almost crude on exquisite lips and contradicting an imputation no one would have indecently made. 'Gracious goodness, I hope not! The man surely doesn't *suppose* you'd traffic.'

She might, while she still smiled at him, have been fairly enjoying the friendly horror she produced. 'I don't quite know what he supposes. But people *have* trafficked; people do; people are trafficking all round.'

'Ah,' Hugh Crimble cried, 'that's what deprives me of my rest and, as a lover of our vast and beneficent art-wealth, poisons my waking hours. That art-wealth is at the mercy of a leak there appears no means of stopping.' She had tapped a spring in him, clearly, and the consequent flood might almost at any moment become copious. 'Precious things are going out of our distracted country at a quicker rate than the very quickest – a century and more ago – of their ever coming in.'

She was sharply struck, but was also unmistakably a person in whom stirred thought soon found connections and relations. 'Well, I suppose our art-wealth came in – save for those awkward Elgin Marbles! – mainly by purchase too, didn't it? We ourselves largely took it away from somewhere, didn't we? We didn't *grow* it all.'

'We grew some of the loveliest flowers – and on the whole to-day the most exposed.' He had been pulled up but for an instant. 'Great Gainsboroughs and Sir Joshuas and Romneys and Sargents, great Turners and Constables and old Cromes and Brabazons, form, you'll recognize, a vast garden in themselves. What have we ever for instance more successfully grown than your splendid "Duchess of Waterbridge"?'

The girl showed herself ready at once to recognize under his eloquence anything he would. 'Yes – it's our Sir Joshua, I believe, that Mr Bender has proclaimed himself particularly "after."'

It brought a cloud to her friend's face. 'Then he'll be capable of anything.'

'Of anything, no doubt, but of making my father capable –! And you haven't at any rate,' she said, 'so much as seen the picture.'

'I beg your pardon – I saw it at the Guildhall three years ago; and am almost afraid of getting again, with a fresh sense of its beauty, a livelier sense of its danger.'

Lady Grace, however, was so far from fear that she could even afford pity. 'Poor baffled Mr Bender!'

'Oh, rich and confident Mr Bender!' Crimble cried. 'Once given his money, his confidence is a horrid engine in itself –

there's the rub! I dare say' – the young man saw it all – 'he has brought his poisonous cheque.'

She gave it her less exasperated wonder. 'One has heard of that, but only in the case of some particularly pushing dealer.'

'And Mr Bender, to do him justice, isn't a particularly pushing dealer?'

'No,' Lady Grace judiciously returned; 'I think he's not a dealer at all, but just what you a moment ago spoke of yourself as being.'

He gave a glance at his possibly wild recent past. 'A fond true lover?'

'As we *all* were in our lucky time – when we rumaged Italy and Spain.'

He appeared to recognize this complication – of Bender's voracious integrity; but only to push it away. 'Well, I don't know whether the best lovers are, or ever were, the best buyers – but I feel to-day that they're the best keepers.'

The breath of his emphasis blew, as her eyes showed, on the girl's dimmer fire. 'It's as if it were suddenly in the air that you've brought us some light or some help – that you may do something really good for us.'

'Do you mean "mark down," as they say at the shops, all your greatest claims?'

His chord of sensibility had trembled all gratefully into derision, and not to seem to swagger he had put his possible virtue at its lowest. This she beautifully showed that she beautifully saw. 'I dare say that if you did even that we should have to take it from you.'

'Then it may very well be,' he laughed back, 'the reason why I feel, under my delightful, wonderful impression, a bit anxious and nervous and afraid.'

'That shows,' she returned, 'that you suspect us of horrors

hiding from justice, and that your natural kindness yet shrinks from handing us over!'

Well, clearly, she might put it as she liked – it all came back to his being more charmed. 'Heaven knows I've wanted a chance at you, but what should you say if, having then at last just taken you in in your so apparent perfection, I should feel it the better part of valour simply to mount my "bike" again and spin away?'

'I should be sure that at the end of the avenue you'd turn right round and come back. You'd think again of Mr Bender.'

'Whom I don't, however, you see – if he's prowling off there – in the least want to meet.' Crimble made the point with gaiety. 'I don't know what I mightn't do to him – and yet it's not of my temptation to violence, after all, that I'm most afraid. It's of the brutal mistake of one's breaking – with one's priggish, precious modernity and one's possibly futile discriminations – into a *general* situation or composition, as we say, so serene and sound and right. What should one do here, out of respect for that felicity, but hold one's breath and walk on tip-toe? The very celebrations and consecrations, as you tell me, instinctively stay outside. I saw that all,' the young man went on with more weight in his ardour, 'I saw it, while we talked in London, as your natural setting and your native air – and now ten minutes on the spot have made it sink into my spirit. You're a case, all together, of enchanted harmony, of perfect equilibrium – there's nothing to be done or said.'

His friend listened to this eloquence with her eyes lowered, then raising them to meet, with a vague insistence, his own; after which something she had seen there appeared to determine in her another motion. She indicated the small landscape that Mr Bender had, by Lady Sandgate's report, rapidly studied and denounced. 'For what do you take that little picture?'

Hugh Crimble went over and looked. 'Why, don't you know? It's a jolly little Vandermeer of Delft.'

'It's not a base imitation?'

He looked again, but appeared at a loss. 'An imitation of Vandermeer?'

'Mr Bender thinks of Cuyp.'

It made the young man ring out: 'Then Mr Bender's doubly dangerous!'

'Singly is enough!' Lady Grace laughed. 'But you see you *have* to speak.'

'Oh, to *him*, rather, after that – if you'll just take me to him.'

'Yes then,' she said; but even while she spoke Lord John, who had returned, by the terrace, from his quarter of an hour passed with Lady Imber, was there practically between them; a fact that she had to notice for her other visitor, to whom she was hastily reduced to naming him.

His lordship eagerly made the most of this tribute of her attention, which had reached his ear; he treated it – her 'Oh Lord John!' – as a direct greeting. 'Ah Lady Grace! I came back particularly to find you.'

She could but explain her predicament. 'I was taking Mr Crimble to see the pictures.' And then more pointedly, as her manner had been virtually an introduction of that gentleman, an introduction which Lord John's mere noncommittal stare was as little as possible a response to: 'Mr Crimble's one of the quite new connoisseurs.'

'Oh, I'm at the very lowest round of the ladder. But I aspire!' Hugh laughed.

'You'll mount!' said Lady Grace with friendly confidence.

He took it again with gay deprecation. 'Ah, if by that time there's anything left here to mount *on!*'

'Let us hope there will be at least what Mr Bender, poor man, won't have been able to carry off.' To which Lady Grace added, as to strike a helpful spark from the personage who had just joined them, but who had the air of wishing to preserve his detachment: 'It's to Lord John that we owe Mr Bender's acquaintance.'

Hugh looked at the gentleman to whom they were so indebted. 'Then do you happen to know, sir, what your friend means to *do* with his spoil?'

The question got itself but dryly treated, as if it might be a commercially calculating or interested one. 'Oh, not sell it again.'

'Then ship it to New York?' the inquirer pursued, defining himself somehow as not snubbed and, from this point, not snubbable.

That appearance failed none the less to deprive Lord John of a betrayed relish for being able to displease Lady Grace's odd guest by large assent. 'As fast as ever he can – and you can land things there *now*, can't you? in three or four days.'

'I dare say. But can't he be induced to have a little mercy?' Hugh sturdily pursued.

Lord John pushed out his lips. 'A "little"? How much do you want?'

'Well, one wants to be able somehow to stay his hand.'

'I doubt if you can any more stay Mr Bender's hand than you can empty his purse.'

'Ah, the Despoilers!' said Crimble with strong expression. 'But it's *we*,' he added, 'who are base.'

'"Base"?' – and Lord John's surprise was apparently genuine.

'To want only to "do business," I mean, with our treasures, with our glories.'

Hugh's words exhaled such a sense of peril as to draw at once Lady Grace. 'Ah, but if we're above that *here*, as you know —!'

He stood smilingly corrected and contrite. 'Of course I know

– but you must forgive me if I have it on the brain. And show me first of all, won't you? the Moretto of Brescia.'

'You know then about the Moretto of Brescia?'

'Why, didn't you tell me yourself?' It went on between them for the moment quite as if there had been no Lord John.

'Probably, yes,' she recalled; 'so how I must have swaggered!' After which she turned to the other visitor with a kindness strained clear of urgency. 'Will you also come?'

He confessed to a difficulty – which his whole face begged her also to take account of. 'I hoped you'd be at leisure – for something I've so at heart!'

This had its effect; she took a rapid decision and turned persuasively to Crimble – for whom, in like manner, there must have been something in *her* face. 'Let Mr Bender himself then show you. And there are things in the library too.'

'Oh yes, there are things in the library.' Lord John, happy in his gained advantage and addressing Hugh from the strong ground of an initiation already complete, quite sped him on the way.

Hugh clearly made no attempt to veil the penetration with which he was moved to look from one of these counsellors to the other, though with a ready 'Thank-you!' for Lady Grace he the next instant started in pursuit of Mr Bender.

V

'Your friend seems remarkably hot!' Lord John remarked to his young hostess as soon as they had been left together.

'He has cycled twenty miles. And indeed,' she smiled, 'he does appear to care for what he cares for!'

Her companion then, during a moment's silence, might have been noting the emphasis of her assent. 'Have you known him long?'

'No – not long.'

'Nor seen him often?'

'Only once – till now.'

'Oh!' said Lord John with another pause. But he soon proceeded. 'Let us leave him then to cool! I haven't cycled twenty miles, but I've motored forty very much in the hope of *this*, Lady Grace – the chance of being able to assure you that I too care very much for what I care for.' To which he added on an easier note, as to carry off a slight awkwardness while she only waited: 'You certainly mustn't let yourself – between us all – be worked to death.'

'Oh, such days as this –!' She made light enough of her burden.

'They don't come often to *me* at least, Lady Grace! I hadn't grasped in advance the scale of your fête,' he went on; 'but since I've the great luck to find you alone –!' He paused for breath, however, before the full sequence.

She helped him out as through common kindness, but it was a trifle colourless. 'Alone or in company, Lord John, I'm always very glad to see you.'

'Then that assurance helps me to wonder if you don't perhaps gently guess what it is I want to say.' This time indeed she left him to his wonder, so that he had to support himself. 'I've tried, all considerately – these three months – to let you see for yourself how I feel. I feel very strongly, Lady Grace; so that at last' – and his impatient sincerity took after another instant the jump – 'well, I regularly worship you. You're my absolute ideal. I think of you the whole time.'

She measured out consideration as if it had been a yard of pretty ribbon. 'Are you sure you *know* me enough?'

'I think I know a perfect woman when I see one!' Nothing now at least could have been more prompt, and while a decent pity for such a mistake showed in her smile he followed it up. 'Isn't what you rather mean that you haven't cared sufficiently to know *me*? If so, that can be little by little mended, Lady Grace.' He was in fact altogether gallant about it. 'I'm aware of the limits of what I have to show or to offer, but I defy you to find a limit to my possible devotion.'

She deferred to that, but taking it in a lower key. 'I believe you'd be very good to me.'

'Well, isn't *that* something to start with?' – he fairly pounced on it. 'I'll do any blest thing in life you like, I'll accept any condition you impose, if you'll only tell me you see your way.'

'Shouldn't I have a little more first to see yours?' she asked. 'When you say you'll do anything in life I like, isn't there anything you yourself want strongly enough to do?'

He cast a stare about on the suggestions of the scene. 'Anything that will make money, you mean?'

'Make money or make reputation – or even just make the time pass.'

'Oh, what I have to look to in the way of a career?' If that was her meaning he could show after an instant that he didn't fear it. 'Well, your father, dear delightful man, has been so good as to give me to understand that he backs me for a decent deserving creature; and I've noticed, as you doubtless yourself have, that when Lord Theign backs a fellow —!'

He left the obvious moral for her to take up – which she did, but all interrogatively. 'The fellow at once comes in for something awfully good?'

'I don't in the least mind your laughing at me,' Lord John returned, 'for when I put him the question of the lift he'd give me by speaking to you first he bade me simply remember the complete personal liberty in which he leaves you, and yet which doesn't come – take my word!' said the young man sagely – 'from his being at all indifferent.'

'No,' she answered – 'father isn't indifferent. But father's "great."'

'Great indeed!' – her friend took it as with full comprehension. This appeared not to prevent, however, a second and more anxious thought. 'Too great for *you?*'

'Well, he makes me feel – even as his daughter – my extreme comparative smallness.'

It was easy, Lord John indicated, to see what she meant. 'He's a *grand seigneur*, and a serious one – that's what he is: the very type and model of it, down to the ground. So you can imagine,' the young man said, 'what he makes me feel – most of all when he's so awfully good-natured to me. His being as "great" as you say and yet backing me – such as I am! – doesn't *that* strike you as a good note for me, the best you could possibly require? For he really *would* like what I propose to you.'

She might have been noting, while she thought, that he had risen to ingenuity, to fineness, on the wings of his argument;

under the effect of which her reply had the air of a concession. 'Yes – he would like it.'

'Then he *has* spoken to you?' her suitor eagerly asked.

'He hasn't needed – he has ways of letting one know.'

'Yes, yes, he has ways; all his own – like everything else he has. He's wonderful.'

She fully agreed. 'He's wonderful.'

The tone of it appeared somehow to shorten at once for Lord John the rest of his approach to a conclusion. 'So you do see your way?'

'Ah –!' she said with a quick sad shrinkage.

'I mean,' her visitor hastened to explain, 'if he does put it to you as the very best idea he has for you. When he does that – as I believe him ready to do – will you really and fairly listen to him? I'm certain, honestly, that when you know me better –!' His confidence in short donned a bravery.

'I've been feeling this quarter of an hour,' the girl returned, 'that I do know you better.'

'Then isn't that all I want? – unless indeed I ought perhaps to ask rather if it isn't all *you* do! At any rate,' said Lord John, 'I may see you again here?'

She waited a moment. 'You must have patience with me.'

'I *am* having it. But *after* your father's appeal.'

'Well,' she said, 'that must come first.'

'Then you won't dodge it?'

She looked at him straight. 'I don't dodge, Lord John.'

He admired the manner of it. 'You look awfully handsome as you say so – and you see what *that* does to me.' As to attentuate a little the freedom of which he went on: 'May I fondly hope that if Lady Imber too should wish to put in another word for me —?'

'Will I listen to her?' – it brought Lady Grace straight down. 'No, Lord John, let me tell you at once that I'll do nothing of the sort. Kitty's quite another affair, and I never listen to her a bit more than I can help.'

Lord John appeared to feel, on this, that he mustn't too easily, in honour, abandon a person who had presented herself to him as an ally. 'Ah, you strike me as a little hard on her. Your father himself – in his looser moments! – takes pleasure in what she says.'

Our young woman's eyes, as they rested on him after this remark, had no mercy for its extreme feebleness. 'If you mean that she's the most reckless rattle one knows, and that she never looks so beautiful as when she's at her worst, and that, always clever for where she makes out her interest, she has learnt to "get round" him till he only sees through her eyes – if you mean *that* I understand you perfectly. But even if you think me horrid for reflecting so on my nearest and dearest, it's not on the side on which he has most confidence in his elder daughter that his youngest is moved to have most confidence in *him*.'

Lord John stared as if she had shaken some odd bright fluttering object in his face; but then recovering himself: 'He hasn't perhaps an absolutely boundless confidence —'

'In any one in the world but himself?' – she had taken him straight up. 'He hasn't indeed, and that's what we must come to; so that even if he likes you as much as you doubtless very justly feel, it won't be because you are right about your being nice, but because *he* is!'

'You mean that if I were wrong about it he would still insist that he isn't?'

Lady Grace was indeed sure. 'Absolutely – if he had begun so! He began so with Kitty – that is with allowing her everything.'

Lord John appeared struck. 'Yes – and he still allows her two thousand.'

'I'm glad to hear it – she has never told me how much!' the girl undisguisedly smiled.

'Then perhaps I oughtn't!' – he glowed with the light of contrition.

'Well, you can't help it now,' his companion remarked with amusement.

'You mean that he ought to allow *you* as much?' Lord John inquired. 'I'm sure you're right, and that he will,' he continued quite as in good faith; 'but I want you to understand that I don't care in the least what it may be!'

The subject of his suit took the longest look at him she had taken yet. 'You're very good to say so!'

If this was ironic the touch fell short, thanks to his perception that they had practically just ceased to be alone. They were in presence of a third figure, who had arrived from the terrace, but whose approach to them was not so immediate as to deprive Lord John of time for another question. 'Will you let *him* tell you, at all events, how good he thinks me? – and then let me come back and have it from you again?'

Lady Grace's answer to this was to turn, as he drew nearer, to the person by whom they were now joined. 'Lord John desires you should tell me, father, how good you think him.'

'"Good," my dear? – good for what?' said Lord Theign a trifle absurdly, but looking from one of them to the other.'

'I feel I must ask *him* to tell you.'

'Then I shall give him a chance – as I should particularly like you to go back and deal with those overwhelming children.'

'Ah, they don't overwhelm *you*, father!'– the girl put it with some point.

'If you mean to say I overwhelmed *them*, I dare say I did,' he replied –'from my view of that vast collective gape of six hundred painfully plain and perfectly expressionless faces. But that was only for the time: I pumped advice – oh *such* advice!

– and they held the large bucket as still as my pet pointer, when I scratch him, holds his back. The bucket, under the stream —'

'Was bound to overflow?' Lady Grace suggested.

'Well, the strong recoil of the wave of intelligence has been not unnaturally followed by the formidable break. You must really,' Lord Theign insisted, 'go and deal with it.'

His daughter's smile, for all this, was perceptibly cold. 'You work people up, father, and then leave others to let them down.'

'The two things,' he promptly replied, 'require different natures.' To which he simply added, as with the habit of authority, though not of harshness, 'Go!'

It was absolute and she yielded; only pausing an instant to look as with a certain gathered meaning from one of the men to the other. Faintly and resignedly sighing she passed away to the terrace and disappeared.

'The nature that *can* let you down – I rather like it, you know!' Lord John threw off. Which, for an airy elegance in them, were perhaps just slightly rash words – his companion gave him so sharp a look as the two were left together.

VI

Face to face with his visitor the master of Dedborough betrayed the impression his daughter appeared to have given him. 'She didn't want to go?' And then before Lord John could reply: 'What the deuce is the matter with her?'

Lord John took his time. 'I think perhaps a little Mr Crimble.'

'And who the deuce is a little Mr Crimble?'

'A young man who was just with her – and whom she appears to have invited.'

'Where is he then?' Lord Theign demanded.

'Off there among the pictures – which he seems partly to have come for.'

'Oh!' – it made his lordship easier. 'Then he's all right – on such a day.'

His companion could none the less just wonder. 'Hadn't Lady Grace told you?'

'That he was coming? Not that I remember.' But Lord Theign, perceptibly preoccupied, made nothing of this. 'We've had other fish to fry, and you know the freedom I allow her.'

His friend had a vivid gesture. 'My dear man, I only ask to profit by it!' With which there might well have been in Lord John's face a light of comment on the pretension in such a quarter to allow freedom.

Yet it was a pretension that Lord Theign sustained – as to show himself far from all bourgeois narrowness. 'She has her friends by the score – at this time of day.' There was clearly a claim here also – to *know* the time of day. 'But in the matter of friends where, by the way, is your own – of whom I've but just heard?'

'Oh, off there among the pictures too; so they'll have met and taken care of each other.' Accounting for this inquirer would be clearly the least of Lord John's difficulties. 'I mustn't appear to Bender to have failed him; but I must at once let you know, before I join him, that, seizing my opportunity, I have just very definitely, in fact very pressingly, spoken to Lady Grace. It hasn't been perhaps,' he continued, 'quite the pick of a chance; but that seemed never to come, and if I'm not too fondly mistaken, at any rate, she listened to me without abhorrence. Only I've led her to expect – for our case – that you'll be so good, without loss of time, as to say the clinching word to her yourself.'

'Without loss, you mean, of – a – my daughter's time?' Lord Theign, confessedly and amiably interested, had accepted these intimations – yet with the very blandness that was not accessible to hustling and was never forgetful of its standing privilege of criticism. He had come in from his public duty, a few minutes before, somewhat flushed and blown; but that had presently dropped – to the effect, we should have guessed, of his appearing to Lord John at least as cool as the occasion required. His appearance, we ourselves certainly should have felt, was in all respects charming – with the great note of it the beautiful restless, almost suspicious, challenge to you, on the part of deep and mixed things in him, his pride and his shyness, his conscience, his taste and his temper, to deny that he was admirably simple. Obviously, at this rate, he had a passion for simplicity – simplicity, above all, of relation with you, and would show you, with the last subtlety of displeasure, his impatience of your attempting anything more with himself.

With such an ideal of decent ease he would, confound you, 'sink' a hundred other attributes – or the recognition at least and the formulation of them – that you might abjectly have taken for granted in him: just to show you that in a beastly vulgar age you had, and small wonder, a beastly vulgar imagination. He sank thus, surely, in defiance of insistent vulgarity, half his consciousness of his advantages, flattering himself that mere facility and amiability, a true effective, a positively ideal suppression of reference in any one to anything that might complicate, alone floated above. This would be quite his religion, you might infer – to cause his hands to ignore in whatever contact any opportunity, however convenient, for an unfair pull. Which habit it was that must have produced in him a sort of ripe and radiant fairness; if it be allowed us, that is, to figure in so shining an air a nobleman of fifty-three, of an undecided rather than a certified frame or outline, of a head thinly though neatly covered and not measureably massive, of an almost trivial freshness, of a face marked but by a fine inwrought line or two and lighted by a merely charming expression. You might somehow have traced back the whole character so presented to an ideal privately invoked – that of his establishing in the formal garden of his suffered greatness such easy seats and short perspectives, such winding paths and natural-looking waters, as would mercifully break up the scale. You would perhaps indeed have reflected at the same time that the thought of so much mercy was almost more than anything else the thought of a great option and a great margin – in fine of fifty alternatives. Which remarks of ours, however, leave his lordship with his last immediate question on his hands.

'Well, yes – *that*, of course, in all propriety,' his companion has meanwhile replied to it. 'But I was thinking a little, you understand, of the importance of our own time.'

Divinably Lord Theign put himself out less, as we may say, for the comparatively matter-of-course haunters of his garden than for interlopers even but slightly accredited. He seemed thus not at all to strain to 'understand' in this particular connection – it would be his familiarly amusing friend Lord John, clearly, who must do most of the work for him. ' "Our own" in the sense of yours and mine?'

'Of yours and mine and Lady Imber's, yes – and a good bit, last not least, in that of my watching and waiting mother's.' This struck no prompt spark of apprehension from his listener, so that Lord John went on: 'The last thing she did this morning was to remind me, with her fine old frankness, that she would like to learn without more delay where, on the whole question, she *is*, don't you know? What she put to me' – the younger man felt his ground a little, but proceeded further – 'what she put to me, with her rather grand way of looking *all* questions straight in the face, you see, was: Do we or don't we, decidedly, take up practically her very handsome offer – "very handsome" being, I mean, what *she* calls it; though it strikes even me too, you know, as rather decent.'

Lord Theign at this point resigned himself to know. 'Kitty has of course rubbed into me how decent she herself finds it. She hurls herself again on me – successfully! – for everything, and it suits her down to the ground. She pays her beastly debt – that is, I mean to say,' and he took himself up, though it was scarce more than perfunctory, 'discharges her obligations – by her sister's fair hand; not to mention a few other trifles for which I naturally provide.'

Lord John, a little unexpectedly to himself on the defensive, was yet but briefly at a loss. 'Of course we take into account, don't we? not only the fact of my mother's desire (intended, I assure you, to be most flattering) that Lady Grace shall enter our family with all honours, but her expressed readiness to facilitate the thing by an understanding over and above —'

'Over and above Kitty's release from her damnable payment?' — Lord Theign reached out to what his guest had left rather in the air. 'Of course we take *everything* into account — or I shouldn't, my dear fellow, be discussing with you at all a business one or two of whose aspects so little appeal to me: especially as there's nothing, you easily conceive, that a daughter of mine can come in for by entering even your family, or any other (*as* a family) that she wouldn't be quite as sure of by just staying in her own. The Duchess's idea, at any rate, if I've followed you, is that if Grace does accept you she settles on you twelve thousand; with the condition —'

Lord John was already all there. 'Definitely, yes, of your settling the equivalent on Lady Grace.'

'And what do you call the equivalent of twelve thousand?'

'Why, tacked on to a value so great and so charming as Lady Grace herself, I dare say such a sum as nine or ten would serve.'

'And where the mischief, if you please, at this highly inconvenient time, am I to pick up nine or ten thousand?'

Lord John declined, with a smiling, a fairly irritating eye for his friend's general resources, to consider that question seriously. 'Surely you can have no difficulty whatever —!'

'Why not? — when you can see for yourself that I've had this year to let poor dear old Hill Street! Do you call it the moment for me to have *liked* to see myself all but cajoled into planking down even such a matter as the very much lower figure of Kitty's horrid incubus?'

'Ah, but the inducement and the *quid pro quo*,' Lord John brightly indicated, 'are here much greater! In the case you speak of you will only have removed the incubus — which, I grant you, she must and you must feel as horrid. In this other you pacify Lady Imber *and* marry Lady Grace: marry her to a man who has set his heart on her and of whom she has just expressed – to himself – a very kind and very high opinion.'

'She has expressed a very high opinion of you?' – Lord Theign scarce glowed with credulity.

But the younger man held his ground. 'She has told me she thoroughly likes me and that – though a fellow feels an ass repeating such things – she thinks me perfectly charming.'

'A tremendous creature, eh, all round? Then,' said Lord Theign, 'what does she want more?'

'She very possibly wants nothing – but I'm to that beastly degree, you see,' his visitor patiently explained, 'in the cleft stick of my fearfully positive mother's wants. Those are her "terms," and I don't mind saying that they're most disagreeable to me – I quite hate 'em: there! Only I think it makes a jolly difference that I wouldn't touch 'em with a long pole if my personal feeling – in respect to Lady Grace – wasn't so immensely enlisted.'

'I assure you I'd chuck 'em out of window, my boy, if I didn't believe you'd be really good to her,' Lord Theign returned with the properest spirit.

It only encouraged his companion. 'You *will* just tell her then, now and here, how good you honestly believe I shall be?'

This appeal required a moment – a longer look at him. 'You truly hold that that friendly guarantee, backed by my parental weight, will do your job?'

'That's the conviction I entertain.'

Lord Theign thought again. 'Well, even if your conviction's just, that still doesn't tell me into which of my very empty pockets it will be of the least use for me to fumble.'

'Oh,' Lord John laughed, 'when a man has such a tremendous assortment of breeches –!' He pulled up, however, as, in his motion, his eye caught the great vista of the open rooms.

'If it's a question of pockets – and what's *in* 'em – here precisely is my man!' This personage had come back from his tour of observation and was now, on the threshold of the hall, exhibited to Lord Theign as well. Lord John's welcome was warm. 'I've had awfully to fail you, Mr Bender, but I was on the point of joining you. Let me, however, still better, introduce you to our host.'

VII

Mr Bender indeed, formidably advancing, scarce had use for this assistance. 'Happy to meet you – especially in your beautiful home, Lord Theign.' To which he added while the master of Dedborough stood good-humouredly passive to his approach: 'I've been round, by your kind permission and the light of nature, and haven't required support; though if I had there's a gentleman there who seemed prepared to allow me any amount.' Mr Bender, out of his abundance, evoked as by a suggestive hand this contributory figure. 'A young, spare, nervous gentleman with eye-glasses – I guess he's an author. A friend of yours too?' he asked of Lord John.

The answer was prompt and emphatic. 'No, the gentleman is no friend at all of mine, Mr Bender.'

'A friend of my daughter's,' Lord Theign easily explained. 'I hope they're looking after him.'

'Oh, they took care he had tea and bread and butter to any extent; and were so good as to move something,' Mr Bender conscientiously added, 'so that he could get up on a chair and see straight into the Moretto.'

This was a touch, however, that appeared to affect Lord John unfavourably. 'Up on a chair? I say!'

Mr Bender took another view. 'Why, I got right up myself – a little more and I'd almost have begun to paw it! He got me quite interested' – the proprietor of the picture would perhaps

care to know – 'in that Moretto.' And it was on these lines that
Mr Bender continued to advance. 'I take it that your biggest
value, however, Lord Theign, is your splendid Sir Joshua.
Our friend there has a great deal to say about that too – but it
didn't lead to our moving any more furniture.' On which he
paused as to enjoy, with a show of his fine teeth, his host's
reassurance. 'It *has* yet, my impression of that picture, sir, led
to something else. Are you prepared, Lord Theign, to entertain
a proposition?'

Lord Theign met Mr Bender's eyes while this inquirer left
these few portentous words to speak for themselves. 'To the
effect that I part to you with "The Beautiful Duchess of Waterbridge"? No, Mr Bender, such a proposition would leave me
intensely cold.'

Lord John had meanwhile had a more headlong cry. 'My
dear Bender, I *envy* you!'

'I guess you don't envy me,' his friend serenely replied, 'as
much as I envy Lord Theign.' And then while Mr Bender and
the latter continued to face each other searchingly and firmly:
'What I allude to is an overture of a strong and simple stamp
– such as perhaps would shed a softer light on the difficulties
raised by association and attachment. I've had some experience
of first shocks, and I'd be glad to meet you as man to man.'

Mr Bender was, quite clearly, all genial and all sincere; he
intended no irony and used, consciously, no great freedom.
Lord Theign, not less evidently, saw this, and it permitted him
amusement. 'As rich man to poor man is how I'm to understand
it? For me to meet *you*,' he added, 'I should have to be tempted
– and I'm not even temptable. So there we are,' he blandly
smiled.

His blandness appeared even for a moment to set an example
to Lord John. ' "The Beautiful Duchess of Waterbridge," Mr
Bender, is a golden apple of one of those great family trees of

which respectable people don't lop off the branches whose venerable shade, in this garish and denuded age, they so much enjoy.'

Mr Bender looked at him as if he had cut some irrelevant caper. 'Then if they don't sell their ancestors where in the world are all the ancestors bought?'

'Doesn't it for the moment sufficiently answer your question,' Lord Theign asked, 'that they're definitely not bought at Dedborough?'

'Why,' said Mr Bender with a wealthy patience, 'you talk as if it were my interest to be *reasonable* – which shows how little you understand. I'd be ashamed – with the lovely ideas I have – if I didn't make you kick.' And his sturdy smile for it all fairly proclaimed his faith. 'Well, I guess I can wait!'

This again in turn visibly affected Lord John: marking the moment from which he, in spite of his cultivated levity, allowed an intenser and more sustained look to keep straying toward their host. 'Mr Bender's bound to *have* something!'

It was even as if after a minute Lord Theign had been reached by his friend's mute pressure. '"Something"?'

'Something, Mr Bender?' Lord John insisted.

It made their visitor rather sharply fix him. 'Why, have *you* an interest, Lord John?'

This personage, though undisturbed by the challenge, if such it was, referred it to Lord Theign. 'Do you authorize me to speak – a little – as if I have an interest?'

Lord Theign gave the appeal – and the speaker – a certain attention, and then appeared rather sharply to turn away from them. 'My dear fellow, you may amuse yourself at my expense as you like!'

'Oh, I don't mean at your expense,' Lord John laughed – 'I mean at Mr Bender's!'

'Well, go ahead, Lord John,' said that gentleman, always

easy, but always too, as you would have felt, aware of everything – 'go ahead, but don't sweetly hope to create in me any desire that doesn't already exist in the germ. The attempt has often been made, over here – has in fact been organized on a considerable scale; but I guess I've got some peculiarity, for it doesn't seem as if the thing could be done. If the germ *is* there, on the other hand,' Mr Bender conceded, 'it develops independently of all encouragement.'

Lord John communicated again as in a particular sense with Lord Theign. 'He thinks I really mean to *offer* him something!'

Lord Theign, who seemed to wish to advertise a degree of detachment from the issue, or from any other such, strolled off, in his restlessness, toward the door that opened to the terrace, only stopping on his way to light a cigarette from a matchbox on a small table. It was but after doing so that he made the remark: 'Ah, Mr Bender may easily be too much for you!'

'That makes me the more sorry, sir,' said his visitor, 'not to have been enough for *you!*'

'I risk it, at any rate,' Lord John went on – 'I put you, Bender, the question of whether you wouldn't "love," as you say, to acquire that Moretto.'

Mr Bender's large face had a commensurate gaze. 'As I say? I haven't said anything of the sort!'

'But you do "love," you know,' Lord John slightly over-grimaced.

'I don't when I don't want to. I'm different from most people – I can love or not as I like. The trouble with that Moretto,' Mr Bender continued, 'is that it ain't what I'm after.'

His 'after' had somehow, for the ear, the vividness of a sharp whack on the resisting surface of things, and was concerned doubtless in Lord John's speaking again across to their host. 'The worst he can do for me, you see, is to refuse it.'

Lord Theign, who practically had his back turned and was fairly dandling about in his impatience, tossed out to the terrace the cigarette he had but just lighted. Yet he faced round to reply: 'It's the very first time in the history of this house (a long one, Mr Bender) that a picture, or anything else in it, has been offered —!'

It was not imperceptible that even if he hadn't dropped Mr Bender mightn't have been markedly impressed. 'Then it must be the very first time such an offer has failed.'

'Oh, it isn't that we in the least press it!' Lord Theign quite naturally laughed.

'Ah, I beg your pardon – I press it very hard!' And Lord John, as taking from his face and manner a cue for further humorous license, went so far as to emulate, though sympathetically enough, their companion's native form. 'You don't mean to say you don't feel the interest of that Moretto?'

Mr Bender, quietly confident, took his time to reply. 'Well, if you had seen me up on that chair you'd have thought I did.'

'Then you must have stepped down from the chair properly impressed.'

'I stepped down quite impressed with that young man.'

'Mr Crimble?' – it came after an instant to Lord John. 'With *his* opinion, really? Then I hope he's aware of the picture's value.'

'You had better ask him,' Mr Bender observed.

'Oh, we don't depend here on the Mr Crimbles!' Lord John returned.

Mr Bender took a longer look at him. 'Are you aware of the value yourself?'

His friend resorted again, as for the amusement of the thing, to their entertainer. 'Am I aware of the value of the Moretto?'

Lord Theign, who had meanwhile lighted another cigarette, appeared, a bit extravagantly smoking, to wish to put an end to his effect of hovering aloof. 'That question needn't trouble us – when I see how much Mr Bender himself knows about it.'

'Well, Lord Theign, I only know what that young man puts it at.' And then as the others waited, 'Ten thousand,' said Mr Bender.

'Ten thousand?' The owner of the work showed no emotion.

'Well,' said Lord John again in Mr Bender's style, 'what's the matter with ten thousand?'

The subject of his gay tribute considered. 'There's nothing the matter with ten thousand.'

'Then,' Lord Theign asked, 'is there anything the matter with the picture?'

'Yes, sir – I guess there is.'

It gave an upward push to his lordship's eyebrows. 'But what in the world —?'

'Well, that's just the question!'

The eyebrows continued to rise. 'Does he pretend there's a question of whether it *is* a Moretto?'

'That's what he was up there trying to find out.'

'But if the value's, according to himself, ten thousand —?'

'Why, of course,' said Mr Bender, 'it's a fine work anyway.'

'Then,' Lord Theign brought good-naturedly out, 'what's the matter with *you*, Mr Bender?'

That gentleman was perfectly clear. 'The matter with me, Lord Theign, is that I've no use for a ten thousand picture.'

'"No use"?' – the expression had an oddity. 'But what's it your idea to do with such things?'

'I mean,' Mr Bender explained, 'that a picture of that rank is not what I'm after.'

'The figure,' said his noble host – speaking thus, under pressure, commercially – 'is beyond what you see your way to?'

But Lord John had jumped at the truth. 'The matter with Mr Bender is that he sees his way much further.'

'Further?' their companion echoed.

'The matter with Mr Bender is that he wants to give millions.'

Lord Theign sounded this abyss with a smile. 'Well, there would be no difficulty about *that*, I think!'

'Ah,' said his guest, 'you know the basis, sir, on which I'm ready to pay.'

'On the basis then of the Sir Joshua,' Lord John inquired, 'how far would you go?'

Mr Bender indicated by a gesture that on a question reduced to a moiety by its conditional form he could give but semi-satisfaction. 'Well, I'd go all the way.'

'He wants, you see,' Lord John elucidated, 'an *ideally* expensive thing.'

Lord Theign appeared to decide after a moment to enter into the pleasant spirit of this; which he did by addressing his younger friend. 'Then why shouldn't I make even the Moretto as expensive as he desires?'

'Because you can't do violence to *that* master's natural modesty,' Mr Bender declared before Lord John had time to speak. And conscious at this moment of the reappearance of his fellow-explorer, he at once supplied a further light. 'I guess this gentleman at any rate can tell you.'

VIII

Hugh Crimble had come back from his voyage of discovery, and it was visible as he stood there flushed and quite radiant that he had caught in his approach Lord Theign's last inquiry and Mr Bender's reply to it. You would have imputed to him on the spot the lively possession of a new idea, the sustaining sense of a message important enough to justify his irruption. He looked from one to the other of the three men, scattered a little by the sight of him, but attached eyes of recognition then to Lord Theign's, whom he remained an instant longer communicatively smiling at. After which, as you might have gathered, he all confidently plunged, taking up the talk where the others had left it. 'I should say, Lord Theign, if you'll allow me, in regard to what you appear to have been discussing, that it depends a good deal on just that question – of what your Moretto, at any rate, may be presumed or proved to "be". Let me thank you,' he cheerfully went on, 'for your kind leave to go over your treasures.'

The personage he so addressed was, as we know, nothing if not generally affable; yet if that was just then apparent it was through a shade of coolness for the slightly heated familiarity of so plain, or at least so free, a young man in eye-glasses, now for the first time definitely apprehended. 'Oh, I've scarcely "treasures" – but I've some things of interest.'

Hugh, however, entering the opulent circle, as it were,

clearly took account of no breath of a chill. 'I think possible, my lord, that you've a great treasure – if you've really so high a rarity as a splendid Mantovano.'

'A "Mantovano"?' You wouldn't have been sure that his lordship didn't pronounce the word for the first time in his life.

'There have been supposed to be only *seven* real examples about the world; so that if by an extraordinary chance you find yourself the possessor of a magnificent eighth —'

But Lord John had already broken in. 'Why, there you *are*, Mr Bender!'

'Oh, Mr Bender, with whom I've made acquaintance,' Hugh returned, 'was there as it began to work in me —'

'That your Moretto, Lord Theign' – Mr Bender took their informant up – 'isn't, after all, a Moretto at all.' And he continued amusedly to Hugh: 'It began to work in you, sir, like very strong drink!'

'Do I understand you to suggest,' Lord Theign asked of the startling young man, 'that my precious picture isn't genuine?'

Well, Hugh knew exactly what he suggested. 'As a picture, Lord Theign, as a great portrait, one of the most genuine things in Europe. But it strikes me as probable that from far back – for reasons! – there has been a wrong attribution; that the work has been, in other words, traditionally, obstinately miscalled. It has passed for a Moretto, and at first I quite took it for one; but I suddenly, as I looked and looked and saw and saw, began to doubt, and now I know *why* I doubted.'

Lord Theign had during this speech kept his eyes on the ground; but he raised them to Mr Crimble's almost palpitating presence for the remark: 'I'm bound to say that I hope you've some very good grounds!'

'I've three or four, Lord Theign; they seem to me of the best

63

– as yet. They made me wonder and wonder – and then light splendidly broke.'

His lordship didn't stint his attention. 'Reflected, you mean, from *other* Mantovanos – that I don't know?'

'I mean from those I know myself,' said Hugh; 'and I mean from fine analogies with one in particular.'

'Analogies that in all these years, these centuries, have so remarkably not been noticed?'

'Well,' Hugh competently explained, 'they're a sort of thing the very sense of, the value and meaning of, are a highly modern – in fact a quite recent growth.'

Lord John at this professed with cordiality that he at least quite understood. 'Oh, we know a lot more about our pictures and things than ever our ancestors did!'

'Well, I guess it's enough for *me*,' Mr Bender contributed, 'that your ancestors knew enough to get 'em!'

'Ah, that doesn't go so far,' cried Hugh, 'unless we ourselves know enough to keep 'em!'

The words appeared to quicken in a manner Lord Theign's view of the speaker. 'Were *your* ancestors, Mr Crimble, great collectors?'

Arrested, it might be, in his general assurance, Hugh wondered and smiled. 'Mine – collectors? Oh, I'm afraid I haven't any – to speak of. Only it has seemed to me for a long time,' he added, 'that on that head we should all feel together.'

Lord Theign looked for a moment as if these were rather large presumptions; then he put them in their place a little curtly. 'It's one thing to keep our possessions for ourselves – it's another to keep them for other people.'

'Well,' Hugh good-humouredly returned, 'I'm perhaps not so absolutely sure of myself, if you press me, as that I sha'n't be glad of a higher and wiser opinion – I mean than my own. It would be awfully interesting, if you'll allow me to say so, to have the judgment of one or two of the great men.'

'You're not yourself, Mr Crimble, one of the great men?' his host asked with tempered irony.

'Well, I guess he's going to be, anyhow,' Mr Bender cordially struck in; 'and this remarkable exhibition of intelligence may just let him loose on the world, mayn't it?'

'Thank you, Mr Bender!' – and Hugh obviously tried to look neither elated nor snubbed. 'I've too much still to learn, but I'm learning every day, and I shall have learnt immensely this afternoon.'

'Pretty well at my expense, however,' Lord Theign laughed, 'if you demolish a name we've held for generations so dear.'

'You may have held the name dear, my lord,' his young critic answered; 'but my whole point is that, if I'm right, you've held the picture itself cheap.'

'Because a Mantovano,' said Lord John, 'is so much greater a value?'

Hugh met his eyes a moment. 'Are you talking of values pecuniary?'

'What values are *not* pecuniary?'

Hugh might, during his hesitation, have been imagined to stand off a little from the question. 'Well, some things have in a higher degree that one, and some have the associational or the factitious, and some the clear artistic.'

'And some,' Mr Bender opined, 'have them *all* – in the highest degree. But what you mean,' he went on, 'is that a Mantovano would come higher under the hammer than a Moretto?'

'Why, sir,' the young man returned, 'there aren't any, as I've just stated, *to* "come." I account – or I easily can – for every one of the very small number.'

'Then do you consider that you account for this one?'

'I believe I shall if you'll give me time.'

'Oh, time!' Mr Bender impatiently sighed. 'But we'll give you all we've got – only I guess it isn't much.' And he appeared freely to invite their companions to join in this estimate. They listened to him, however, they watched him, for the moment, but in silence, and with the next he had gone on: 'How much higher – if your idea *is* correct about it – would Lord Theign's picture come?'

Hugh turned to that nobleman. 'Does Mr Bender mean come to *him*, my lord?'

Lord Theign looked again hard at Hugh, and then harder than he had done yet at his other invader. 'I don't know *what* Mr Bender means!' With which he turned off.

'Well, I guess I mean that it would come higher to me than to any one! But how *much* higher?' the American continued to Hugh.

'How much higher to *you*?'

'Oh, I can size *that*. How much higher as a Mantovano?'

Unmistakably – for us at least – our young man was gaining time; he had the instinct of circumspection and delay. 'To any one?'

'To any one.'

'Than as a Moretto?' Hugh continued.

It even acted on Lord John's nerves. 'That's what we're talking about – really!'

But Hugh still took his ease; as if, with his eyes first on Bender and then on Lord Theign, whose back was practically presented, he were covertly studying signs. 'Well,' he presently said, 'in view of the very great interest combined with the very great rarity, more than – ah more than can be estimated off-hand.'

It made Lord Theign turn round. 'But a fine Moretto has a very great rarity and a very great interest.'

'Yes – but not on the whole the same amount of either.'

'No, not on the whole the same amount of either!' – Mr Bender judiciously echoed it. 'But how,' he freely pursued, 'are you going to find out?'

'Have I your permission, Lord Theign,' Hugh brightly asked, 'to attempt to find out?'

The question produced on his lordship's part a visible, a natural anxiety. 'What would it be your idea then to *do* with my property?'

'Nothing at all here – it could all be done, I think, at Verona. What besets, what quite haunts me,' Hugh explained, 'is the vivid image of a Mantovano – one of the glories of the short list – in a private collection in that place. The conviction grows in me that the two portraits must be of the same original. In fact I'll bet my head,' the young man quite ardently wound up, 'that the wonderful subject of the Verona picture, a very great person clearly, is none other than the very great person of yours.'

Lord Theign had listened with interest. 'Mayn't he be that and yet from another hand?'

'It isn't another hand' – oh Hugh was quite positive. 'It's the hand of the very same painter.'

'How can you prove it's the same?'

'Only by the most intimate internal evidence, I admit – and evidence that of course has to be estimated.'

'Then who,' Lord Theign asked, 'is to estimate it?'

'Well,' – Hugh was all ready – 'will you let Pappendick, one of the first authorities in Europe, a good friend of mine, in fact more or less my master, and who is generally to be found at Brussels? I happen to know he knows your picture – he once spoke to me of it; and he'll go and look again at the Verona one, he'll go and judge our issue, if I apply to him, in the light of certain new tips that I shall be able to give him.'

Lord Theign appeared to wonder. 'If you "apply" to him?'

'Like a shot, I believe, if I ask it of him – as a service.'

'A service to *you?* He'll be very obliging,' his lordship smiled.

'Well, I've obliged *him!*' Hugh readily retorted.

'The obligation will be to *me*' – Lord Theign spoke more formally.

'Well, the satisfaction,' said Hugh, 'will be to all of us. The things Pappendick has seen he intensely, ineffaceably keeps in mind, to every detail; so that he'll tell me – as no one else really can – if the Verona man is *your* man.'

'But then,' asked Mr Bender, 'we've got to believe anyway what he says?'

'The market,' said Lord John with emphasis, 'would have to believe it – that's the point.'

'Oh,' Hugh returned lightly, 'the market will have nothing to do with it, I hope; but I think you'll feel when he has spoken that you really know where you are.'

Mr Bender couldn't doubt of that. 'Oh, if he gives us a bigger thing we won't complain. Only, how long will it take him to get there? I want him to start right away.'

'Well, as I'm sure he'll be deeply interested —'

'We *may*' – Mr Bender took it straight up – 'get news next week?'

Hugh addressed his reply to Lord Theign; it was already a little too much as if he and the American between them were snatching the case from that possessor's hands. 'The day I hear from Pappendick you shall have a full report. And,' he conscientiously added, 'if I'm proved to have been unfortunately wrong —!'

His lordship easily pointed the moral. 'You'll have caused me some inconvenience.'

'Of course I shall,' the young man unreservedly agreed – 'like a wanton meddling ass!' His candour, his freedom had decidedly a note of their own. 'But my conviction, after those moments with your picture, was too strong for me not to speak – and, since you allow it, I face the danger and risk the test.'

'I allow it of course in the form of business.'

This produced in Hugh a certain blankness. '"Business"?'

'If I consent to the inquiry I pay for the inquiry.'

Hugh demurred. 'Even if I turn out mistaken?'

'You make me in any event your proper charge.'

The young man thought again, and then as for vague accommodation: 'Oh, my charge won't be high!'

'Ah,' Mr Bender protested, 'it ought to be handsome if the thing's marked *up!*' After which he looked at his watch. 'But I guess I've got to go, Lord Theign, though your lovely old Duchess – for it's to *her* I've lost my heart – does cry out for me again.'

'You'll find her then still there,' Lord John observed with emphasis, but with his eyes for the time on Lord Theign; 'and if you want another look at her I'll presently come and take one too.'

'I'll order your car to the garden-front,' Lord Theign added to this; 'you'll reach it from the saloon, but I'll see you again first.'

Mr Bender glared as with the round full force of his pair of motor lamps. 'Well, if you're ready to talk about anything, I am. Good-bye, Mr Crimble.'

'Good-bye, Mr Bender.' But Hugh, addressing their host while his fellow-guest returned to the saloon, broke into the familiarity of confidence. 'As if you *could* be ready to "talk"!'

This produced on the part of the others present a mute exchange that could only have denoted surprise at all the irrepressible young outsider thus projected upon them took for granted. 'I've an idea,' said Lord John to his friend, 'that you're quite ready to talk with *me*.'

Hugh then, with his appetite so richly quickened, could but rejoice. 'Lady Grace spoke to me of things in the library.'

'You'll find it *that* way' – Lord Theign gave the indication.

'Thanks,' said Hugh elatedly, and hastened away.

Lord John, when he had gone, found relief in a quick comment. 'Very sharp, no doubt – but he wants taking down.'

The master of Dedborough wouldn't have put it so crudely, but the young expert did bring certain things home. 'The people my daughters, in the exercise of a wild freedom, do pick up —!'

'Well, don't you see that all you've got to do – on the question we're dealing with – is to claim your very own wild freedom? Surely I'm right in feeling you,' Lord John further remarked, 'to have jumped at once to my idea that Bender is heaven-sent – and at what they call the psychologic moment, don't they? – to point that moral. Why look anywhere else for a sum of money that – smaller or greater – you can find with perfect ease in that extraordinarily bulging pocket?'

Lord Theign, slowly pacing the hall again, threw up his hands. 'Ah, with "perfect ease" can scarcely be said!'

'Why not? – when he absolutely thrusts his dirty dollars down your throat.'

'Oh, I'm not talking of ease to *him*,' Lord Theign returned – 'I'm talking of ease to myself. I shall have to make a sacrifice.'

'Why not then – for so great a convenience – gallantly make it?'

'Ah, my dear chap, if you want me to sell my Sir Joshua —!'

But the horror in the words said enough, and Lord John felt its chill. 'I don't make a point of that – God forbid! But there are other things to which the objection wouldn't apply.'

'You see how it applies – in the case of the Moretto – for

him. A mere Moretto,' said Lord Theign, 'is too cheap – for a Yankee "on the spend."'

'Then the Mantovano wouldn't be.'

'It remains to be proved that it *is* a Mantovano.'

'Well,' said Lord John, 'go into it.'

'Hanged if I won't!' his friend broke out after a moment. 'It *would* suit me. I mean' – the explanation came after a brief intensity of thought – 'the possible size of his cheque would.'

'Oh,' said Lord John gaily, 'I guess there's no limit to the possible size of his cheque!'

'Yes, it would suit me, it would suit me!' the elder man, standing there, audibly mused. But his air changed and a lighter question came up to him as he saw his daughter reappear at the door from the terrace. 'Well, the infant horde?' he immediately put to her.

Lady Grace came in, dutifully accounting for them. 'They've marched off – in a huge procession.'

'Thank goodness! And our friends?'

'All playing tennis,' she said – 'save those who are sitting it out.' To which she added, as to explain her return: 'Mr Crimble has gone?'

Lord John took upon him to say. 'He's in the library, to which you addressed him – making discoveries.'

'Not then, I hope,' she smiled, 'to our disadvantage!'

'To your very great honour and glory.' Lord John clearly valued the effect he might produce. 'Your Moretto of Brescia – do you know what it really and spendidly is?' And then as the girl, in her surprise, but wondered: 'A Mantovano, neither more nor less. Ever so much more swagger.'

'A Mantovano?' Lady Grace echoed. 'Why, how tremendously jolly!'

Her father was struck. 'Do you know the artist – of whom I had never heard?'

'Yes, something of the little that is known.' And she rejoiced as her knowledge came to her. 'He's a tremendous swell, because, great as he was, there are but seven proved examples —'

'With this of yours,' Lord John broke in, 'there are eight.'

'Then why haven't I known about him?' Lord Theign put it as if so many other people were guilty for this.

His daughter was the first to plead for the vague body. 'Why, I suppose in order that you should have exactly this pleasure, father.'

'Oh, pleasures not desired are like acquaintances not sought – they rather bore one!' Lord Theign sighed. With which he moved away from her.

Her eyes followed him an instant – then she smiled at their guest. 'Is he bored at having the higher prize – if you're sure it is the higher?'

'Mr Crimble is sure – because if he isn't,' Lord John added, 'he's a wretch.'

'Well,' she returned, 'as he's certainly not a wretch it must be true. And fancy,' she exclaimed further, though as more particularly for herself, 'our having suddenly incurred this immense debt to him!'

'Oh, I shall pay Mr Crimble!' said her father, who had turned round.

The whole question appeared to have provoked in Lord John a rise of spirits and a flush of humour. 'Don't you let him stick it on.'

His host, however, bethinking himself, checked him. 'Go *you* to Mr Bender straight!'

Lord John saw the point. 'Yes – till he leaves. But I shall find you here, shan't I?' he asked with all earnestness of Lady Grace.

She had an hesitation, but after a look at her father she assented. 'I'll wait for you.'

'Then *à tantôt!*'[2] It made him show for happy as, waving his hand at her, he proceeded to seek Mr Bender in presence of the object that most excited that gentleman's appetite – to say nothing of the effect involved on Lord John's own.

IX

Lord Theign, when he had gone, revolved – it might have been nervously – about the place a little, but soon broke ground. 'He'll have told you, I understand, that I've promised to speak to you for him. But I understand also that he has found something to say for himself.'

'Yes, we talked – a while since,' the girl said. 'At least *he* did.'

'Then if you listened I hope you listened with a good grace.'

'Oh, he speaks very well – and I've never disliked him.'

It pulled her father up. 'Is that *all* – when I think so much of him?'

She seemed to say that she had, to her own mind, been liberal and gone far; but she waited a little. 'Do you think very, *very* much?'

'Surely I've made my good opinion clear to you!'

Again she had a pause. 'Oh yes, I've seen you like him and believe in him – and I've found him pleasant and clever.'

'He has never had,' Lord Theign more or less ingeniously explained, 'what I call a real show.' But the character under discussion could after all be summed up without searching analysis. 'I consider nevertheless that there's plenty in him.'

It was a moderate claim, to which Lady Grace might assent. 'He strikes me as naturally quick and – well, nice. But I agree with you that he hasn't had a chance.'

'Then if you can see your way by sympathy and confidence to help him to one I dare say you'll find your reward.'

For a third time she considered, as if a certain curtness in her companion's manner rather hindered, in such a question, than helped. Didn't he simplify too much, you would have felt her ask, and wasn't his visible wish for brevity of debate a sign of his uncomfortable and indeed rather irritated sense of his not making a figure in it? 'Do you desire it very particularly?' was, however, all she at last brought out.

'I should like it exceedingly – if you act from conviction. Then of course only; but of one thing I'm myself convinced – of what he thinks of yourself and feels for you.'

'Then would you mind my waiting a little?' she asked. 'I mean to be absolutely sure of myself.' After which, on his delaying to agree, she added frankly, as to help her case: 'Upon my word, father, I should like to do what would please you.'

But it determined in him a sharper impatience. 'Ah, what would please *me!* Don't put it off on "me"! Judge absolutely for yourself' – he slightly took himself up – 'in the light of my having consented to do for him what I always *hate* to do: deviate from my normal practice of never intermeddling. If I've deviated now you can judge. But to do so all round, of course, take – in reason! – your time.'

'May I ask then,' she said, 'for still a little more?'

He looked for this, verily, as if it was not in reason. 'You know,' he then returned, 'what he'll feel that a sign of.'

'Well, I'll tell him what I mean.'

'Then I'll send him to you.'

He glanced at his watch and was going, but after a 'Thanks, father,' she had stopped him. 'There's one thing more.' An embarrassment showed in her manner, but at the cost of some effect of earnest abruptness she surmounted it. 'What does your American – Mr Bender – want?'

Lord Theign plainly felt the challenge. '"My" American? He's none of mine!'

'Well then Lord John's.'

'He's none of his either – more, I mean, than any one else's. He's every one's American, literally – to all appearance; and I've not to tell *you*, surely, with the freedom of your own visitors, how people stalk in and out here.'

'No, father – certainly,' she said. 'You're splendidly generous.'

His eyes seemed rather sharply to ask her then how he could improve on that; but he added as if it were enough: 'What the man must by this time want more than anything else is his car.'

'Not then anything of ours?' she still insisted.

'Of "ours"?' he echoed with a frown. 'Are you afraid he has an eye to something of *yours*?'

'Why, if we've a new treasure – which we certainly have if we possess a Mantovano – haven't we all, even I, an immense interest in it?' And before he could answer, 'Is *that* exposed?' she asked.

Lord Theign, a little unready, cast about at his storied halls; any allusion to the 'exposure' of the objects they so solidly sheltered was obviously unpleasant to him. But then it was as if he found at a stroke both his own reassurance and his daughter's. 'How can there be a question of it when he only wants Sir Joshuas?'

'He wants ours?' the girl gasped.

'At absolutely any price.'

'But you're not,' she cried, 'discussing it?'

He hesitated as between chiding and contenting her – then he handsomely chose. 'My dear child, for what do you take me?' With which he impatiently started, through the long and stately perspective, for the saloon.

She sank into a chair when he had gone; she sat there some moments in a visible tension of thought, her hands clasped in her lap and her dropped eyes fixed and unperceiving; but she sprang up as Hugh Crimble, in search of her, again stood before her. He presented himself as with winged sandals.

'What luck to find you! I must take my spin back.'

'You've seen everything as you wished?'

'Oh,' he smiled, 'I've seen wonders.'

She showed her pleasure. 'Yes, we've got some things.'

'So Mr Bender says!' he laughed. 'You've got five or six —'

'Only five or six?' she cried in bright alarm.

'"Only"?' he continued to laugh. 'Why, that's enormous, five or six things of the first importance! But I think I ought to mention to you,' he added, 'a most barefaced "Rubens" there in the library.'

'It isn't a Rubens?'

'No more than I'm a Ruskin.'

'Then you'll brand us – expose us for it?'

'No, I'll let you off – I'll be quiet if you're good, if you go straight. I'll only hold it *in terrorem*.[3] One can't be sure in these dreadful days – that's always to remember; so that if you're not good I'll come down on you with it. But to balance against that threat,' he went on, 'I've made the very grandest find. At least I believe I have!'

She was all there for this news. 'Of the Mantovano – hidden in the other thing?'

Hugh wondered – almost as if she had been before him. 'You don't mean to say *you've* had the idea of that?'

'No, but my father has told me.'

'And is your father,' he eagerly asked, 'really gratified?'

With her conscious eyes on him – her eyes could clearly be very conscious about her father – she considered a moment. 'He always prefers old associations and appearances to new;

but I'm sure he'll resign himself if you see your way to a certainty.'

'Well, it will be a question of the weight of expert opinion that I shall invoke. But I'm not afraid,' he resolutely said, 'and I shall make the thing, from its splendid rarity, the crown and flower of your glory.'

Her serious face shone at him with a charmed gratitude. 'It's awfully beautiful then your having come to us so. It's awfully beautiful your having brought us this way, in a flash – as dropping out of a chariot of fire – more light and what you apparently feel with myself as more honour.'

'Ah, the beauty's in your having yourself done it!' he returned. He gave way to the positive joy of it. 'If I've brought the "light" and the rest – that's to say the very useful information – who in the world was it brought *me*?'

She had a gesture of protest. 'You'd have come in some other way.'

'I'm not so sure! I'm beastly shy – little as I may seem to show it: save in great causes, when I'm horridly bold and hideously offensive. Now at any rate I only know what *has* been.' She turned off for it, moving away from him as with a sense of mingled things that made for unrest; and he had the next moment grown graver under the impression. 'But does anything in it all,' he asked, 'trouble you?'

She faced about across the wider space, and there was a different note in what she brought out. 'I don't know what forces me so to *tell* you things.'

'"Tell" me?' he stared. 'Why, you've told me nothing more monstrous than that I've been welcome!'

'Well, however that may be, what did you mean just now by the chance of our not "going straight"? When you said you'd expose our bad – or is it our false? – Rubens in the event of a certain danger.'

'Oh, in the event of your ever being bribed' – he laughed again as with relief. And then as her face seemed to challenge the word: 'Why, to let anything – of your best! – ever leave Dedborough. By which I mean really of course leave the country.' She turned again on this, and something in her air made him wonder. 'I hope you don't feel there *is* such a danger? I understood from you half an hour ago that it was unthinkable.'

'Well, it *was*, to me, half an hour ago,' she said as she came nearer. 'But if it has since come up?'

'"If" it has! But *has* it? In the form of that monster? What Mr Bender wants is the great Duchess,' he recalled.

'And my father won't sell *her*? No, he won't sell the great Duchess – there I feel safe. But he greatly needs a certain sum of money – or he thinks he does – and I've just had a talk with him.'

'In which he has told you that?'

'He has told me nothing,' Lady Grace said – 'or else told me quite other things. But the more I think of them the more it comes to me that he feels urged or tempted —'

'To despoil and denude these walls?' Hugh broke in, looking about in his sharper apprehension.

'Yes, to satisfy, to save my sister. *Now* do you think our state so ideal?' she asked – but without elation for her hint of triumph.

He had no answer for this save 'Ah. but you terribly interest me. May I ask what's the matter with your sister?'

Oh, she wanted to go on straight now! 'The matter is – in the first place – that she's too dazzlingly, dreadfully beautiful.'

'More beautiful than you?' his sincerity easily risked.

'Millions of times.' Sad, almost sombre, she hadn't a shade of coquetry. 'Kitty has debts – great heaped-up gaming debts.'

'But to such amounts?'

'Incredible amounts it appears. And mountains of others too. She throws herself all on our father.'

'And he *has* to pay them? There's no one else?' Hugh asked.

She waited as if he might answer himself, and then as he apparently didn't, 'He's only afraid there *may* be some else – that's how she makes him do it,' she said. And 'Now do you think,' she pursued, 'that I don't tell you things?'

He turned them over in his young perception and pity, the things she told him. 'Oh, oh, oh!' And then, in the great place, while as, just spent by the effort of her disclosure, she moved from him again, he took them all in. 'That's the situation that, as you say, may force his hand.'

'It absolutely, I feel, does force it.' And the renewal of her appeal brought her round. 'Isn't it too lovely?'

His frank disgust answered. 'It's too damnable!'

'And it's you,' she quite terribly smiled, 'who – by the "irony of fate"! – have given him help.'

He smote his head in the light of it. 'By the Mantovano?'

'By the possible Mantovano – as a substitute for the impossible Sir Joshua. You've made him aware of a value.'

'Ah, but the value's to be fixed!'

'Then Mr Bender will fix it!'

'Oh, but – as he himself would say – I'll fix Mr Bender!' Hugh declared. 'And he won't buy a pig in a poke.'

This cleared the air while they looked at each other; yet she had already asked: 'What in the world can you do, and how in the world can you do it?'

Well, he was too excited for decision. 'I don't quite see now, but give me time.' And he took out his watch as already to measure it. 'Oughtn't I before I go to say a word to Lord Theign?'

'Is it your idea to become a lion in his path?'

'Well, say a cub – as that's what I'm afraid he'll call me! But I think I should speak to him.'

She drew a conclusion momentarily dark. 'He'll have to learn in that case that I've told you of my fear.'

'And is there any good reason why he shouldn't?'

She kept her eyes on him and the darkness seemed to clear. 'No!' she at last replied, and, having gone to touch an electric bell, was with him again. 'But I think I'm rather sorry for you.'

'Does that represent a reason why I should be so for you?'

For a little she said nothing; but after that: 'None whatever!'

'Then is the sister of whom you speak Lady Imber?'

Lady Grace, at this, raised her hand in caution: the butler had arrived, with due gravity, in answer to her ring; to whom she made known her desire. 'Please say to his lordship – in the saloon or wherever – that Mr Crimble must go.' When Banks had departed, however, accepting the responsibility of this mission, she answered her friend's question. 'The sister of whom I speak is Lady Imber.'

'She loses then so heavily at bridge?'

'She loses more than she wins.'

Hugh gazed as with interest at these oddities of the great. 'And yet she still plays?'

'What else, in her set, should she do?'

This he was quite unable to say; but he could after a moment's exhibition of the extent to which he was out of it put a question instead. 'So *you're* not in her set?'

'I'm not in her set.'

'Then decidedly,' he said, 'I don't want to save her. I only want —'

He was going on, but she broke in: 'I know what you want!'

He kept his eyes on her till he had made sure – and this deep exchange between them had a beauty. 'So you're now *with* me?'

'I'm now *with* you!'

'Then,' said Hugh, 'shake hands on it.'

He offered her his hand, she took it, and their grasp became, as you would have seen in their fine young faces, a pledge in which they stood a minute locked. Lord Theign came upon them from the saloon in the midst of the process; on which they separated as with an air of its having consisted but of Hugh's leave-taking. With some such form of mere civility, at any rate, he appeared, by the manner in which he addressed himself to Hugh, to have supposed them occupied.

'I'm sorry my daughter can't keep you; but I must at least thank you for your interesting view of my picture.'

Hugh indulged in a brief and mute, though very grave, acknowledgment of this expression; presently speaking, however, as on a resolve taken with a sense of possibly awkward consequences: 'May I – before you're sure of your indebtedness – put you rather a straight question, Lord Theign?' It sounded doubtless, and of a sudden, a little portentous – as was in fact testified to by his lordship's quick stiff stare, full of wonder at so free a note. But Hugh had the courage of his undertaking. 'If I contribute in my modest degree to establishing the true authorship of the work you speak of, may I have from you an assurance that my success isn't to serve as a basis for any peril – or possibility – of its leaving the country?'

Lord Theign was visibly astonished, but had also, independently of this, turned a shade pale. 'You ask of me an "assurance"?'

Hugh had now, with his firmness and his strained smile, quite the look of having counted the cost of his step. 'I'm afraid I *must*, you see.'

It pressed at once in his host the spring of a very grand manner. 'And pray by what right here do you do anything of the sort?'

'By the right of a person from whom you, on your side, are accepting a service.'

Hugh had clearly determined in his opponent a rise of what is called spirit. 'A service that you half an hour ago thrust on me, sir – and with which you may take it from me that I'm already quite prepared to dispense.'

'I'm sorry to appear indiscreet,' our young man returned; 'I'm sorry to have upset you in any way. But I can't overcome my anxiety —'

Lord Theign took the words from his lips. 'And you therefore invite me – at the end of half an hour in this house! – to account to you for my personal intentions and my private affairs and make over my freedom to your hands?'

Hugh stood there with his eyes on the black and white pavement that stretched about him – the great lozenged marble floor that might have figured that ground of his own vision which he had made up his mind to 'stand.' 'I can only see the matter as I see it, and I should be ashamed not to have seized any chance to appeal to you.' Whatever difficulty he had had shyly to face didn't exist for him now. 'I entreat you to think again, to think *well*, before you deprive us of such a source of just envy.'

'And you regard your entreaty as helped,' Lord Theign asked, 'by the beautiful threat you are so good as to attach to it?' Then as his monitor, arrested, exchanged a searching look with Lady Grace, who, showing in her face all the pain of the business, stood off at the distance to which a woman instinctively retreats when a scene turns to violence as precipitately as this one appeared to strike her as having turned: 'I ask you that not less than I should like to know whom you speak of as "deprived" of property that happens – for reasons that I don't suppose you also quarrel with! – to be mine.'

'Well, I know nothing about threats, Lord Theign,' Hugh

said, 'but I speak of *all* of us – of all the people of England; who would deeply deplore such an act of alienation, and whom, for the interest they bear you, I beseech you mercifully to consider.'

'The interest they bear me?' – the master of Dedborough fairly bristled with wonder. 'Pray how the devil do they show it?'

'I think they show it in all sorts of ways' – and Hugh's critical smile, at almost any moment hovering, played over the question in a manner seeming to convey that he meant many things.

'Understand then, please,' said Lord Theign with every inch of his authority, 'that they'll show it best by minding their own business while I very particularly mind mine.'

'You simply do, in other words,' Hugh explicitly concluded, 'what happens to be convenient to you.'

'In very distinct preference to what happens to be convenient to *you!* So that I need no longer detain you,' Lord Theign added with the last dryness and as if to wind up their brief and thankless connection.

The young man took his dismissal, being able to do no less, while, unsatisfied and unhappy, he looked about mechanically for the cycling-cap he had laid down somewhere in the hall on his arrival. 'I apologize, my lord, if I seem to you to have ill repaid your hospitality. But,' he went on with his uncommended cheer, 'my interest in your picture remains.'

Lady Grace, who had stopped and strayed and stopped again as a mere watchful witness, drew nearer hereupon, breaking her silence for the first time. 'And please let me say, father, that mine also grows and grows.'

It was obvious that this parent, surprised and disconcerted by her tone, judged her contribution superfluous. 'I'm happy to hear it, Grace – but yours is another affair.'

'I think on the contrary that it's quite the same one,' she returned – 'since it's on my hint to him that Mr Crimble has said to you what he has.' The resolution she had gathered while she awaited her chance sat in her charming eyes, which met, as she spoke, the straighter paternal glare. 'I let him know that I supposed you to think of profiting by the importance of Mr Bender's visit.'

'Then you might have spared, my dear, your – I suppose and hope well-meant – interpretation of my mind.' Lord Theign showed himself at this point master of the beautiful art of righting himself as without having been in the wrong. 'Mr Bender's visit will terminate – as soon as he has released Lord John – without my having profited in the smallest particular.'

Hugh meanwhile evidently but wanted to speak for his friend. 'It was Lady Grace's anxious inference, she will doubtless let me say for her, that my idea about the Moretto would add to your power – well,' he pushed on not without awkwardness, 'of "realizing" advantageously on such a prospective rise.'

Lord Theign glanced at him as for positively the last time, but spoke to Lady Grace. 'Understand then, please, that, as I detach myself from any association with this gentleman's ideas – whether about the Moretto or about anything else – his further application of them ceases from this moment to concern us.'

The girl's rejoinder was to address herself directly to Hugh, across their companion. 'Will you make your inquiry for *me* then?'

The light again kindled in him. 'With all the pleasure in life!' He had found his cap and, taking them together, bowed to the two, for departure, with high emphasis of form. Then he marched off in the direction from which he had entered.

Lord Theign scarce waited for his disappearance to turn in

wrath to Lady Grace. 'I denounce the indecency, wretched child, of your public defiance of me!'

They were separated by a wide interval now, and though at her distance she met his reproof so unshrinkingly as perhaps to justify the terms into which it had broken, she became aware of a reason for his not following it up. She pronounced in quick warning 'Lord John!' – for their friend, released from among the pictures, was rejoining them, was already there.

He spoke straight to his host on coming into sight. 'Bender's at last off, but' – he indicated the direction of the garden front – 'you may still find him, out yonder, prolonging the agony with Lady Sandgate.'

Lord Theign remained a moment, and the heat of his resentment remained. He looked with a divided discretion, the pain of his indecision, from his daughter's suitor and his approved candidate to that contumacious young woman and back again; then choosing his course in silence he had a gesture of almost desperate indifference and passed quickly out by the door to the terrace.

It had left Lord John gaping. 'What on earth's the matter with your father?'

'What on earth indeed?' Lady Grace unaidingly asked. 'Is he discussing with that awful man?'

'Old Bender? Do you think him so awful?' Lord John showed surprise – which might indeed have passed for harmless amusement; but he shook everything off in view of a nearer interest. He quite waved old Bender away. 'My dear girl, what do *we* care —?'

'I care immensely, I assure you,' she interrupted, 'and I ask of you, please, to tell me!'

Her perversity, coming straight and which he had so little expected, threw him back so that he looked at her with sombre eyes. 'Ah, it's not for such a matter I'm here, Lady Grace – I'm here with that fond question of my own.' And then as she turned away, leaving him with a vehement motion of protest: 'I've come for your kind answer – the answer your father instructed me to count on.'

'I've no kind answer to give you!' – she raised forbidding hands. 'I entreat you to leave me alone.'

There was so high a spirit and so strong a force in it that he stared as if stricken by violence. 'In God's name then what has happened – when you almost gave me your word?'

'What has happened is that I've found it impossible to listen to you.' And she moved as if fleeing she scarce knew whither before him.

He had already hastened around another way, however, as to meet her in her quick circuit of the hall. 'That's all you've got to say to me after what has passed between us?'

He had stopped her thus, but she had also stopped him, and her passionate denial set him a limit. 'I've got to say – sorry as I am – that if you *must* have an answer it's this: that never, Lord John, never, can there be anything more between us.' And her gesture cleared her path, permitting her to achieve her flight. 'Never, no, never,' she repeated as she went – 'never, never, never!' She got off by the door at which she had been aiming to some retreat of her own, while aghast and defeated, left to make the best of it, he sank after a moment into a chair and remained quite pitiably staring before him, appealing to the great blank splendour.

BOOK SECOND

I

Lady Sandgate, on a morning late in May, entered her drawing-room by the door that opened at the right of that charming retreat as a person coming in faced Bruton Street; and she met there at this moment Mr Gotch, her butler, who had just appeared in the much wider doorway forming opposite the Bruton Street windows an apartment not less ample, lighted from the back of the house and having its independent connection with the upper floors and the lower. She showed surprise at not immediately finding the visitor to whom she had been called.

'But Mr Crimble —?'

'Here he is, my lady.' And he made way for that gentleman, who emerged from the back room; Gotch observing the propriety of a prompt withdrawal.

'I went in for a minute, with your servant's permission,' Hugh explained, 'to see your famous Lawrence – which is splendid; he was so good as to arrange the light.' The young man's dress was of a form less relaxed than on the occasion of his visit to Dedborough; yet the soft felt hat that he rather restlessly crumpled as he talked marked the limit of his sacrifice to vain appearances.

Lady Sandgate was at once interested in the punctuality of his reported act. 'Gotch thinks as much of my grandmother as

I do – and even seems to have ended by taking her for his very own.'

'One sees, unmistakably, from her beauty, that you at any rate are of her line,' Hugh allowed himself, not without confidence, the amusement of replying; 'and I must make sure of another look at her when I've a good deal more time.'

His hostess heard him as with a lapse of hope. 'You hadn't then come *for* the poor dear?' And then as he obviously hadn't, but for something quite else: 'I thought, from so prompt an interest, that she might be coveted –!' It dropped with a yearning sigh.

'You imagined me sent by some prowling collector?' Hugh asked. 'Ah, I shall never do their work – unless to betray them: *that* I shouldn't in the least mind! – and I'm here, frankly, at this early hour, to ask your consent to my seeing Lady Grace a moment on a particular business, if she can kindly give me time.'

'You've known then of her being with me?'

'I've known of her coming to you straight on leaving Dedborough,' he explained; 'of her wishing not to go to her sister's, and of Lord Theign's having proceeded, as they say, or being on the point of proceeding, to some foreign part.'

'And you've learnt it from having seen her – these three or four weeks?'

'I've met her – but just barely – two or three times: at a "private view," at the opera, in the lobby, and that sort of thing. But she hasn't told you?'

Lady Sandgate neither affirmed nor denied; she only turned on him her thick lustre. 'I wanted to see how much *you'd* tell.' She waited even as for more, but this not coming she helped herself. 'Once again at dinner?'

'Yes, but alas not near her!'

'Once then at a private view? – when, with the squash they usually are, you might have been very near her indeed!'

The young man, his hilarity quickened, took but a moment for the truth. 'Yes – it *was* a squash!'

'And once,' his hostess pursued, 'in the lobby of the opera?'

'After "Tristan" – yes; but with some awful grand people I didn't know.'

She recognized; she estimated the grandeur. 'Oh, the Pennimans are nobody! But now,' she asked, 'you've come, you say, on "business"?'

'Very important, please – which accounts for the hour I've ventured and the appearance I present.'

'I don't ask you too much to "account,"' Lady Sandgate kindly said; 'but I can't not wonder if she hasn't told you what things have happened.'

He cast about. 'She has had no chance to tell me anything – beyond the fact of her being here.'

'Without the reason?'

'"The reason"?' he echoed.

She gave it up, going straighter. 'She's with me then as an old firm friend. Under my care and protection.'

'I see' – he took it, with more penetration than enthusiasm, as a hint in respect to himself. 'She puts you on your guard.'

Lady Sandgate expressed it more graciously. 'She puts me on my honour – or at least her father does.'

'As to her seeing *me?*'

'As to *my* seeing at least – what may happen to her.'

'Because – you say – things *have* happened?'

His companion fairly sounded him. 'You've only talked – when you've met – of "art"?'

'Well,' he smiled, '"art is long"!'

'Then I hope it may see you through! But you should know first that Lord Theign is presently due —'

'*Here*, back already from abroad?' – he was all alert.

'He has not yet gone – he comes up this morning to start.'

'And stops here on his way?'

'To take the *train de luxe* this afternoon to his annual Salso-maggiore.[4] But with so little time to spare,' she went on reassuringly, 'that, to simplify – as he wired me an hour ago from Dedborough – he has given rendezvous here to Mr Bender, who is particularly to wait for him.'

'And who may therefore arrive at any moment?'

She looked at her bracelet watch. 'Scarcely before noon. So you'll just have your chance —'

'Thank the powers then!' – Hugh grasped at it. 'I shall have it best if you'll be so good as to tell me first – well,' he faltered, 'what it is that, to my great disquiet, you've further alluded to; what it is that has occurred.'

Lady Sandgate took her time, but her good-nature and other sentiments pronounced. 'Haven't you at least guessed that she has fallen under her father's extreme reprobation?'

'Yes, so much as that – that she must have greatly annoyed him – I have been supposing. But isn't it by her having asked me to act for her? I mean about the Mantovano – which I *have* done.'

Lady Sandgate wondered. 'You've "acted"?'

'It's what I've come to tell her at last – and I'm all impatience.'

'I see, I see' – she had caught a clue. 'He hated that – yes; but you haven't really made out,' she put to him, 'the *other* effect of your hour at Dedborough?' She recognized, however, while she spoke, that his divination had failed, and she didn't trouble him to confess it. 'Directly you had gone she "turned down" Lord John. Declined, I mean, the offer of his hand in marriage.'

Hugh was clearly as much mystified as anything else. 'He proposed there —?'

'He had spoken, that day, *before* – before your talk with Lord Theign, who had every confidence in her accepting him. But you came, Mr Crimble, you went; and when her suitor reappeared, just after you *had* gone, for his answer —'

'She wouldn't have him?' Hugh asked with a precipitation of interest.

But Lady Sandgate could humour almost any curiosity. 'She wouldn't look at him.'

He bethought himself. 'But had she said she would?'

'So her father indignantly considers.'

'That's the *ground* of his indignation?'

'He had his reasons for counting on her, and it has determined a painful crisis.'

Hugh Crimble turned this over – feeling apparently for something he didn't find. 'I'm sorry to hear such things, but where's the connection with *me?*'

'Ah, you know best yourself, and if you don't see any –!' In that case, Lady Sandgate's motion implied, she washed her hands of it.

Hugh had for a moment the air of a young man treated to the sweet chance to guess a conundrum – which he gave up. 'I really don't see any, Lady Sandgate. But,' he a little inconsistently said, 'I'm greatly obliged to you for telling me.'

'Don't mention it! – though I think it *is* good of me,' she smiled, 'on so short an acquaintance.' To which she added more gravely: 'I leave you the situation – but I'm willing to let you know that I'm all on Grace's side.'

'So am I, *rather!* – please let me frankly say.'

He clearly refreshed, he even almost charmed her. 'It's the very least you can say! – though I'm not sure whether you say it as the simplest or as the very subtlest of men. But in case you don't know as I do how little the particular candidate I've named —'

'Had a right or a claim to succeed with her?' he broke in – all quick intelligence here at least. 'No, I don't perhaps know as well as you do – but I think I know as well as I just yet require.'

'There you are then! And if you did prevent,' his hostess maturely pursued, 'what wouldn't have been – well, good or nice, I'm quite on your side too.'

Our young man seemed to feel the shade of ambiguity, but he reached at a meaning. 'You're with me in my plea for our defending at any cost of effort or ingenuity —'

'The precious picture Lord Theign exposes?' – she took his presumed sense faster than he had taken hers. But she hung fire a moment with her reply to it. 'Well, will you keep the secret of everything I've said or say?'

'To the death, to the stake, Lady Sandgate!'

'Then,' she momentously returned, 'I only want, too, to make Bender impossible. If you ask me,' she pursued, 'how I arrange that with my deep loyalty to Lord Theign —'

'I don't ask you anything of the sort,' he interrupted – 'I wouldn't ask you for the world; and my own bright plan for achieving the *coup* you mention —'

'You'll have time, at the most,' she said, consulting afresh her bracelet watch, 'to explain to Lady Grace.' She reached an electric bell, which she touched – facing then her visitor again with an abrupt and slightly embarrassed change of tone. 'You do think *my* great portrait splendid?'

He had strayed far from it and all too languidly came back. 'Your Lawrence there? As I said, magnificent.'

But the butler had come in, interrupting, straight from the lobby; of whom she made her request. 'Let her ladyship know – Mr Crimble.'

Gotch looked hard at Hugh and the crumpled hat – almost as if having an option. But he resigned himself to repeating, with a distinctness that scarce fell short of the invidious, 'Mr Crimble,' and departed on his errand.

Lady Sandgate's fair flush of diplomacy had meanwhile not faded. 'Couldn't you, with your immense cleverness and power, get the Government to do something?'

'About your picture?' Hugh betrayed on this head a graceless detachment. 'You too then want to sell?'

Oh she righted herself. 'Never to a private party!'

'Mr Bender's not after it?' he asked – though scarce lighting his reluctant interest with a forced smile.

'Most intensely after it. But never,' cried the proprietress, 'to a bloated alien!'

'Then I applaud your patriotism. Only why not,' he asked, 'carrying that magnanimity a little further, set us all an example as splendid as the object itself?'

'Give it you for nothing?' She threw up shocked hands. 'Because I'm an aged female pauper and can't make *every* sacrifice.'

Hugh pretended – none too convincingly – to think. 'Will you let them have it very cheap?'

'Yes – for less than such a bribe as Bender's.'

'Ah,' he said expressively, 'that might be, and still —!'

Well, she had a flare of fond confidence. 'I'll find out what he'll offer – if you'll on your side do what you can – and then ask them a third less.' And she followed it up – as if suddenly conceiving him a prig. 'See here, Mr Crimble, I've been – and this very first time! – charming to you.'

'You have indeed,' he returned; 'but you throw back on it a lurid light if it has all been for *that!*'

'It has been – well, to keep things as I want them; and if I've given you precious information mightn't you on your side —'

'Estimate its value in cash?' – Hugh sharply took her up. 'Ah, Lady Sandgate, I *am* in your debt, but if you really bargain

97

for your precious information I'd rather we assume that I haven't enjoyed it.'

She made him, however, in reply, a sign for silence; she had heard Lady Grace enter the other room from the back landing, and, reaching the nearer door, she disposed of the question with high gay bravery. 'I won't bargain with the Treasury!' – she had passed out by the time Lady Grace arrived.

II

As Hugh recognized in this friend's entrance and face the light of welcome he went, full of his subject, straight to their main affair. 'I haven't been able to wait, I've wanted so much to tell you – I mean how I've just come back from Brussels, where I saw Pappendick, who was free and ready, by the happiest chance, to start for Verona, which he must have reached some time yesterday.'

The girl's responsive interest fairly broke into rapture. 'Ah, the dear sweet thing!'

'Yes, he's a brick – but the question now hangs in the balance. Allowing him time to have got into relation with the picture, I've begun to expect his wire, which will probably come to my club; but my fidget, while I wait, has driven me' – he threw out and dropped his arms in expression of his soft surrender – 'well, just to do *this*: to come to you here, in my fever, at an unnatural hour and uninvited, and at least let you know I've "acted."'

'Oh, but I simply rejoice,' Lady Grace declared, 'to be acting *with* you.'

'Then if you are, if you *are*,' the young man cried, 'why everything's beautiful and right!'

'It's all I care for and think of now,' she went on in her bright devotion, 'and I've only wondered and hoped!'

Well, Hugh found for it all a rapid, abundant lucidity. 'He

was away from home at first, and I had to wait – but I crossed last week, found him and settled it; coming home by Paris, where I had a grand four days' jaw with the fellows there and saw *their* great specimen of our master: all of which has given him time.'

'And now his time's up?' the girl eagerly asked.

'It *must* be – and we shall see.' But Hugh postponed that question to a matter of more moment still. 'The thing is that at last I'm able to tell you how I feel the trouble I've brought you.'

It made her, quickly colouring, rest grave eyes on him. 'What do you know – when I haven't told you – about my "trouble"?'

'Can't I have guessed, with a ray of intelligence?' – he had his answer ready. 'You've sought asylum with this good friend from the effects of your father's resentment.'

' "Sought asylum" is perhaps excessive,' Lady Grace returned – 'though it wasn't pleasant with him after that hour, no,' she allowed. 'And I couldn't go, you see, to Kitty.'

'No indeed, you couldn't go to Kitty.' He smiled at her hard as he added: 'I should have liked to see you go to Kitty! Therefore exactly is it that I've set you adrift – that I've darkened and poisoned your days. You're paying with your comfort, with your peace, for having joined so gallantly in my grand remonstrance.'

She shook her head, turning from him, but then turned back again – as if accepting, as if even relieved by, this version of the prime cause of her state. 'Why do you talk of it as "paying" – if it's all to come back to my *being* paid? I mean by your blest success – if you really do what you want.'

'I have your word for it,' he searchingly said, 'that our really pulling it off together will make up to you —?'

'I should be ashamed if it didn't, for everything!' – she took the question from his mouth. 'I believe in such a cause exactly as you do – and found a lesson, at Dedborough, in your frankness and your faith.'

'Then you'll help me no end,' he said all simply and sincerely.

'You've helped *me* already' – that she gave him straight back. And on it they stayed a moment, their strenuous faces more intensely communing.

'You're very wonderful – for a girl!' Hugh brought out.

'One *has* to be a girl, naturally, to be a daughter of one's house,' she laughed; 'and that's all I am of ours – but a true and a right and a straight one.'

He glowed with his admiration. 'You're splendid!'

That might be or not, her light shrug intimated; she gave it, at any rate, the go-by and more exactly stated her case. 'I see our situation.'

'So do I, Lady Grace!' he cried with the strongest emphasis. 'And your father only doesn't.'

'Yes,' she said for intelligent correction – 'he sees it, there's nothing in life he sees so much. But unfortunately he sees it all wrong.'

Hugh seized her point of view as if there had been nothing of her that he wouldn't have seized. 'He sees it all wrong then! My appeal the other day he took as a rude protest. And any protest —'

'Any protest,' she quickly and fully agreed, 'he takes as an offence, yes. It's his theory that he still has rights,' she smiled, 'though he *is* a miserable peer.'

'How should he not have rights,' said Hugh, 'when he has really everything on earth?'

'Ah, he doesn't even *know* that – he takes it so much for granted.' And she sought, though as rather sadly and despairingly, to explain. 'He lives all in his own world.'

'He lives all in his own, yes; but he does business all in ours

– quite as much as the people who come up to the city in the Tube.' With which Hugh had a still sharper recall of the stiff actual. 'And he must be here to do business to-day.'

'You know,' Lady Grace asked, 'that he's to meet Mr Bender?'

'Lady Sandgate kindly warned me, and,' her companion saw as he glanced at the clock on the chimney, 'I've only ten minutes, at best. The "Journal" won't have been good for him,' he added – 'you doubtless have seen the "Journal"?'

'No' – she was vague. 'We live by the "Morning Post."'

'That's why our friend here didn't speak then,' Hugh said with a better light – 'which, out of a dim consideration for her, I didn't do, either. But they've a leader this morning about Lady Lappington and her Longhi, and on Bender and his hauls, and on the certainty – if we don't do something energetic – of more and more Benders to come: such a conquering horde as invaded the old civilization, only armed now with huge cheque-books instead of with spears and battle-axes. They refer to the rumour current – as too horrific to believe – of Lord Theign's putting up his Moretto; with the question of how properly to qualify any such sad purpose in him should the further report prove true of a new and momentous opinion about the picture entertained by several eminent authorities.'

'Of whom,' said the girl, intensely attached to this recital, 'you're of course seen as not the least.'

'Of whom, of course, Lady Grace, I'm as yet – however I'm "seen" – the whole collection. But we've time' – he rested on that. 'The fat, if you'll allow me the expression, is on the fire – which, as I see the matter, is where this particular fat *should* be.'

'Is the article, then,' his companion appealed, 'very severe?'

'I prefer to call it very enlightened and very intelligent – and the great thing is that it immensely "marks," as they say. It will have made a big public difference – from this day; though it's of course aimed not so much at persons as at conditions; which it calls upon us all somehow to tackle.'

'Exactly' – she was full of the saving vision; 'but as the conditions are directly embodied in persons —'

'Oh, of course it here and there bells the cat; which means that it bells three or four.'

'Yes,' she richly brooded – 'Lady Lappington *is* a cat!'

'She will have been "belled," at any rate, with your father,' Hugh amusedly went on, 'to the certainty of a row; and a row can only be good for us – I mean for *us* in particular.' Yet he had to bethink himself. 'The case depends a good deal of course on how your father *takes* such a resounding rap.'

'Oh, I know how he'll take it!' – her perception went all the way.

'In the very highest and properest spirit?'

'Well, you'll see.' She was as brave as she was clear. 'Or at least *I* shall!'

Struck with all this in her he renewed his homage. 'You *are*, yes, splendid!'

'I even,' she laughed, 'surprise myself.'

But he was already back at his calculations. 'How early do the papers get to you?'

'At Dedborough? Oh, quite for breakfast – which isn't, however, very early.'

'Then that's what has caused his wire to Bender.'

'But how will such talk strike *him*?' the girl asked.

Hugh meanwhile, visibly, had not only followed his train of thought, he had let it lead him to certainty. 'It will have moved Mr Bender to absolute rapture.'

'Rather,' Lady Grace wondered, 'than have put him off?'

'It will have put him prodigiously *on!* Mr Bender – as he said to me at Dedborough of his noble host there,' Hugh pursued – 'is "a very nice man"; but he's a product of the world of advertisement, and advertisement is all he sees and aims at. He lives in it as a saint in glory or a fish in water.'

She took it from him as half doubting. 'But mayn't advertisement, in so special a case, turn, on the whole, against him?'

Hugh shook a negative forefinger with an expression he might have caught from foreign comrades. 'He rides the biggest whirlwind – he has got it saddled and bitted.'

She faced the image, but cast about. 'Then where does our success come in?'

'In our making the beast, all the same, bolt with him and throw him.' And Hugh further pointed the moral. 'If in such proceedings all he knows is publicity the thing is to give him publicity, and it's only a question of giving him enough. By the time he has enough for himself, you see, he'll have too much for every one else – so that we shall "up" in a body and slay him.'

The girl's eyebrows, in her wondering face, rose to a question. 'But if he has meanwhile got the picture?'

'We'll slay him before he gets it!' He revelled in the breadth of his view. 'Our own policy must be to *organize* to that end the inevitable outcry. Organize Bender himself – organize him to scandal.' Hugh had already even pity to spare for their victim. 'He won't know it from a boom.'

Though carried along, however, Lady Grace could still measure. 'But that will be only if he wants and decides for the picture.'

'We must make him then want and decide for it – decide, that is, for "ours." To save it we must work him up – he'll in that case want it so indecently much. Then *we* shall have to want it more!'

'Well,' she anxiously felt it her duty to remind him, 'you can take a horse to water —!'

'Oh, trust me to make him drink!'

There appeared a note in this that convinced her. 'It's you, Mr Crimble, who are "splendid"!'

'Well, I shall be – with my jolly wire!' And all on that scent again, 'May I come back to you from the club with Pappendick's news?' he asked.

'Why, rather, of course, come back!'

'Only not,' he debated, 'till your father has left.'

Lady Grace considered too, but sharply decided. 'Come when you *have* it. But tell me first,' she added, 'one thing.' She hung fire a little while he waited, but she brought it out. 'Was it you who got the "Journal" to speak?'

'Ah, one scarcely "gets" the "Journal"!'

'Who then gave them their "tip"?'

'About the Mantovano and its peril?' Well, he took a moment – but only not to say; in addition to which the butler had reappeared, entering from the lobby. 'I'll tell you,' he laughed, 'when I come back!'

Gotch had his manner of announcement while the visitor was mounting the stairs. 'Mr Breckenridge Bender!'

'Ah then I go,' said Lady Grace at once.

'I'll stay three minutes.' Hugh turned with her, alertly, to the easier issue, signalling hope and cheer from that threshold as he watched her disappear; after which he faced about with as brave a smile and as ready for immediate action as if she had there within kissed her hand to him. Mr Bender emerged at the same instant, Gotch withdrawing and closing the door behind him; and the former personage, recognizing his young friend, threw up his hands for friendly pleasure.

III

'Ah, Mr Crimble,' he cordially inquired, 'you've come with your great news?'

Hugh caught the allusion, it would have seemed, but after a moment. 'News of the Moretto? No, Mr Bender, I haven't news *yet*.' But he added as with high candour for the visitor's motion of disappointment: 'I think I warned you, you know, that it would take three or four weeks.'

'Well, in *my* country,' Mr Bender returned with disgust, 'it would take three or four minutes! Can't you make 'em step more lively?'

'I'm expecting, sir,' said Hugh good-humouredly, 'a report from hour to hour.'

'Then will you let me have it right off?'

Hugh indulged in a pause; after which very frankly: 'Ah, it's scarcely for you, Mr Bender, that I'm acting!'

The great collector was but briefly checked. 'Well, can't you just act for Art?'

'Oh, you're doing that yourself so powerfully,' Hugh laughed, 'that I think I had best leave it to you!'

His friend looked at him as some inspector on circuit might look at a new improvement. 'Don't you want to go round acting *with* me?'

'Go "on tour," as it were? Oh, frankly, Mr Bender,' Hugh said, 'if I had any weight —!'

'You'd add it to your end of the beam? Why, what have I done that *you* should go back on me – after working me up so down there? The worst I've done,' Mr Bender continued, 'is to refuse that Moretto.'

'Has it deplorably been *offered* you?' our young man cried, unmistakably and sincerely affected. After which he went on, as his fellow-visitor only eyed him hard, not, on second thoughts, giving the owner of the great work away: 'Then why are you – as if you were a banished Romeo – so keen for news from Verona?' To this odd mixture of business and literature Mr Bender made no reply, contenting himself with but a large vague blandness that wore in him somehow the mark of tested utility; so that Hugh put him another question: 'Aren't you here, sir, on the chance of the Mantovano?'

'I'm here,' he then imperturbably said, 'because Lord Theign has wired me to meet him. Ain't you here for that yourself?'

Hugh betrayed for a moment his enjoyment of a 'big' choice of answers. 'Dear, no! I've but been in, by Lady Sandgate's leave, to see that grand Lawrence.'

'Ah yes, she's very kind about it – one does go "in."' After which Mr Bender had, even in the atmosphere of his danger, a throb of curiosity. 'Is any one *after* that grand Lawrence?'

'Oh, I hope not,' Hugh laughed, 'unless you again dreadfully are: wonderful thing as it is and so just in its right place there.'

'You call it,' Mr Bender impartially inquired, 'a *very* wonderful thing?'

'Well, as a Lawrence, it has quite bowled me over' – Hugh spoke as for the strictly æsthetic awkwardness of that. 'But you know I take my pictures hard.' He gave a punch to his hat, pressed for time in this connection as he was glad truly to appear to his friend. 'I must make my little *rapport*.'[5] Yet before it he did seek briefly to explain. 'We're a band of young men who care – and we watch the great things. Also – for I must give you the real truth about myself – we watch the great people.'

'Well, I guess I'm used to being watched – if that's the worst you can do.' To which Mr Bender added in his homely way: 'But you know, Mr Crimble, what I'm *really* after.'

Hugh's strategy on this would again have peeped out for us. 'The man in this morning's "Journal" appears at least to have discovered.'

'Yes, the man in this morning's "Journal" has discovered three or four weeks – as it appears to take you here for everything – after my beginning to talk. Why, they knew I was talking *that* time ago on the other side.'

'Oh, they know things in the States,' Hugh cheerfully agreed, 'so independently of their happening! But you must have talked loud.'

'Well, I haven't so much talked as raved,' Mr Bender conceded – 'for I'm afraid that when I do want a thing I rave till I get it. You heard me at Dedborough, and your enterprising daily press has at last caught the echo.'

'Then they'll make up for lost time! But have you done it,' Hugh asked, 'to prepare an alibi?'

'An alibi?'

'By "raving," as you say, the saddle on the wrong horse. I don't think you at all believe you'll get the Sir Joshua – but meanwhile we shall have cleared up the question of the Moretto.'

Mr Bender, imperturbable, didn't speak till he had done justice to this picture of his subtlety. 'Then, why on earth do you want to boom the Moretto?'

'You ask that,' said Hugh, 'because it's the boomed thing that's most in peril.'

'Well, it's the big, the bigger, the biggest things, and if you drag their value to the light why shouldn't we want to grab them and carry them off – the same as all of *you* originally did?'

'Ah, not quite the same,' Hugh smiled – 'that I *will* say for you!'

'Yes, you stick it on now – you *have* got an eye for the rise in values. But I grant you your unearned increment, and you ought to be mighty glad that, to such a tune, I'll pay it you.'

Our young man kept, during a moment's thought, his eyes on his companion, and then resumed with all intensity and candour: 'You may easily, Mr Bender, be too much for me – as you appear too much for far greater people. But may I ask you, very earnestly, for your word on *this*, as to any case in which that happens – that when precious things, things we are to lose here, *are* knocked down to you, you'll let us at least take leave of them, let us have a sight of them in London, before they're borne off?'

Mr Bender's big face fell almost with a crash. 'Hand them over, you mean, to the sandwich men on Bond Street?'

'To one or other of the placard and poster men – I don't insist on the inserted human slice! Let the great values, as a compensation to us, be on view for three or four weeks.'

'You ask me,' Mr Bender returned, 'for a *general* assurance to that effect?'

'Well, a particular one – so it be particular enough,' Hugh said – 'will do just for now. Let me put in my plea for the issue – well, of the value that's actually in the scales.'

'The Mantovano-Moretto?'

'The Moretto-Mantovano!'

Mr Bender carnivorously smiled. 'Hadn't we better know which it is first?'

Hugh had a motion of practical indifference for this. 'The public interest – playing so straight on the question – may help to settle it. By which I mean that it will profit enormously

– the question of probability, of identity itself will – by the discussion it will create. The discussion will promote certainty —'

'And certainty,' Mr Bender massively mused, 'will kick up a row.'

'*Of course* it will kick up a row!' – Hugh thoroughly guaranteed that. 'You'll be, for the month, the best-abused man in England – if you venture to remain here at all; except, naturally, poor Lord Theign.'

'Whom it won't be my interest, at the same time, to worry into backing down.'

'But whom it will be exceedingly *mine* to practise on' – and Hugh laughed as at the fun before them – 'if I may entertain the sweet hope of success. The only thing is – from my point of view,' he went on – 'that backing down before what he will call vulgar clamour isn't in the least in his traditions, nothing less so; and that if there should be really too much of it for his taste or his nerves he'll set his handsome face as a stone and never budge an inch. But at least again what I appeal to you for will have taken place – the picture will have been seen by a lot of people who'll care.'

'It will have been seen,' Mr Bender amended – 'on the mere contingency of my acquisition of it – only if its present owner consents.'

'"Consents"?' Hugh almost derisively echoed; 'why, he'll propose it himself, he'll insist on it, he'll put it through, once he's angry enough – as angry, I mean, as almost any public criticism of a personal act of his will be sure to make him; and I'm afraid the striking criticism, or at least animadversion, of this morning, will have blown on his flame of bravado.'

Inevitably a student of character, Mr Bender rose to the occasion. 'Yes, I guess he's pretty mad.'

'They've imputed to him' – Hugh but wanted to abound in that sense – 'an intention of which after all he isn't guilty.'

'So that' – his listener glowed with interested optimism – 'if they don't look out, if they impute it to him again, I guess he'll just go and be guilty!'

Hugh might at this moment have shown to an initiated eye as fairly elated by the sense of producing something of the effect he had hoped. 'You entertain the fond vision of lashing them up to that mistake, oh fisher in troubled waters?' And then with a finer art, as his companion, expansively bright but crudely acute, eyed him in turn as if to sound *him*: 'The strongest thing in such a type – one does make out – is his resentment of a liberty taken; and the most natural furthermore is quite that he should feel almost anything you do take uninvited from the groaning board of his banquet of life to *be* such a liberty.'

Mr Bender participated thus at his perceptive ease in the exposed aristocratic illusion. 'Yes, I guess he has always lived as he likes, the way those of you who have got things fixed for them *do*, over here; and to have to quit it on account of unpleasant remark –' But he gave up thoughtfully trying to express what this must be; reduced to the mere synthetic interjection 'My!'

'That's it, Mr Bender,' Hugh said for the consecration of such a moral; 'he won't quit it without a hard struggle.'

Mr Bender hereupon at last gave himself quite gaily away as to his high calculation of impunity. 'Well, I guess he won't struggle too hard for me to hold on to him if I *want* to!'

'In the thick of the conflict then, however that may be,' Hugh returned, 'don't forget what I've urged on you – the claim of our desolate country.'

But his friend had an answer to this. 'My natural interest,

Mr Crimble – considering what I do for it – is in the claim of ours. But I wish you were on my side!'

'Not so much,' Hugh hungrily and truthfully laughed, 'as I wish you were on mine!' Decidedly, none the less, he had to go. 'Good-bye – for another look here!'

He reached the doorway of the second room, where, however, his companion, freshly alert at this, stayed him by a gesture. 'How much is she really worth?'

'"She"?' Hugh, staring a moment, was miles at sea. 'Lady Sandgate?'

'Her great-grandmother.'

A responsible answer was prevented – the butler was again with them; he had opened wide the other door and he named to Mr Bender the personage under his convoy. 'Lord John!'

Hugh caught this from the inner threshold, and it gave him his escape. 'Oh, ask *that* friend!' With which he sought the further passage to the staircase and street, while Lord John arrived in charge of Mr Gotch, who, having remarked to the two occupants of the front drawing-room that her ladyship would come, left them together.

IV

'Then Theign's not yet here!' Lord John had to resign himself as he greeted his American ally. 'But he told me I should find you.'

'He has kept me waiting,' that gentleman returned – 'but what's the matter with him anyway?'

'The matter with him' – Lord John treated such ignorance as irritating – 'must of course be this beastly thing in the "Journal."'

Mr Bender proclaimed, on the other hand, his incapacity to seize such connections. 'What's the matter with the beastly thing?'

'Why, aren't you aware that the stiffest bit of it is a regular dig at you?'

'If you call *that* a regular dig you can't have had much experience of the Papers. I've known them to dig much deeper.'

'I've had *no* experience of such horrid attacks, thank goodness; but do you mean to say,' asked Lord John with the surprise of his own delicacy, 'that you don't unpleasantly feel it?'

'Feel it where, my dear sir?'

'Why, God bless me, such impertinence, everywhere!'

'All over me at once?' – Mr Bender took refuge in easy humour. 'Well, I'm a large man – so when I want to feel so much I look out for something good. But what, if he suffers from the blot on his ermine – ain't that what you wear? – does our friend propose to do about it?'

Lord John had a demur, which was immediately followed by the apprehension of support in his uncertainty. Lady Sandgate was before them, having reached them through the other room, and to her he at once referred the question. 'What *will* Theign propose, do you think, Lady Sandgate, to do about it?'

She breathed both her hospitality and her vagueness. 'To "do" —?'

'Don't you know about the thing in the "Journal" – awfully offensive all round?'

'There'd be even a little pinch for *you* in it,' Mr Bender said to her – 'if you were bent on fitting the shoe!'

Well, she met it all as gaily as was compatible with a firm look at her elder guest while she took her place with them. 'Oh, the shoes of such monsters as that are much too big for poor *me!*' But she was more specific for Lord John. 'I know only what Grace has just told me; but since it's a question of footgear dear Theign will certainly – what you may call – take his stand!'

Lord John welcomed this assurance. 'If I know him he'll take it splendidly!'

Mr Bender's attention was genial, though rather more detached. 'And what – while he's about it – will he take it particularly *on?*'

'Oh, we've plenty of things, thank heaven,' said Lady Sandgate, 'for a man in Theign's position to hold fast by!'

Lord John freely confirmed it. 'Scores and scores – rather! And I will say for us that, with the rotten way things seem going, the fact may soon become a real convenience.'

Mr Bender seemed struck – and not unsympathetic. 'I see that your system would be rather a fraud if you hadn't pretty well fixed *that!*'

Lady Sandgate spoke as one at present none the less substantially warned and convinced. 'It doesn't, however, alter the fact that we've thus in our ears the first growl of an outcry.'

'Ah,' Lord John concurred, 'we've unmistakably the first growl of an outcry!'

Mr Bender's judgment on the matter paused at sight of Lord Theign, introduced and announced, as Lord John spoke, by Gotch; but with the result of his addressing directly the person so presenting himself. 'Why, they tell me that what this means, Lord Theign, is the first growl of an outcry!'

The appearance of the most eminent figure in the group might have been held in itself to testify to some such truth; in the sense at least that a certain conscious radiance, a gathered light of battle in his lordship's aspect would have been explained by his having taken the full measure – an inner success with which he glowed – of some high provocation. He was flushed, but he bore it as the ensign of his house; he was so admirably, vividly dressed, for the morning hour and for his journey, that he shone as with the armour of a knight; and the whole effect of him, from head to foot, with every jerk of his unconcern and every flash of his ease, was to call attention to his being utterly unshaken and knowing perfectly what he was about. It was at this happy pitch that he replied to the prime upsetter of his peace.

'I'm afraid I don't know what anything means to *you*, Mr Bender – but it's exactly to find out that I've asked you, with our friend John, kindly to meet me here. For a very brief conference, dear lady, by your good leave,' he went on to Lady Sandgate; 'at which I'm only too pleased that you yourself should assist. The "first growl" of any outcry, I may mention to you all, affects me no more than the last will —!'

'So I'm delighted to gather' – Lady Sandgate took him straight up – 'that you don't let go your inestimable Cure.'

He at first quite stared superior – '"Let go"?' – but then treated it with a lighter touch. 'Upon my honour I might, you know – that dose of the daily press has made me feel so fit! I arrive at any rate,' he pursued to the others and in particular to Mr Bender, 'I arrive with my decision taken – which I've thought may perhaps interest you. If that tuppeny rot *is* an attempt at an outcry I simply nip it in the bud.'

Lord John rejoicingly approved. 'Absolutely the only way – with the least self-respect – to treat it!'

Lady Sandgate, on the other hand, sounded a sceptical note. 'But are you sure it's so easy, Theign, to hush up a *real* noise?'

'It ain't what I'd call a real one, Lady Sandgate,' Mr Bender said; 'you can generally distinguish a real one from the squeak of two or three mice! But granted mice do affect you, Lord Theign, it will interest me to hear what sort of a trap – by what you say – you propose to set for them.'

'You must allow me to measure, myself, Mr Bender,' his lordship replied, 'the importance of a gross freedom publicly used with my absolutely personal proceedings and affairs; to the cause and origin of any definite report of which – in such circles! – I'm afraid I rather wonder if you yourself can't give me a clue.'

It took Mr Bender a minute to do justice to these stately remarks. 'You rather wonder if I've talked of how I feel about your detaining in your hands my Beautiful Duchess —?'

'Oh, if you've already published her as "yours" – with your *power* of publication!' Lord Theign coldly laughed, – 'of course I trace the connection!'

Mr Bender's acceptance of responsibility clearly cost him no shade of a pang. 'Why, I haven't for quite a while talked of a blessed other thing – and I'm capable of growing more profane over my *not* getting her than I guess any one would dare to be if I did.'

'Well, you'll certainly not "get" her, Mr Bender,' Lady Sandgate, as for reasons of her own, bravely trumpeted; 'and even if there were a chance of it don't you see that your way wouldn't be publicly to abuse our noble friend?'

Mr Bender but beamed, in reply, upon that personage. 'Oh, I guess our noble friend knows I *have* to talk big about big things. You understand, sir, the scream of the eagle!'

'I'll forgive you,' Lord Theign civilly returned, 'all the big talk you like if you'll now understand *me*. My retort to that hireling pack shall be at once to dispose of a picture.'

Mr Bender rather failed to follow. 'But that's what you wanted to do before.'

'Pardon me,' said his lordship – 'I make a difference. It's what you wanted me to do.'

The mystification, however, continued. 'And you were *not* – as you seemed then – willing?'

Lord Theign waived cross-questions. 'Well, I'm willing *now* – that's all that need concern us. Only, once more and for the last time,' he added with all authority, 'you can't have our Duchess!'

'You can't have our Duchess!' – and Lord John, as before the altar of patriotism, wrapped it in sacrificial sighs.

'You can't have our Duchess!' Lady Sandgate repeated, but with a grace that took the sting from her triumph. And she seemed still all sweet sociability as she added: 'I wish he'd tell you too, you dreadful rich thing, that you can't have anything at all!'

Lord Theign, however, in the interest of harmony, deprecated that rigour. 'Ah, what then would become of my happy retort?'

'And what – as it *is*,' Mr Bender asked – 'becomes of my unhappy grievance?'

'Wouldn't a really great capture make up to you for that?'

'Well, I take more interest in what I want than in what I have – and it depends, don't you see, on how you measure the size.'

Lord John had at once in this connection a bright idea. 'Shouldn't you like to go back there and take the measure yourself?'

Mr Bender considered him as through narrowed eyelids. 'Look again at that tottering Moretto?'

'Well, its size – as you say – isn't in *any* light a negligible quantity.'

'You mean that – big as it is – it hasn't yet stopped growing?'

The question, however, as he immediately showed, resided in what Lord Theign himself meant. 'It's more to the purpose,' he said to Mr Bender, 'that I should mention to you the leading feature, or in other words the very essence, of my plan of campaign – which is to put the picture at once on view.' He marked his idea with a broad but elegant gesture. 'On view as a thing definitely disposed of.'

'I say, I say, I say!' cried Lord John, moved by this bold stroke to high admiration.

Lady Sandgate's approval was more qualified. 'But on view, dear Theign, how?'

'With one of those pushing people in Bond Street.' And then as for the crushing climax of his policy: 'As a Mantovano pure and simple.'

'But my dear man,' she quavered, 'if it *isn't* one?'

Mr Bender at once anticipated; the wind had suddenly risen for him and he let out sail. 'Lady Sandgate, it's going, by all that's – well, interesting, to *be* one!'

Lord Theign took him up with pleasure. 'You seize me? We *treat* it as one!'

Lord John eagerly borrowed the emphasis. 'We *treat* it as one!'

Mr Bender meanwhile fed with an opened appetite on the thought – he even gave it back larger. 'As the long-lost Number Eight!'

Lord Theign happily seized *him*. 'That will be it – to a charm!'

'It will make them,' Mr Bender asked, 'madder than anything?'

His patron – if not his client – put it more nobly. 'It will markedly affirm my attitude.'

'Which will in turn the more markedly create discussion.'

'It may create all it will!'

'Well, if *you* don't mind it, *I* don't!' Mr Bender concluded. But though bathed in this high serenity he was all for the rapid application of it elsewhere. 'You'll put the thing on view right off?'

'As soon as the proper arrangement —'

'You put off your journey to *make* it?' Lady Sandgate at once broke in.

Lord Theign bethought himself – with the effect of a gracious confidence in the others. 'Not if these friends will act.'

'Oh, I guess we'll *act!*' Mr Bender declared.

'Ah, *won't* we though!' Lord John re-echoed.

'You understand then I have an interest?' Mr Bender went on to Lord Theign.

His lordship's irony met it. 'I accept that complication – which so much simplifies!'

'And yet also have a liberty?'

'Where else would be those you've taken? The point is,' said Lord Theign, 'that *I* have a show.'

It settled Mr Bender. 'Then I'll *fix* your show.' He snatched up his hat. 'Lord John, come right round!'

Lord John had of himself reached the door, which he opened to let the whirlwind tremendously figured by his friend pass out first. Taking leave of the others he gave it even his applause. 'The fellow can do anything anywhere!' And he hastily followed.

V

Lady Sandgate, left alone with Lord Theign, drew the line at their companion's enthusiasm. 'That may be true of Mr Bender – for it's dreadful how he bears one down. But I simply find him a terror.'

'Well,' said her friend, who seemed disposed not to fatigue the question, 'I dare say a terror will help me.' He had other business to which he at once gave himself. 'And now, if you please, for that girl.'

'I'll send her to you,' she replied, 'if you can't stay to luncheon.'

'I've three or four things to do,' he pleaded, 'and I lunch with Kitty at one.'

She submitted in that case – but disappointedly. 'With Berkeley Square then you've time. But I confess I don't quite grasp the so odd inspiration that you've set those men to carry out.'

He showed surprise and regret, but even greater decision. 'Then it needn't trouble you, dear – it's enough that I myself go straight.'

'Are you so very convinced it's straight?' – she wouldn't be a bore to him, but she couldn't not be a blessing.

'What in the world else is it,' he asked, 'when, having good reasons, one acts on 'em?'

'You must have an immense array,' she sighed, 'to fly so in the face of Opinion!'

'"Opinion"?' he commented – 'I fly in its face? Why, the vulgar thing, as I'm taking my quiet walk, flies in mine! I give it a whack with my umbrella and send it about its business.' To which he added with more reproach: 'It's enough to have been dished by Grace – without *your* falling away!'

Sadly and sweetly she defended herself. 'It's only my great affection – and all that these years have been for us: *they* it is that make me wish you weren't so proud.'

'I've a perfect sense, my dear, of what these years have been for us – a very charming matter. But "proud" is it you find me of the daughter who does her best to ruin me, or of the one who does her best to humiliate?'

Lady Sandgate, not undiscernibly, took her choice of ignoring the point of this. 'Your surrenders to Kitty are your own affair – but are you sure you can really bear to see Grace?'

'I seem expected indeed to bear much,' he said with more and more of his parental bitterness, 'but I don't know that I'm yet in a funk before my child. Doesn't she *want* to see me, with any contrition, after the trick she has played me?' And then as his companion's answer failed: 'In spite of which trick you suggest that I should leave the country with no sign of her explaining —?'

His hostess raised her head. 'She does want to see you, I know; but you must recall the sequel to that bad hour at Dedborough – when it was you who declined to see *her*.'

'Before she left the house with you, the next day, for this?' – he was entirely reminiscent. 'What I recall is that even if I had condoned – that evening – her deception of *me*, in my folly, I still loathed, for my friend's sake, her practical joke on poor John.'

Lady Sandgate indulged in the shrug conciliatory. 'It was

your very complaint that your own appeal to her *became* an appeal from herself.'

'Yes,' he returned, so well he remembered, 'she was about as civil to me then – picking a quarrel with me on such a trumped-up ground! – as that devil of a fellow in the newspaper; the taste of whose elegant remarks, for that matter, she must now altogether enjoy!'

His good friend showily balanced and might have been about to reply with weight; but what she in fact brought out was only: 'I see you're right about it: I must let her speak for herself.'

'That I shall greatly prefer to her speaking – as she did so extraordinarily, out of the blue, at Dedborough, upon my honour – for the wonderful friends she picks up: the picture-man introduced by her (what was his name?) who regularly 'cheeked' me, as I suppose he'd call it, in my own house, and whom I hope, by the way, that under this roof she's not able to be quite so thick with!'

If Lady Sandgate winced at that vain dream she managed not to betray it, and she had, in any embarrassment on this matter, the support, as we know, of her own tried policy. 'She leads her life under this roof very much as under yours; and she's not of an age, remember, for me to pretend either to watch her movements or to control her contacts.' Leaving him however thus to perform his pleasure the charming woman had before she went an abrupt change of tone. 'Whatever your relations with others, dear friend, don't forget that *I'm* still here.'

Lord Theign accepted the reminder, though, the circumstances being such, it scarce moved him to ecstasy. 'That you're here, thank heaven, is of course a comfort – or would be if you understood.'

'Ah,' she submissively sighed, 'if I don't always "understand" a spirit so much higher than mine and a situation so much more complicated, certainly, I at least always defer, I at least always – well, what can I say but worship?' And then as he remained not other than finely passive, 'The old altar, Theign,' she went on – 'and a spark of the old fire!'

He had not looked at her on this – it was as if he shrank, with his preoccupations, from a tender passage; but he let her take his left hand. 'So I feel!' he was, however, kind enough to answer.

'Do feel!' she returned with much concentration. She raised the hand to her pressed lips, dropped it and with a rich 'Good-bye!' reached the threshold of the other room.

'May I smoke?' he asked before she had disappeared.

'Dear, yes!'

He had meanwhile taken out his cigarette case and was looking about for a match. But something else occurred to him. 'You must come to Victoria.'

'Rather!' she said with intensity; and with that she passed away.

VI

Left alone he had a moment's meditation where he stood; it found issue in an articulate 'Poor dear thing!' – an exclamation marked at once with patience and impatience, with resignation and ridicule. After which, waiting for his daughter, Lord Theign slowly and absently roamed, finding matches at last and lighting his cigarette – all with an air of concern that had settled on him more heavily from the moment of his finding himself alone. His luxury of gloom – if gloom it was – dropped, however, on his taking heed of Lady Grace, who, arriving on the scene through the other room, had had just time to stand and watch him in silence.

'Oh!' he jerked out at sight of her – which she had to content herself with as a parental greeting after separation, his next words doing little to qualify its dryness. 'I take it for granted that you know I'm within a couple of hours of leaving England under a necessity of health.' And then as drawing nearer, she signified without speaking her possession of this fact: 'I've thought accordingly that before I go I should – on this first possible occasion since that odious occurrence at Dedborough – like to leave you a little more food for meditation, in my absence, on the painfully false position in which you there placed me.' He carried himself restlessly even perhaps with a shade of awkwardness, to which her stillness was a contrast; she just waited, wholly passive – possibly indeed a trifle portentous. 'If you had plotted and planned it in advance,' he none the less firmly pursued, 'if you had acted from some uncanny or malignant motive, you couldn't have arranged more perfectly to incommode, to disconcert and, to all intents and purposes, make light of me and insult me.' Even before this charge she made no sign; with her eyes now attached to the ground she let him proceed. 'I had practically guaranteed to our excellent, our charming friend, your favourable view of his appeal – which you yourself too, remember, had left him in so little doubt of! – so that, having by your performance so egregiously failed him, I have the pleasure of their coming down on me for explanations, for compensations, and for God knows what besides.'

Lady Grace, looking up at last, left him in no doubt of the rigour of her attention. 'I'm sorry indeed, father, to have done you any wrong; but may I ask whom, in such a connection, you refer to as "they"?'

'"They"?' he echoed in the manner of a man who has had handed back to his more careful eye, across the counter, some questionable coin that he has tried to pass. 'Why, your own sister to begin with – whose interest in what may make for your happiness I suppose you decently recognize; and *his* people, one and all, the delightful old Duchess in particular, who only wanted to be charming to you, and who are as good people, and as pleasant and as clever, damn it, when all's said and done, as any others that are likely to come your way.' It clearly did his lordship good to work out thus his case, which grew more and more coherent to him and glowed with irresistible colour. 'Letting alone gallant John himself, most amiable of men, about whose merits and whose claims you appear to have pretended to agree with me just that you might, when he presumed, poor chap, ardently to urge them, deal him with the more cruel effect that calculated blow on the mouth!'

It was clear that in the girl's great gravity embarrassment had no share. 'They so come down on you I understand then, father, that you're obliged to come down on *me*?'

'Assuredly – for some better satisfaction than your just moping here without a sign!'

'But a sign of what, father?' she asked – as helpless as a lone islander scanning the horizon for a sail.

'Of your appreciating, of your in some degree dutifully considering, the predicament into which you've put me!'

'Hasn't it occurred to you in the least that you've rather put *me* into one?'

He threw back his head as from exasperated nerves. 'I put you certainly in the predicament of your receiving by my care a handsome settlement in life – which all the elements that would make for your enjoying it had every appearance of successfully commending to you.' The perfect readiness of which on his lips had, like a higher wave, the virtue of lifting and dropping him to still more tangible ground. 'And if I understand you aright as wishing to know whether I apologize for that zeal, why you take a most preposterous view of our relation as father and daughter.'

'You understand me no better than I fear I understand you,' Lady Grace returned, 'if what you expect of me is really to take back my words to Lord John.' And then as he didn't answer, while their breach gaped like a jostled wound, 'Have you seriously come to propose – and from *him* again,' she added – 'that I shall reconsider my resolute act and lend myself to your beautiful arrangement?'

It had so the sound of unmixed ridicule that he could only, for his dignity, not give way to passion. 'I've come, above all, for *this*, I may say, Grace: to remind you of whom you're addressing when you jibe at me, and to make of you assuredly a plain demand – exactly as to whether you judged us to have

127

actively *incurred* your treatment of our unhappy friend, to have brought it upon us, he and I, by my refusal to discuss with you at such a crisis the question of my disposition of a particular item of my property. I've only to look at you, for that matter,' Lord Theign continued – always with a finer point and a higher consistency as his rehearsal of his wrongs broadened – 'to have my inquiry, as it seems to me, eloquently answered. You flounced away from poor John, you took, as he tells me, "his head off," just to repay me for what you chose to regard as my snub on the score of your challenging my entertainment of a possible purchaser; a rebuke launched at me, practically, in the presence of a most inferior person, a stranger and an intruder, from whom you had all the air of taking your cue for naming me the great condition on which you'd gratify my hope. Am I to understand, in other words,' – and his lordship mounted to a climax – 'that you sent us about our business because I failed to gratify *your* hope: that of my knocking under to your sudden monstrous pretension to lay down the law for my choice of ways and means of raising, to my best convenience, a considerable sum of money? You'll be so good as to understand, once for all, that I recognize there no right of interference from any quarter – and also to let that knowledge govern your behaviour in my absence.'

Lady Grace had thus for some minutes waited on his words – waited even as almost with anxiety for the safe conduct he might look to from some of the more extravagant of them. But he at least felt at the end – if it was an end – all he owed them; so that there was nothing for her but to accept as achieved his dreadful felicity. 'You're very angry with me, and I hope you won't feel me simply "aggravating" if I say that, thinking everything over, I've done my best to allow for that. But I *can* answer your question if I do answer it by saying that my discovery of your possible sacrifice of one of our most beautiful things didn't predispose me to decide in favour of a person – however "backed" by you – for whose benefit the sacrifice was to take place. Frankly,' the girl pushed on, 'I did quite hate, for the moment, everything that might make for such a mistake; and took the darkest view, let me also confess, of every one, without exception, connected with it. I interceded with you, earnestly, for our precious picture, and you wouldn't on any terms *have* my intercession. On top of that Lord John blundered in, without timeliness or tact – and I'm afraid that, as I hadn't been the least in love with him even before, he did have to take the consequence.'

Lord Theign, with an elated swing of his person, greeted this as all he could possibly want. 'You recognize then that your reception of him *was* purely vindictive! – the meaning of which is that unless my conduct of my private interests, of which you know nothing whatever, happens to square with your superior wisdom you'll put me under boycott all round! While you chatter about mistakes and blunders, and about our charming friend's lack of the discretion of which you yourself set so grand an example, what account have you to offer of the scene you made me there before that fellow – your confederate, as he had all the air of being! – by giving it me with such effrontery that, if I had eminently done with him after his remarkable display, you at least were but the more determined to see him keep it up?'

The girl's justification, clearly, was very present to her, and not less obviously the truth that to make it strong she must, avoiding every side-issue, keep it very simple. 'The only account I can give you, I think, is that I could but speak at such a moment as I felt, and that I felt – well, how can I say how deeply? If you can really bear to know, I feel so still I care in fact more than ever that we shouldn't do such things. I care, if you like, to indiscretion – I care, if you like, to offence, to arrogance, to folly. But even as my last word to you before you leave England on the conclusion of such a step, I'm ready to cry out to you that you oughtn't, you oughtn't, you oughtn't!'

Her father, with wonder-moved, elevated brows and high commanding hand, checked her as in an act really of violence – save that, like an inflamed young priestess, she had already, in essence, delivered her message. 'Hallo, hallo, hallo, my distracted daughter – no "crying out," if you please!' After which, while arrested but unabashed, she still kept her lighted eyes on him, he gave back her conscious stare for a minute, inwardly and rapidly turning things over, making connections, taking, as after some long and lamentable lapse of observation, a new strange measure of her: all to the upshot of his then speaking with a difference of tone, a recognition of still more of the odious than he had supposed, so that the case might really call for some coolness. 'You keep bad company, Grace – it pays the devil with your sense of proportion. If you make this row when I sell a picture, what will be left to you when I forge a cheque?'

'If you had arrived at the necessity of forging a cheque,' she answered, 'I should then resign myself to that of your selling a picture.'

'But not short of that!'

'Not short of that. Not one of ours.'

'But I couldn't,' said his lordship with his best and coldest amusement, 'sell one of somebody else's!'

She was, however, not disconcerted. 'Other people do other things – they appear to have done them, and to be doing them, all about us. But *we* have been so decently different – always and ever. We've never done anything disloyal.'

'"Disloyal"?' – he was more largely amazed and even interested now.

Lady Grace stuck to her word. 'That's what it seems to *me!*'

'It seems to you' – and his sarcasm here was easy – 'more disloyal to sell a picture than to buy one? Because we didn't paint 'em all ourselves, you know!'

She threw up impatient hands. 'I don't ask you either to paint or to buy —!'

'Oh, *that's* a mercy!' he interrupted, riding his irony hard; 'and I'm glad to hear you at least let me off *such* efforts! However, if it strikes you as gracefully filial to apply to your father's conduct so invidious a word,' he went on less scathingly, 'you must take from him, in your turn, his quite other view of what makes disloyalty – understanding distinctly, by the same token, that he enjoins on you not to give an odious illustration of it, while he's away, by discussing and deploring with any *one* of your extraordinary friends any aspect or feature whatever of his walk and conversation. That – pressed as I am for time,' he went on with a glance at his watch while she remained silent – 'is the main sense of what I have to say to you; so that I count on your perfect conformity. When you have told me that I *may* so count' – and casting about for his hat he espied it and went to take it up – 'I shall more cordially bid you good-bye.'

His daughter looked as if she had been for some time expecting the law thus imposed upon her – had been seeing where he must come out; but in spite of this preparation she made him wait for his reply in such tension as he had himself created. 'To Kitty I've practically said nothing – and she herself can tell you why: I've in fact scarcely seen her this fortnight. Putting aside then Amy Sandgate, the only person to whom I've spoken – of your "sacrifice," as I suppose you'll let me call it? – is Mr Hugh Crimble, whom you talk of as my "confederate" at Dedborough.'

Lord Theign recovered the name with relief. 'Mr Hugh Crimble – that's it! – whom you so amazingly caused to be present, and apparently invited to be active, at a business that so little concerned him.'

'He certainly took upon himself to be interested, as I had hoped he would. But it was because I had taken upon *my* self—'

'To act, yes,' Lord Theign broke in, 'with the grossest want of delicacy! Well, it's from that exactly that you'll now forbear; and "interested" as he may be – for which I'm deucedly obliged to him! – you'll not speak to Mr Crimble again.'

'Never again?' – the girl put it as for full certitude.

'Never of the question that I thus exclude. You may chatter your fill,' said his lordship curtly, 'about any others.'

'Why, the particular question you forbid,' Grace returned with great force, but as if saying something very reasonable – 'that question is *the* question we care about: it's our very ground of conversation.'

'Then,' her father decreed, 'your conversation will please to *dispense* with a ground; or you'll perhaps, better still – if that's the only way! – dispense with your conversation.'

Lady Grace took a moment as if to examine this more closely. 'You require of me not to communicate with Mr Crimble at all?'

'Most assuredly I require it – since it's to that you insist on reducing me.' He didn't look reduced, the master of Dedborough, as he spoke – which was doubtless precisely because he held his head so high to affirm what he suffered. 'Is it so essential to your comfort,' he demanded, 'to hear him, or to make him, abuse me?'

'"Abusing" you, father dear, has nothing whatever to do with it!' – his daughter had fairly lapsed, with a despairing gesture, to the tenderness involved in her compassion for his perversity. 'We look at the thing in a much larger way,' she pursued, not heeding that she drew from him a sound of scorn for her 'larger.' 'It's of our Treasure itself we talk – and of what can be *done* in such cases; though with a close application, I admit, to the case that you embody.'

'Ah,' Lord Theign asked as with absurd curiosity, 'I embody a case?'

'Wonderfully, father – as you do everything; and it's the fact of its being exceptional,' she explained, 'that makes it so difficult to deal with.'

His lordship had a gape for it. '"To deal with"? You're undertaking to "deal" with me?'

She smiled more frankly now, as for a rift in the gloom. 'Well, how can we help it if you *will* be a case?' And then as her tone but visibly darkened his wonder: 'What we've set our hearts on is saving the picture.'

'What you've set your hearts on, in other words, is working straight against me?'

But she persisted without heat. 'What we've set our hearts on is working for England.'

'And pray who in the world's "England,"' he cried in his stupefaction, 'unless *I* am?'

'Dear, dear father,' she pleaded, 'that's all we *want* you to be! I mean' – she didn't fear firmly to force it home – 'in the real, the right, the grand sense; the sense that, you see, is so intensely ours.'

'"Ours"?' – he couldn't but again throw back her word at her. 'Isn't it, damn you, just *in* ours —?'

'No, no,' she interrupted – 'not in *ours!*' She smiled at him still, though it was strained, as if he really ought to perceive.

But he glared as at a senseless juggle. 'What and who the devil are you talking about? What are "we," the whole blest lot of us, pray, but the best and most English thing in the country: people walking – and riding! – straight; doing, disin-terestedly, most of the difficult and all the thankless jobs;

minding their own business, above all, and expecting others to mind theirs?' So he let her 'have' the stout sound truth, as it were – and so the direct force of it clearly might, by his view, have made her reel. 'You and I, my lady, and your two decent brothers, God be thanked for them, and mine into the bargain, and all the rest, the jolly lot of us, take us together – make us numerous enough without any foreign aid or mixture: if that's what I understand you to mean!'

'You don't understand me at all – evidently; and above all I see you don't want to!' she had the bravery to add. 'By "our" sense of what's due to the nation in such a case I mean Mr Crimble's and mine – and nobody's else at all; since, as I tell you, it's only with him I've talked.'

It gave him then, every inch of him showed, the full, the grotesque measure of the scandal he faced. 'So that "you and Mr Crimble" represent the standard, for me, in your opinion, of the proprieties and duties of our house?'

Well, she was too earnest – as she clearly wished to let him see – to mind his perversion of it. 'I express to you the way we feel.'

'It's most striking to hear, certainly, what you express' – he had positively to laugh for it; 'and you speak of him, with your insufferable "we," as if you were presenting him as your – God knows what! You've enjoyed a large exchange of ideas, I gather, to have arrived at such unanimity.' And then, as if to fall into no trap he might somehow be laying for her, she dropped all eagerness and rebutted nothing: 'You must see a great deal of your fellow-critic not to be able to speak of yourself without him!'

'Yes, we're fellow-critics, father' – she accepted this opening. 'I perfectly adopt your term.' But it took her a minute to go further. 'I saw Mr Crimble here half an hour ago.'

'Saw him "here"?' Lord Theign amazedly asked. 'He *comes* to you here – and Amy Sandgate has been silent?'

'It wasn't her business to tell you – since, you see, she could leave it to me. And I quite expect,' Lady Grace then produced, 'that he'll come again.'

It brought down with a bang all her father's authority. 'Then I simply exact of you that you don't see him.'

The pause of which she paid it the deference was charged like a brimming cup. 'Is that what you *really* meant by your condition just now – that when I do see him I shall not speak to him?'

'What I "really meant" is what I really mean – that you bow to the law I lay upon you and drop the man altogether.'

'Have nothing to do with him at all?'

'Have nothing to do with him at all.'

'In fact' – she took it in – 'give him wholly up.'

He had an impatient gesture. 'You sound as if I asked you to give up a fortune!' And then, though she had phrased his idea without consternation – verily as if it had been in the balance for her – he might have been moved by something that gathered in her eyes. 'You're so wrapped up in him that the precious sacrifice is like *that* sort of thing?'

Lady Grace took her time – but showed, as her eyes continued to hold him, what *had* gathered. 'I like Mr Crimble exceedingly, father – I think him clever, intelligent, good; I want what he wants – I want it, I think, really, as much; and I don't at all deny that he has helped to make me so want it. But that doesn't matter. I'll wholly cease to see him, I'll give him up forever, if – if –!' She faltered, however, she hung fire with a smile that anxiously, intensely appealed. Then she began and stopped again, 'If – if –!' while her father caught her up with irritation.

'"If," my lady? If *what*, please?'

'If you'll withdraw the offer of our picture to Mr Bender – and never make another to any one else!'

He stood staring as at the size of it – then translated it into his own terms. 'If I'll obligingly announce to the world that I've made an ass of myself you'll kindly forbear from your united effort – the charming pair of you – to show me up for one?'

Lady Grace, as if consciously not caring or attempting to answer this, simply gave the first flare of his criticism time to drop. It wasn't till a minute passed that she said: 'You don't agree to my compromise?'

Ah, the question but fatally sharpened at a stroke the stiffness of his spirit. 'Good God, I'm to "compromise" on top of everything? – I'm to let you browbeat me, haggle and bargain with me, over a thing that I'm entitled to settle with you as things have ever *been* settled among us, by uttering to you my last parental word?'

'You don't care enough then for what you name?' – she took it up as scarce heeding now what he said.

'For putting an end to your odious commerce –? I give you the measure, on the contrary,' said Lord Theign, 'of how much I care: as you give me, very strangely indeed, it strikes me, that of what it costs you –!' But his other words were lost in the hard long look at her from which he broke off in turn as for disgust.

It was with an effect of decently shielding herself – the unuttered meaning came so straight – that she substituted words of her own. 'Of what it costs me to redeem the picture?'

'To lose your tenth-rate friend' – he spoke without scruple now.

She instantly broke into ardent deprecation, pleading at once and warning. 'Father, father, oh –! You hold the thing in your hands.'

He pulled up before her again as to thrust the responsibility straight back. 'My orders then are so much rubbish to you?'

Lady Grace held her ground, and they remained face to face in opposition and accusation, neither making the other the sign of peace. But the girl at least *had*, in her way, held out the olive-branch, while Lord Theign had but reaffirmed his will. It was for her acceptance of this that he searched her, her last word not having yet come. Before it had done so, however, the door from the lobby opened and Mr Gotch had regained their presence. This appeared to determine in Lady Grace a view of the importance of delay, which she signified to her companion in a 'Well – I must think!' For the butler positively resounded, and Hugh was there.

'Mr Crimble!' Mr Gotch proclaimed – with the further extravagance of projecting the visitor straight upon his lordship.

VII

Our young man showed another face than the face his friend had lately seen him carry off, and he now turned it distressfully from that source of inspiration to Lord Theign, who was flagrantly, even from this first moment, no such source at all, and then from his noble adversary back again, under pressure of difficulty and effort, to Lady Grace, whom he directly addressed. 'Here I am again, you see – and I've got my news, worse luck!' But his manner to her father was the next instant more brisk. 'I learned you were here, my lord; but as the case is important I told them it was all right and came up. I've been to my club,' he added for the girl, 'and found the tiresome thing –!' But he broke down breathless.

'And it isn't good?' she cried with the highest concern.

Ruefully, yet not abjectly, he confessed, 'Not so good as I hoped. For I assure you, my lord, I *counted* —'

'It's the report from Pappendick about the picture at Verona,' Lady Grace interruptingly explained.

Hugh took it up, but, as we should well have seen, under embarrassment dismally deeper; the ugly particular defeat he had to announce showing thus, in his thought, for a more awkward force than any reviving possibilities that he might have begun to balance against them. 'The man I told *you* about also,' he said to his formidable patron; 'whom I went to Brussels to talk with and who, most kindly, has gone for us to Verona.

He has been able to get straight at *their* Mantovano, but the brute horribly wires me that he doesn't quite see the thing; see, I mean' – and he gathered his two hearers together now in his overflow of chagrin, conscious, with his break of the ice, more exclusively of that – 'my vivid vital point, the absolute screaming identity of the two persons represented. I still hold,' he persuasively went on, 'that our man is their man, but Pappendick decides that he isn't – and as Pappendick has so *much* to be reckoned with of course I'm awfully abashed.'

Lord Theign had remained what he had begun by being, immeasurably and inaccessibly detached – only with his curiosity more moved than he could help and as, on second thought, to see what sort of a still more offensive fool the heated youth would really make of himself. 'Yes – you seem indeed remarkably abashed!'

Hugh clearly was thrown again, by the cold 'cut' of this, colder than any mere social ignoring, upon a sense of the damnably poor figure he did offer; so that, while he straightened himself and kept a mastery of his manner and a control of his reply, we should yet have felt his cheek tingle. 'I backed my own judgment strongly, I know – and I've got my snub. But I don't in the least knock under.'

'Only the first authority in Europe doesn't care, I suppose, whether you do or not!'

'He isn't *the* first authority in Europe, thank God,' the young man returned – 'though he is, I admit, one of the three or four first. And I mean to appeal – I've another shot in my locker,' he went on with his rather painfully forced smile to Lady Grace. 'I had already written, you see, to dear old Bardi.'

'Bardi of Milan?' – she recognized, it was admirably manifest, the appeal of his directness to her generosity, awkward as their predicament was also for her herself, and spoke to him as she might have spoken without her father's presence.

It would have shown for beautiful, on the spot, had there been any one to perceive it, that he devoutly recorded her intelligence. 'You know of him? – how delightful of you! For the Italians, I now feel,' he quickly explained, 'he must have *most* the instinct – and it has come over me since that he'd have been more our man. Besides of course his so knowing the Verona picture.'

She had fairly hung on his lips. 'But does he know ours?'

'No – not ours yet. That is' – he consciously and quickly took himself up – 'not yours! But as Pappendick went to Verona for us I've asked Bardi to do us the great favour to come here – if Lord Theign will be so good,' he said, bethinking himself with a turn, 'as to let him examine the Moretto.' He faced again to the personage he mentioned, who, simply standing off and watching, in concentrated interest as well as detachment, this interview of his cool daughter and her still cooler guest, had plainly 'elected,' as it were, to give them rope to hang themselves. Staring very hard at Hugh he met his appeal, but in a silence clearly calculated; against which, however, the young man, bearing up, made such head as he could. He offered his next word, that is, equally to the two companions. 'It's not at all impossible – for such curious effects have been! – that the Dedborough picture seen *after* the Verona will point a different moral from the Verona seen after the Dedborough.'

'And so awfully *long* after – wasn't it?' Lady Grace asked.

'Awfully long after – it was years ago that Pappendick, being in this country for such purposes, was kindly admitted to your house when none of you were there, or at least visible.'

'Oh of course we don't see *every one!*' – she heroically kept it up.

'You don't see every one,' Hugh bravely laughed, 'and that makes it all the more charming that you did, and that you still do, see me. I shall really get Bardi,' he pursued, 'to go again to Verona —'

'The last thing before coming here?' – she had guessed before he could say it; and still she sustained it, so that he could shine at her for assent. 'How happy they should like so to work for you!'

'Ah, we're a band of brothers,' he returned – ' "we few, we happy few[6]" – from country to country'; to which he added, gaining more ease for an eye at Lord Theign: 'though we do have our little rubs and disputes, like Pappendick and me now. The thing, you see, is the ripping *interest* of it all; since,' he developed and explained, for his elder friend's benefit, with pertinacious cheer and an assurance superficially at least recovered, 'when we're really "hit" over a case we'll do almost anything in life.'

Lady Grace, recklessly throbbing in the breath of it all, immediately appropriated what her father let alone. 'It must be so lovely to *feel* so hit!'

'It does spoil one,' Hugh laughed, 'for milder joys. Of course what I have to consider is the chance – putting it at the *merest* chance – of Bardi's own wet blanket! But that's again so very small – though,' he pulled up with a drop to the comparative dismal, which he offered as an almost familiar tribute to Lord Theign, 'you'll retort upon me naturally that I promised you the possibility of Pappendick's veto would be: all on the poor dear old basis, you'll claim, of the wish father to the thought. Well, I do wish to be right as much as I believe I am. Only give me time!' he sublimely insisted.

'How can we prevent your using it?' Lady Grace again interrupted; 'or the fact either that if the worst comes to the worst —'

'The thing' – he at once pursued – 'will always be at the least the greatest of Morettos? Ah,' he cried so cheerily that there was still a freedom in it toward any it might concern, 'the worst sha'n't come to the worst, but the best to the best: my conviction of which it is that supports me in the deep regret I have to express' – and he faced Lord Theign again – 'for any inconvenience I may have caused you by my abortive undertaking. That, I vow here before Lady Grace, I will yet more than make up!'

Lord Theign, after the longest but the blankest contemplation of him, broke hereupon, for the first time, that attitude of completely sustained and separate silence which he had yet made compatible with his air of having deeply noted every element of the scene – so that it was of this full view his participation had effectively consisted. 'I haven't the least idea, sir, what you're talking about!' And he squarely turned his back, strolling toward the other room, the threshold of which he the next moment had passed, remaining scantily within, however, and in sight of the others, not to say of ourselves; even though averted and ostensibly lost in some scrutiny that might have had for its object the great enshrined Lawrence.

There ensued upon his words and movement a vivid mute passage, the richest of commentaries, between his companions; who, deeply divided by the width of the ample room, followed him with their eyes and then used for their own interchange these organs of remark, eloquent now over Hugh's unmistakable dismissal at short order, on which obviously he must at once act. Lady Grace's young arms conveyed to him by a despairing contrite motion of surrender that she had done for him all she could do in his presence and that, however sharply doubtful the result, he was to leave the rest to herself. They communicated thus, the strenuous pair, for their full moment, without speaking; only with the prolonged, the charged give and take of their gaze and, it might well have been imagined, of their passion. Hugh had for an instant a show of hesitation

– of the arrested impulse, while he kept her father within range, to launch at that personage before going some final remonstrance. It was the girl's raised hand and gesture of warning that waved away for him such a mistake; he decided, under her pressure, and after a last searching and answering look at her reached the door and let himself out. The stillness was then prolonged a minute by the further wait of the two others, Lord Theign where he had been standing and his daughter on the spot from which she had not moved. It presently ended in his lordship's turn about as if inferring by the silence that the intruder had withdrawn.

'Is that young man your lover?' he said as he drew again near.

Lady Grace waited a little, but spoke as quietly as if she had been prepared. 'Has the question a bearing on the promise you a short time ago demanded of me?'

'It has a bearing on the so extraordinary appearance of your intimacy with him!'

'You mean that if he *should* be – what you ask me about – your exaction would then be modified?'

'My request that you break it short off? That request would, on the contrary,' Lord Theign pronounced, 'rest on an immense new ground. Therefore I insist on your telling me the truth.'

'Won't the truth be before you, father, if you'll *think* a moment – without extravagance?' After which, while, as stiffly as ever – and it probably seemed to her impatience as stupidly – he didn't rise to it, she went on: 'If I *offered* you not again to see him, does that make for you the appearance —?'

'If you offered it, you mean, on your condition – my promising not to sell? I promised,' said Lord Theign, 'absolutely nothing at all!'

She took him up with all expression. 'So I promised as little!

But that I should have been able to say what I did sufficiently meets your curiosity.'

She might, wronged as she held herself, have felt him stupid not to see *how* wronged; but he was in any case acute for an evasion. 'You risked your offer for the great equivalent over which you've so wildly worked yourself up.'

'Yes, I've worked myself – that, I grant you and don't blush for! But hardly so much as to renounce my "lover" – if,' she prodigiously smiled, 'I were so fortunate as to have one!'

'You renounced poor John mightily easily – whom you were so fortunate as to have!'

Her brows rose as high as his own had ever done. 'Do you call Lord John my lover?'

'He was your suitor most assuredly,' Lord Theign inimitably said, though without looking at her; 'and as strikingly encouraged as he was respectfully ardent!'

'Encouraged by *you*, dear father, beyond doubt!'

'Encouraged – er – by every one: because you were (yes, you *were!*) encouraging. And what I ask of you now is a word of common candour as to whether you didn't, on your honour, turn him off because of your just then so stimulated views on the person who has been with us.'

Grace replied but after an instant, as moved by more things than she could say – moved above all, in her trouble and her pity for him, by other things than harshness: 'Oh father, father, father —!'

He searched her through all the compassion of her cry, but appeared to give way to her sincerity. 'Well then if I *have* your denial I take it as answering my whole question – in a manner that satisfies me. If there's nothing, on your word, of that sort between you, you can all the more drop him.'

'But you said a moment ago that I should all the more in the other case – that of there *being* something!'

He brushed away her logic-chopping. 'If you're so keen then for past remarks I take up your own words – I accept your own terms for your putting an end to Mr Crimble.' To which, while, turning pale, she said nothing, he added: 'You recognize that you profess yourself ready —'

'Not again to see him,' she now answered, 'if you tell me the picture's safe? Yes, I recognize that I *was* ready – as well as how scornfully little you then were!'

'Never mind what I then was – the question's of what I actually am, since I close with you on it. The picture's therefore as safe as you please,' Lord Theign pursued, 'if you'll do what you just now engaged to.'

'I engaged to do nothing,' she replied after a pause; and the face she turned to him had grown suddenly tragic. 'I've no word to take back, for none passed between us; but I *won't* do what I mentioned and what you at once laughed at. Because,' she finished, 'the case is different.'

'Different?' he almost shouted – '*how*, different?'

She didn't look at him for it, but she was none the less strongly distinct. 'He has *been* here – and that has done it. He knows,' she admirably emphasized.

'Knows what I think of him, no doubt – for a brazen young prevaricator! But what else?'

She still kept her eyes on a far-off point. 'What he will have seen – that I feel we're too good friends.'

'Then your denial of it's false,' her father fairly thundered – 'and you *are* infatuated?'

It made her the more quiet. 'I like him very much.'

'So that your row about the picture,' he demanded with passion, 'has been all a blind?' And then as her quietness still held her: 'And his a blind as much – to help him to get *at* you?'

She looked at him again now. 'He must speak for himself. I've said what I mean.'

'But what the devil *do* you mean?' Lord Theign, taking in the hour, had reached the door as in supremely baffled conclusion and with a sense of time lamentably lost.

Their eyes met upon it all dreadfully across the wide space, and, hurried and incommoded as she saw him, she yet made him still stand a minute. Then she let everything go. 'Do what you like with the picture!'

He jerked up his arm and guarding hand as before a levelled blow at his face, and with the other hand flung open the door, having done with her now and immediately lost to sight. Left alone she stood a moment looking before her; then with a vague advance, held apparently by a quickly growing sense of the implication of her act, reached a table where she remained a little, deep afresh in thought – only the next thing to fall into a chair close to it and there, with her elbows on it, yield to the impulse of covering her flushed face with her hands.

BOOK THIRD

I

Hugh Crimble waited again in the Bruton Street drawing-room
– this time at the afternoon hour; he restlessly shifted his place,
looked at things about him without seeing them; all he saw,
all he outwardly studied, was his own face and figure as he
stopped an instant before a long glass suspended between two
windows. Just as he turned from that brief and perhaps not
wholly gratified inspection Lady Grace – that he had sent up
his name to whom was immediately apparent – presented
herself at the entrance from the other room. These young
persons had hereupon no instant exchange of words; their
exchange was mute – they but paused where they were; while
the silence of each evidently tested the other for full confidence.
A measure of this comfort came first, it would have appeared,
to Hugh; though he then at once asked for confirmation of it.

'Am I right, Lady Grace, am I right? – to have *come*, I mean,
after so many days of not hearing, not knowing, and perhaps,
all too stupidly, not trying.' And he went on as, still with her
eyes on him, she didn't speak; though, only, we should have
guessed, from her stress of emotion. 'Even if I'm wrong, let me
tell you, I don't care – simply because, whatever new difficulty
I may have brought about for you here a fortnight ago, there's
something that to-day adds to my doubt and my fear too great
a pang, and that has made me feel I can scarce bear the
suspense of them as they are.'

The girl came nearer, and if her grave face expressed a pity it yet declined a dread. 'Of what suspense do you speak? Your still being without the other opinion —?'

'Ah, that worries me, yes; and all the more, at this hour, as I say, that —' He dropped it, however: 'I'll tell you in a moment! My *real* torment, all the while, has been not to know, from day to day, what situation, what complication that last scene of ours with your father here has let you in for; and yet at the same time – having no sign nor sound from you! – to see the importance of not making anything possibly worse by approaching you again, however discreetly. I've been in the dark,' he pursued, 'and feeling that I must leave *you* there; so that now – just brutally turning up once more under personal need and at any cost – I don't know whether I most want or most fear what I may learn from you.'

Lady Grace, listening and watching, appeared to choose between different ways of meeting this appeal; she had a pacifying, postponing gesture, marked with a beautiful authority, a sign of the value for her of what she gave precedence to and which waved off everything else. 'Have you had – first of all – any news yet of Bardi?'

'That I have is what has driven me straight *at* you again – since I've shown you before how I turn to you at a crisis. He has come as I hoped and like a regular good 'un,' Hugh was able to state; 'I've just met him at the station, but I pick him up again, at his hotel in Clifford Street, at five. He stopped, on his way from Dover this morning, to my extreme exasperation, to "sample" Canterbury, and I leave him to a bath and a change and tea. Then swooping down I whirl him round to Bond Street, where his very first apprehension of the thing (an apprehension, oh I guarantee you, so quick and clean and fine and wise) will be the flash-light projected – well,' said the young man, to wind up handsomely, but briefly and reasonably, 'over the whole field of our question.'

She panted with comprehension. 'That of the two portraits being but the one sitter!'

'That of the two portraits being but the one sitter. With everything so to the good, more and more, that bangs in, up to the head, the golden nail of authenticity, and' – he quite glowed through his gloom for it – 'we take our stand in glory on the last Mantovano in the world.'

It was a presumption his friend visibly yearned for – but over which, too, with her eyes away from him, she still distinguished the shadow of a cloud. 'That is if the flash-light comes!'

'That is if it comes indeed, confound it!' – he had to enlarge a little under the recall of past experience. 'So now, at any rate, you see my tension!'

She looked at him again as with a vision too full for a waste of words. 'While you on your side of course keep well in view Mr Bender's.'

'Yes, while I keep well in view Mr Bender's; though he doesn't know, you see, of Bardi's being at hand.'

'Still,' said the girl, always all lucid for the case, 'if the "flash-light" does presently break —!'

'It will first take him in the eye?' Hugh had jumped to her idea, but he adopted it only to provide: 'It might if he didn't now wear goggles, so to say! – clapped on him too hard by Pappendick's so damnably perverse opinion.' With which, however, he quickly bethought himself. 'Ah, of course, these wretched days, you haven't known of Pappendick's personal visit. After that wire from Verona I wired him back defiance —'

'And that brought him?' she cried.

'To do the honest thing, yes – I *will* say for him: to renew, for full assurance, his early memory of our picture.'

She hung upon it. 'But only to stick then to what he had telegraphed?'

'To declare that for *him*, lackaday! our thing's a pure Moretto – and to declare as much, moreover, with all the weight of his authority, to Bender himself, who of course made a point of seeing him.'

'So that Bender' – she followed and wondered – 'is, as a consequence, wholly off?'

It made her friend's humour play up in his acuteness. 'Bender, Lady Grace, is, by the law of his being, never "wholly" off – or on! – anything. He lives, like the moon, in mid-air, shedding his silver light on earth; never quite gone, yet never *all* there – save for inappreciable moments. He *would* be in eclipse as a peril, I grant,' Hugh went on – 'if the question had struck him as really closed. But luckily the blessed Press – which is a pure heavenly joy and now quite immense on it – keeps it open as wide as Piccadilly.'

'Which makes, however,' Lady Grace discriminated, 'for the danger of a grab.'

'Ah, but all the more for the shame of a surrender! Of course I admit that when it's a question of a life spent, like his, in waiting, acquisitively, for the cat to jump, the only thing for one, at a given moment, as against that signal, is to be found one's self by the animal in the line of its trajectory. That's exactly,' he laughed, 'where we are!'

She cast about as intelligently to note the place. 'Your great idea, you mean, *has* so worked – with the uproar truly as loud as it has seemed to come to us here?'

'All beyond my wildest hope,' Hugh returned; 'since the sight of the picture, flocked to every day by thousands, so beautifully *tells*. That we must at any cost keep it, that the nation must, and hang on to it tight, is the cry that fills the air – to the tune of ten letters a day in the Papers, with every three days a gorgeous leader; to say nothing of more and more passionate talk all over the place, some of it awfully wild, but all of it wind in our sails.'

'I suppose it was that wind then that blew me round there to see the thing in its new light,' Lady Grace said. 'But I couldn't stay – for tears!'

'Ah,' Hugh insisted on his side for comfort, 'we'll crow loudest yet! And don't meanwhile, just *don't*, those splendid strange eyes of the fellow seem consciously to plead? The women, bless them, adore him, cling to him, and there's talk of a "Ladies' League of Protest" – all of which keeps up the pitch.'

'Poor Amy and I are a ladies' league,' the girl joylessly joked – 'as we now take in the "Journal" regardless of expense.'

'Oh then you practically *have* it all – since,' Hugh added after a brief hesitation, 'I suppose Lord Theign himself doesn't languish uninformed.'

'At far-off Salsomaggiore – by the papers? No doubt indeed he isn't spared even the worst,' said Lady Grace – 'and no doubt too it's a drag on his cure.'

Her companion seemed struck with her lack of assurance. 'Then you don't – if I may ask – hear from him?'

'I? Never a word.'

'He doesn't write?' Hugh allowed himself to insist.

'He doesn't write. And I don't write either.'

'And Lady Sandgate?' Hugh once more ventured.

'Doesn't *she* write?'

'Doesn't she hear?' said the young man, treating the other form of the question as a shade evasive.

'I've asked her not to tell me,' his friend replied – 'that is if he simply holds out.'

'So that as she doesn't tell you' – Hugh was clear for the inference – 'he of course does hold out.' To which he added almost accusingly while his eyes searched her: 'But your case is really bad.'

She confessed to it after a moment, but as if vaguely enjoying it. 'My case is really bad.'

He had a vividness of impatience and contrition. 'And it's I who – all too blunderingly! – have made it so?'

'I've made it so myself,' she said with a high head-shake, 'and you, on the contrary –!' But here she checked her emphasis.

'Ah, I've so *wanted*, through our horrid silence, to help you!' And he pressed to get more at the truth. 'You've so quite fatally displeased him?'

'To the last point – as I tell you. But it's not to that I refer,' she explained; 'it's to the ground of complaint I've given *you*.' And then as this but left him blank, 'It's time – it was at once time – that you should know,' she pursued; 'and yet if it's hard for me to speak, as you see, it was impossible for me to write. But there it is.' She made her sad and beautiful effort. 'The last thing before he left us I let the picture go.'

'You mean –?' But he could only wonder – till, however, it glimmered upon him. 'You gave up your protest?'

'I gave up my protest. I told him that – so far as I'm concerned! – he might do as he liked.'

Her poor friend turned pale at the sharp little shock of it; but if his face thus showed the pang of too great a surprise he yet wreathed the convulsion in a gay grimace. 'You leave me to struggle alone?'

'I leave you to struggle alone.'

He took it in bewilderingly, but tried again, even to the heroic, for optimism. 'Ah well, you decided, I suppose, on some new personal ground.'

'Yes; a reason came up, a reason I hadn't to that extent looked for and which of a sudden – quickly, before he went – I *had* somehow to deal with. So to give him my word in the

dismal sense I mention was my only way to meet the strain.'
She paused; Hugh waited for something further, and 'I gave
him my word I wouldn't help you,' she wound up.

He turned it over. 'To *act* in the matter – I see.'

'To act in the matter' – she went through with it – 'after the
high stand I had taken.'

Still he studied it. 'I see – I see. It's between you and your
father.'

'It's between him and me – yes. An engagement not again
to trouble him.'

Hugh, from his face, might have feared a still greater complication; so he made, as he would probably have said, a jolly lot
of this. 'Ah, that was nice of you. And natural. *That's* all right!'

'No' – she spoke from a deeper depth – 'it's altogether
wrong. For whatever happens I must now accept it.'

'Well, say you must' – he really declined not to treat it
almost as rather a 'lark' – 'if we can at least go on talking.'

'Ah, we *can* at least go on talking!' she perversely sighed. 'I
can say anything I like so long as I don't say it to *him!*' she
almost wailed. But she added with more firmness: 'I can still
hope – and I can still pray.'

He set free again with a joyous gesture all his confidence.
'Well, what more *could* you do, anyhow? So isn't that enough?'

It took her a moment to say, and even then she didn't. 'Is it
enough for *you*, Mr Crimble?'

'What *is* enough for me' – he could for his part readily name
it – 'is the harm done you at our last meeting by my irruption;
so that if you got his consent to see me —!'

'I didn't get his consent!' – she had turned away from the
searching eyes, but she faced them again to rectify: 'I see you
against his express command.'

'Ah then thank God I came!' – it was like a bland breath on
a *feu de joie*:[7] he flamed so much higher.

'Thank God you've come, yes – for my deplorable exposure.' And to justify her name for it before he could protest, 'I *offered* him here not to see you,' she rigorously explained.

'"Offered him?" – Hugh did drop for it. 'Not to see me – ever again?'

She didn't falter. 'Never again.'

Ah then he understood. 'But he wouldn't let that serve —?'

'Not for the price I put on it.'

'His yielding on the picture?'

'His yielding on the picture.'

Hugh lingered before it all. 'Your proposal wasn't "good enough"?'

'It wasn't good enough.'

'I see,' he repeated – 'I see.' But he was in that light again mystified. 'Then why are you therefore not free?'

'Because – just after – you came back, and I *did* see you again!'

Ah, it was all present. 'You found you were too sorry for me?'

'I found I was too sorry for you – as he himself found I was.'

Hugh had got hold of it now. 'And *that*, you mean, he couldn't stomach?'

'So little that when you had gone (and *how* you had to go you remember) he at once proposed, rather than that I should receive you in a way so different from his own —'

'To do all we want of him?'

'To do all I did at least.'

'And it was *then*,' he took in, 'that you wouldn't deal?'

'Well' – try though she might to keep the colour out, it all came straighter and straighter now – 'those moments had brought you home to me as they had also brought *him*; making such a difference, I felt, for what he veered round to agree to.'

'The difference' – Hugh wanted it so adorably definite – 'that you didn't see your way to accepting —?'

'No, not to accepting the condition he named.'

'Which was that he'd keep the picture for you if you'd treat me as too "low" —?'

'If I'd treat you,' said Lady Grace with her eyes on his fine young face, 'as impossible.'

He kept her eyes – he clearly liked so to make her repeat it. 'And not even for the sake of the picture –?' After he had given her time, however, her silence, with her beautiful look in it, seemed to admonish him not to force her for his pleasure; as if what she had already told him didn't make him throb enough for the wonder of it. He *had* it, and let her see by his high flush how he made it his own – while, the next thing, as it was but part of her avowal, the rest of that illumination called for a different intelligence. 'Your father's reprobation of me personally is on the ground that you're all such great people?'

She spared him the invidious answer to this as, a moment before, his eagerness had spared her reserve; she flung over the 'ground' that his question laid bare the light veil of an evasion. '"Great people," I've learned to see, mustn't – to remain great – do what my father's doing.'

'It's indeed on the theory of their not so behaving,' Hugh returned, 'that we see them – all the inferior rest of us – in the grand glamour of their greatness!'

If he had spoken to meet her admirable frankness half-way, that beauty in her almost brushed him aside to make at a single step the rest of the journey. 'You won't see them in it for long – if they don't now, under such tests and with such opportunities, begin to take care.'

This had given him, at a stroke, he clearly felt, all freedom for the closer criticism. 'Lord Theign perhaps recognizes some such canny truth, but "takes care," with the least trouble to himself and the finest short cut – does it, if you'll let me say so, rather on the cheap – by finding "the likes" of me, as his daughter's trusted friend, out of the question.'

'Well, you won't mind that, will you?' Lady Grace asked, 'if he finds his daughter herself, in any such relation to you, quite as much so.'

'Different enough, from position to position and person to person,' he brightly brooded, 'is the view that gets itself *most* comfortably taken of the implications of Honour!'

'Yes,' the girl returned; 'my father, in the act of despoiling us all, all who are interested, without apparently the least unpleasant consciousness, keeps the balance showily even, to his mostly so fine, so delicate sense, by suddenly discovering that he's scandalized at my caring for your friendship.'

Hugh looked at her, on this, as with the gladness verily of possession promised and only waiting – or as if from that moment forth he had her assurance of everything that most concerned him and that might most inspire. 'Well, isn't the moral of it all simply that what his perversity of pride, as we can only hold it, will have most done for us is to bring us – and to keep us – blessedly together?'

She seemed for a moment to question his 'simply.' 'Do you regard us as so much "together" when you remember where, in spite of everything, I've put myself?'

'By telling him to do what he likes?' he recalled without embarrassment. 'Oh, that wasn't in spite of "everything" – it was only in spite of the Mantovano.'

'"Only"?' she flushed – 'when I've given the picture up?'

'Ah,' Hugh cried, 'I don't care a hang for the picture!' And then as she let him, closer, close to her with this, possess himself of her hands: 'We both only care, don't we, that we're given to each other thus? We both only care, don't we, that nothing can keep us apart?'

'Oh, if you've forgiven me –!' she sighed into his fond face.

'Why, since you gave the thing up *for* me,' he pleadingly laughed, 'it isn't as if you had given *me* up —!'

'For anything, anything? Ah never, never!' she breathed.

'Then why aren't we all right?'

'Well, if you will —!'

'Oh for ever and ever and ever!' – and with this ardent cry of his devotion his arms closed in their strength and she was clasped to his breast and to his lips.

The next moment, however, she had checked him with the warning 'Amy Sandgate!' – as if she had heard their hostess enter the other room. Lady Sandgate was in fact almost already upon them – their disjunction had scarce been effected and she had reached the nearer threshold. They had at once put the widest space possible between them – a little of the flurry of which transaction agitated doubtless their clutch at composure. They gave back a shade awkwardly and consciously, on one side and the other, the speculative though gracious attention she for a few moments made them and their recent intimate relation the subject of; from all of which indeed Lady Grace sought and found cover in a prompt and responsible address to Hugh. 'Mustn't you go without more delay to Clifford Street?'

He came back to it all alert. 'At once!' He had recovered his hat and reached the other door, whence he gesticulated farewell to the elder lady. 'Please pardon me' – and he disappeared.

Lady Sandgate hereupon stood for a little silently confronted with the girl. 'Have you freedom of mind for the fact that your father's suddenly at hand?'

'He has come back?' – Lady Grace was sharply struck.

'He arrives this afternoon and appears to go straight to Kitty – according to a wire that I find downstairs on coming back late from my luncheon. He has returned with a rush – as,' said his correspondent in the elation of triumph, 'I was *sure* he would!'

Her young friend was more at sea. 'Brought back, you mean, by the outcry – even though he so hates it?'

But she was more and more all lucidity – save in so far as she was now almost all authority. 'Ah, hating still more to seem afraid, he has come back to face the music!'

Lady Grace, turning away as in vague despair for the manner in which the music might affect him, yet wheeled about again, after thought, to a positive recognition and even to quite an inconsequent pride. 'Yes – that's dear old father!'

And what was Lady Sandgate moreover but mistress now of the subject? 'At the point the row has reached he couldn't stand it another day; so he has thrown up his cure and – lest we should oppose him! – not even announced his start.'

'Well,' her companion returned, 'now that I've *done* it all I shall never oppose him again!'

Lady Sandgate appeared to show herself as still under the impression she might have received on entering. 'He'll only oppose *you!*'

'If he does,' said Lady Grace, 'we're at present two to bear it.'

'Heaven save us then' – the elder woman was quick, was even cordial, for the sense of this – 'your good friend *is* clever!'

Lady Grace honoured the remark. 'Mr Crimble's remarkably clever.'

'And you've arranged —?'

'We haven't arranged – but we've understood. So that, dear Amy, if *you* understand –!' Lady Grace paused, for Gotch had come in from the hall.

'His lordship has arrived?' his mistress immediately put to him.

'No, my lady, but Lord John has – to know if he's expected *here*, and in that case, by your ladyship's leave, to come up.'

Her ladyship turned to the girl. 'May Lord John – as we do await your father – come up?'

'As suits *you*, please!'

'He may come up,' said Lady Sandgate to Gotch. 'His lord-ship's expected.' She had a pause till they were alone again, when she went on to her companion: 'You asked me just now if I understood. Well – I do understand!'

Lady Grace, with Gotch's withdrawal, which left the door open, had reached the passage to the other room. 'Then you'll excuse me!' – she made her escape.

II

Lord John, reannounced the next instant from the nearest quarter and quite waiving salutations, left no doubt of the high pitch of his eagerness and tension as soon as the door had closed behind him. 'What on earth then do you suppose he has come back to *do* –?' To which he added while his hostess's gesture impatiently disclaimed conjecture: 'Because when a fellow really finds himself the centre of a cyclone —!'

'Isn't it just at the centre,' she interrupted, 'that you keep remarkably still, and only in the suburbs that you feel the rage? I count on dear Theign's doing nothing in the least foolish —!'

'Ah, but he can't have chucked everything for nothing,' Lord John sharply returned; 'and wherever you place him in the rumpus he can't not meet somehow, hang it, such an assault on his character as a great nobleman and good citizen.'

'It's his luck to have become with the public of the news-papers the scapegoat-in-chief: for the sins, so-called, of a lot of people!' Lady Sandgate inconclusively sighed.

'Yes,' Lord John concluded for her, 'the mercenary millions on whose traffic in their trumpery values – when they're so lucky as to have any! – *this* isn't a patch!'

'Oh, there are cases *and* cases: situations and responsibilities so intensely differ!' – that appeared on the whole, for her ladyship, the moral to be gathered.

'Of course everything differs, all round, from everything,' Lord John went on; 'and who in the world knows anything of his own case but the victim of circumstances exposing himself, for the highest and purest motives, to be literally torn to pieces?'

'Well,' said Lady Sandgate as, in her strained suspense, she freshly consulted her bracelet watch, 'I hope he isn't already torn – if you tell me you've been to Kitty's.'

'Oh, he was all right so far: he had arrived and gone out again,' the young man explained, 'as Lady Imber hadn't been at home.'

'Ah cool Kitty!' his hostess sighed again – but diverted, as she spoke, by the reappearance of her butler, this time positively preceding Lord Theign, whom she met, when he presently stood before her, his garb of travel exchanged for consummate afternoon dress, with yearning tenderness and compassionate curiosity. 'At last, dearest friend – what a joy! But with Kitty not at home to receive you?'

That young woman's parent made light of it for the indulged creature's sake. 'Oh I knew my Kitty! I dressed and I find her at five-thirty.' To which he added as he only took in further, without expression, Lord John: 'But Bender, who came there before my arrival – he hasn't tried for me here?'

It was a point on which Lord John himself could at least be expressive. 'I met him at the club at luncheon; he had had your letter – but for which chance, my dear man, I should have known nothing. You'll see him all right at this house; but I'm glad, if I may say so, Theign,' the speaker pursued with some emphasis – 'I'm glad, you know, to get hold of you first.'

Lord Theign seemed about to ask for the meaning of this remark, but his other companion's apprehension had already overflowed. 'You haven't come back, have you – to whatever it may be! – for *trouble* of any sort with Breckenridge?'

His lordship transferred his penetration to this fair friend. 'Have you become so intensely absorbed – these remarkable days! – in "Breckenridge"?'

She felt the shadow, you would have seen, of his claimed right, or at least privilege, of search – yet easily, after an instant, emerged clear. 'I've thought and dreamt but of *you* – suspicious man! – in proportion as the clamour has spread; and Mr Bender meanwhile, if you want to know, hasn't been near me once!'

Lord John came in a manner, and however unconsciously, to her aid. 'You'd have seen, if he had been, what's the matter with him, I think – and what perhaps Theign has seen from his own letter: since,' he went on to his fellow-visitor, 'I understood him a week ago to have been much taken up with writing you.'

Lord Theign received this without comment, only again with an air of expertly sounding the speaker; after which he gave himself afresh for a moment to Lady Sandgate. 'I've not come home for any clamour, as you surely know me well enough to believe; or to notice for a minute the cheapest insolence and aggression – which frankly scarce reached me out there; or which, so far as it did, I was daily washed clean of by those blest waters. I returned on Mr Bender's letter,' he then vouchsafed to Lord John – 'three extraordinarily vulgar pages about the egregious Pappendick!'

'About his having suddenly turned up in person, yes, and, as Breckenridge says, marked the picture down?' – the young man was clearly all-knowing. 'That *has* of course weighed on Bender – being confirmed apparently, on the whole, by the drift of public opinion.'

Lord Theign took, on this, with a frank show of reaction from some of his friend's terms, a sharp turn off; he even ironically indicated the babbler or at least the blunderer in question to Lady Sandgate. 'He too has known me so long, and he comes here to talk to me of "the drift of public opinion"!' After which he quite charged at his vain informant. 'Am I to tell you again that I snap my fingers at the drift of public opinion? – which is but another name for the chatter of all the fools one doesn't know, in addition to all those (and plenty of 'em!) one damnably does.'

Lady Sandgate, by a turn of the hand, dropped oil from her golden cruse. 'Ah, you did *that*, in your own grand way, before you went abroad!'

'I don't speak of the matter, my dear man, in the light of its effect on *you*,' Lord John importantly explained – 'but in the light of its effect on Bender; who so consumedly wants the picture, if he *is* to have it, to be a Mantovano, but seems unable to get it taken at last for anything but the fine old Moretto that of course it has always been.'

Lord Theign, in growing disgust at the whole beastly complication, betrayed more and more the odd pitch of the temper that had abruptly restored him with such incalculable weight to the scene of action. 'Well, isn't a fine old Moretto good enough for him; confound him?'

It pulled up not a little Lord John, who yet made his point. 'A fine old Moretto, you know, was exactly what he declined at Dedborough – for its comparative, strictly comparative, insignificance; and he only thought of the picture when the wind began to rise for the enormous rarity —'

'That that mendacious young cad who has bamboozled Grace,' Lord Theign broke in, 'tried to befool us, for his beggarly reasons, into claiming for it?'

Lady Sandgate renewed her mild influence. 'Ah, the knowing people haven't had their last word – the possible Mantovano isn't exploded *yet!*'

Her noble friend, however, declined the offered spell. 'I've had enough of the knowing people – the knowing people are serpents! My picture's to take or to leave – and it's what I've come back, if you please, John, to say to your man to his face.'

This declaration had a report as sharp and almost as multiplied as the successive cracks of a discharged revolver; yet when the light smoke cleared Lady Sandgate at least was still left standing and smiling. 'Yes, why in mercy's name can't he choose *which*? – and why does he write him, dreadful Breckenridge, such tiresome argumentative letters?'

Lord John took up her idea as with the air of something that had been working in him rather vehemently, though under due caution too, as a consequence of this exchange, during which he had apprehensively watched his elder. 'I don't think I quite see *how*, my dear Theign, the poor chap's letter was so offensive.'

In that case his dear Theign could tell him. 'Because it was a tissue of expressions that may pass current – over counters and in awful newspapers – in *his* extraordinary world or country, but that I decline to take time to puzzle out here.'

'If he didn't make himself understood,' Lord John took leave to laugh, 'it must indeed have been an unusual production for Bender.'

'Oh, I often, with the wild beauty, if you will, of so many of his turns, haven't a notion,' Lady Sandgate confessed with an equal gaiety, 'of what he's talking about.'

'I think I never miss his weird sense,' her younger guest again loyally contended – 'and in fact as a general thing I rather like it!'

'I happen to like nothing that I don't enjoy,' Lord Theign rejoined with some asperity – 'and so far as I do follow the fellow he assumes on my part an interest in his expenditure of purchase-money that I neither feel nor pretend to. He doesn't want – by what I spell out – the picture he refused at Dedborough; he may possibly want – if one reads it so – the picture on view in Bond Street; and he yet appears to make, with great emphasis, the stupid ambiguous point that these two "articles" (the greatest of Morettos an "article"!) haven't been "by now" proved different; as if I engaged with him that I myself would so prove them!'

Lord John indulged in a pause – but also in a suggestion. 'He must allude to your hoping – when you allowed us to place the picture with Mackintosh[8] – that it would show to all London in the most precious light conceivable.'

'Well, if it hasn't so shown' – and Lord Theign stared as if mystified – 'what in the world's the meaning of this preposterous racket?'

'The racket is largely,' his young friend explained, 'the vociferation of the people who contradict each other about it.'

On which their hostess sought to enliven the gravity of the question. 'Some – yes – shouting on the housetops that's a Mantovano of the Mantovanos, and others shrieking back at them that they're donkeys if not criminals.'

'He may take it for whatever he likes,' said Lord Theign, heedless of these contributions, 'he may father it on Michael Angelo himself if he'll but clear out with it and let me alone!'

'What he'd *like* to take it for,' Lord John at this point saw his way to remark, 'is something in the nature of a Hundred Thousand.'

'A Hundred Thousand?' cried his astonished friend.

'Quite, I dare say, a Hundred Thousand' – the young man enjoyed clearly handling even by the lips so round a sum.

Lady Sandgate disclaimed however with agility any appearance of having gaped. 'Why, haven't you yet realized, Theign, that those are the American figures?'

His lordship looked at her fixedly and then did the same by Lord John, after which he waited a little. 'I've nothing to do with the American figures – which seem to me, if you press me, you know, quite intolerably vulgar.'

'Well, I'd be as vulgar as anybody for a Hundred Thousand!' Lady Sandgate hastened to proclaim.

'Didn't he let us know at Dedborough,' Lord John asked of the master of that seat, 'that he had no use, as he said, for lower values?'

'I've heard him remark myself,' said their companion, rising to the monstrous memory, 'that he wouldn't take a cheap picture – even though a "handsome" one – as a present.'

'And does he call the thing round the corner a cheap picture?' the proprietor of the work demanded.

Lord John threw up his arms with a grin of impatience. 'All he wants to do, don't you see? is to prevent your *making* it one!'

Lord Theign glared at this imputation to him of a low ductility. 'I offered the thing, as it was, at an estimate worthy of it – and of *me*.'

'My dear reckless friend,' his young adviser protested, 'you named no figure *at all* when it came to the point —!'

'It *didn't* come to the point! Nothing came to the point but that I put a Moretto on view; as a thing, yes, perfectly' – Lord Theign accepted the reminding gesture – 'on which a rich American had an eye and in which he had, so to speak, an interest. That was what I wanted, and so we left it – parting each of us ready but neither of us bound.'

'Ah, Mr Bender's bound, as he'd say,' Lady Sandgate interposed – '"bound" to make you swallow the enormous luscious plum that your appetite so morbidly rejects!'

'My appetite, as morbid as you like' – her old friend had shrewdly turned on her – 'is my own affair, and if the fellow must deal in enormities I warn him to carry them elsewhere!'

Lord John, plainly, by this time, was quite exasperated at

the absurdity of him. 'But how can't you see that it's only a plum, as she says, for a plum and an eye for an eye – since the picture itself, with this huge ventilation, is now quite a different affair?'

'How the deuce a different affair when just what the man himself confesses is that, in spite of all the chatter of the prigs and pedants, there's no really established ground for treating it as anything but the same?' On which, as having so unanswerably spoken, Lord Theign shook himself free again, in his high petulance, and moved restlessly to where the passage to the other room appeared to offer his nerves an issue; all moreover to the effect of suggesting to us that something still other than what he had said might meanwhile work in him behind and beneath that quantity. The spectators of his trouble watched him, for the time, in uncertainty and with a mute but associated comment on the perversity and oddity he had so suddenly developed; Lord John giving a shrug of almost bored despair and Lady Sandgate signalling caution and tact for their action by a finger flourished to her lips, and in fact at once proceeding to apply these arts. The subject of her attention had still remained as in worried thought; he had even mechanically taken up a book from a table – which he then, after an absent glance at it, tossed down.

'You're so detached from reality, you adorable dreamer,' she began – 'and unless you stick to *that* you might as well have done nothing. What you call the pedantry and priggishness and all the rest of it is exactly what poor Breckenridge asked almost on his knees, wonderful man, to be *allowed* to pay you for; since even if the meddlers and chatterers haven't settled anything for those who know – though which of the elect themselves after all *does* seem to know? – it's a great service rendered him to have started such a hare to run!'

Lord John took freedom to throw off very much the same

idea. 'Certainly his connection with the whole question and agitation makes no end for his glory.'

It didn't, that remark, bring their friend back to him, but it at least made his indifference flash with derision. 'His "glory" – Mr Bender's glory? Why, they quite universally loathe him – judging by the stuff they print!'

'Oh, here – as a corrupter of our morals and a promoter of our decay, even though so many are flat on their faces to him – yes! But it's another affair over there where the eagle screams like a thousand steam-whistles and the newspapers flap like the leaves of the forest: *there* he'll be, if you'll only let him, the biggest thing going; since sound, in that air, seems to mean size, and size to be all that counts. If he said of the thing, as you recognize,' Lord John went on, '"It's going to be a Mantovano," why you can bet your life that it *is* – that it has *got* to be some kind of a one.'

His fellow-guest, at this, drew nearer again, irritated, you would have been sure, by the unconscious infelicity of the pair – worked up to something quite openly wilful and passionate. 'No kind of a furious flaunting one, under *my* patronage, that I can prevent, my boy! The Dedborough picture in the market – owing to horrid little circumstances that regard myself alone – is the Dedborough picture at a decent, sufficient, civilized Dedborough price, and nothing else whatever; which I beg you will take as my last word on the subject.'

Lord John, trying whether he *could* take it, momentarily mingled his hushed state with that of their hostess, to whom he addressed a helpless look; after which, however, he appeared to find that he could only reassert himself. 'May I nevertheless reply that I think you'll not be able to prevent *anything*? – since the discussed object will completely escape your control in New York!'

'And almost any discussed object' – Lady Sandgate rose to

the occasion also – 'is in New York, by what one hears, easily *worth* a Hundred Thousand!'

Lord Theign looked from one of them to the other. 'I sell the man a Hundred Thousand worth of swagger and advertisement; and of fraudulent swagger and objectionable advertisement at that?'

'Well' – Lord John was but briefly baffled – 'when the picture's his you can't help its doing what it can and what it will for him anywhere!'

'Then it isn't his yet,' the elder man retorted – 'and I promise you never will be if he has *sent* you to me with his big drum!'

Lady Sandgate turned sadly on this to her associate in patience, as if the case were now really beyond them. 'Yes, how indeed can it ever *become* his if Theign simply won't let him pay for it?'

Her question was unanswerable. 'It's the first time in all my life I've known a man feel insulted, in such a piece of business, by happening *not* to be, in the usual way, more or less swindled!'

'Theign is unable to take it in,' her ladyship explained, 'that – as I've heard it said of all these money-monsters of the new type – Bender simply can't *afford* not to be cited and celebrated as the biggest buyer who ever lived.'

'Ah, cited and celebrated at my *expense* – say it at once and have it over, that I may enjoy what you all want to do to me!'

'The dear man's inimitable – at his "expense"!' It was more than Lord John could bear as he fairly flung himself off in his derisive impotence and addressed his wail to Lady Sandgate.

'Yes, at my expense is exactly what I mean,' Lord Theign asseverated – 'at the expense of my modest claim to regulate my behaviour by my own standards. There you perfectly *are* about the man, and it's precisely what I say – that he's to hustle and harry me *because* he's a money-monster: which I never for

171

a moment dreamed of, please understand, when I let you, John, thrust him at me as a pecuniary resource at Dedborough. I didn't put my property on view that *he* might blow about it —!'

'No, if you like it,' Lady Sandgate returned; 'but you certainly didn't so arrange' – she seemed to think her point somehow would help – 'that you might blow about it yourself!'

'Nobody wants to "blow,"' Lord John more stoutly interposed, 'either hot or cold, I take it; but I really don't see the harm of Bender's liking to be known for the scale of his transactions – actual or merely imputed even, if you will; since that scale is really so magnificent.'

Lady Sandgate half accepted, half qualified this plea. 'The only question perhaps is why he doesn't try for some precious work that somebody – less delicious than dear Theign – *can* be persuaded on bended knees to accept a hundred thousand for.'

'"Try" for one?' – her younger visitor took it up while her elder more attentively watched him. 'That was exactly what he did try for when he pressed you so hard in vain for the great Sir Joshua.'

'Oh well, he mustn't come back to *that* – must he, Theign?' her ladyship cooed.

That personage failed to reply, so that Lord John went on, unconscious apparently of the still more suspicious study to which he exposed himself. 'Besides which there *are* no things of that magnitude knocking about, don't you know? – they've *got* to be worked up first if they're to reach the grand publicity of the Figure! Would you mind,' he continued to his noble monitor, 'an agreement on some such basis as *this*? – that you shall resign yourself to the biggest equivalent you'll squeamishly consent to take, if it's at the same time the smallest he'll squeamishly consent to offer; but that, that done, you shall leave him free —'

Lady Sandgate took it up straight, rounding it off, as their companion only waited. 'Leave him free to talk about the sum offered and the sum taken as practically one and the same?'

'Ah, you know,' Lord John discriminated, 'he doesn't "talk" so much himself – there's really nothing blatant or crude about poor Bender. It's the rate at which – by the very way he's "fixed": an awful way indeed, I grant you! – a perfect army of reporter-wretches, close at his heels, are always talking for him and of him.'

Lord Theign spoke hereupon at last with the air as of an impulse that had been slowly gathering force. '*You* talk for him, my dear chap, pretty well. You urge his case, my honour, quite as if you were assured of a commission on the job – on a fine ascending scale! Has he put you up to that proposition, eh? *Do* you get a handsome percentage and *are* you to make a good thing of it?'

The young man coloured under this stinging pleasantry – whether from a good conscience affronted or from a bad one made worse; but he otherwise showed a bold front, only bending his eyes a moment on his watch. 'As he's to come to you himself – and I don't know why the mischief he doesn't come! – he will answer you that graceful question.'

'Will he answer it,' Lord Theign asked, 'with the veracity that the suggestion you've just made on his behalf represents him as so beautifully adhering to?' On which he again quite fiercely turned his back and recovered his detachment, the others giving way behind him to a blanker dismay.

Lord John, in spite of this however, pumped up a tone. 'I don't see why you should speak as if I were urging some abomination.'

'Then I'll tell you why!' – and Lord Theign was upon him again for the purpose. 'Because I had rather give the cursed thing away outright and for good and all than that it should

173

hang out there another day in the interest of such equivocations!'

Lady Sandgate's dismay yielded to her wonder, and her wonder apparently in turn to her amusement. '"Give it away," my dear friend, to a man who only longs to smother you in gold?'

Her dear friend, however, had lost patience with her levity. 'Give it away – just for a luxury of protest and a stoppage of chatter – to some cause as unlike as possible that of Mr Bender's power of sound and his splendid reputation: to the Public, to the Authorities, to the Thingumbob, to the Nation!'

Lady Sandgate broke into horror while Lord John stood sombre and stupefied. 'Ah, my dear creature, you've flights of extravagance —!'

'One thing's very certain,' Lord Theign quite heedlessly pursued – 'that the thought of my property on view there does give intolerably on my nerves, more and more every minute that I'm conscious of it; so that, hang it, if one thinks of it, why shouldn't I, for my relief, do again, damme,[9] *what I like?* – that is bang the door in their faces, have the show immediately stopped?' He turned with the attraction of this idea from one of his listeners to the other. 'It's *my* show – it isn't Bender's, surely! – and I can do just as I choose with it.'

'Ah, but isn't that the very point?' – and Lady Sandgate put it to Lord John. 'Isn't it Bender's show much more than his?'

Her invoked authority, however, in answer to this, made but a motion of disappointment and disgust at so much rank folly – while Lord Theign, on the other hand, followed up his happy thought. 'Then if it's Bender's show, or if he claims it is, there's all the more reason!' And it took his lordship's inspiration no longer to flower. 'See here, John – do this: go right round there this moment, please, and tell them from me to shut straight down!'

' "Shut straight down"?' the young man abhorrently echoed.

'Stop it *to-night* – wind it up and end it: see?' The more the entertainer of that vision held it there the more charm it clearly took on for him. 'Have the picture removed from view and the incident closed.'

'You seriously ask *that* of me!' poor Lord John quavered.

'Why in the world shouldn't I? It's a jolly lot less than you asked of me a month ago at Dedborough.'

'What then am I to say to them?' Lord John spoke but after a long moment, during which he had only looked hard and – an observer might even then have felt – ominously at his taskmaster.

That personage replied as if wholly to have done with the matter. 'Say anything that comes into your clever head. I don't really see that there's anything else *for* you!' Lady Sandgate sighed to the messenger, who gave no sign save of positive stiffness.

The latter seemed still to weigh his displeasing obligation; then he eyed his friend significantly – almost portentously. 'Those are absolutely your sentiments?'

'Those are absolutely my sentiments' – and Lord Theign brought this out as with the force of a physical push.

'Very well then!' But the young man, indulging in a final, a fairly sinister, study of such a dealer in the arbitrary, made sure of the extent, whatever it was, of his own wrong. 'Not one more day?'

Lord Theign only waved him away. 'Not one more hour!'

He paused at the door, this reluctant spokesman, as if for some supreme protest; but after another prolonged and decisive engagement with the two pairs of eyes that waited, though differently, on his performance, he clapped on his hat as in the rage of his resentment and departed on his mission.

III

'He can't bear to do it, poor man!' Lady Sandgate ruefully remarked to her remaining guest after Lord John had, under extreme pressure, dashed out to Bond Street.

'I dare say not!' – Lord Theign, flushed with the felicity of self-expression, made little of that. 'But he goes too far, you see, and it clears the air – pouah! Now therefore' – and he glanced at the clock – 'I must go to Kitty.'

'Kitty – with what Kitty wants,' Lady Sandgate opined – 'won't thank you for *that!*'

'She never thanks me for anything' – and the fact of his resignation clearly added here to his bitterness. 'So it's no great loss!'

'Won't you at any rate,' his hostess asked, 'wait for Bender?'

His lordship cast it to the winds. 'What have I to do with him now?'

'Why surely if he'll accept your own price —!'

Lord Theign thought – he wondered; and then as if fairly amused at himself: 'Hanged if I know what *is* my own price!' After which he went for his hat. 'But there's one thing,' he remembered as he came back with it: 'where's my too, *too* unnatural daughter?'

'If you mean Grace and really want her I'll send and find out.'

'Not now' – he bethought himself. 'But does she *see* that chatterbox?'

'Mr Crimble? Yes, she sees him.'

He kept his eyes on her. 'Then how far has it gone?'

Lady Sandgate overcame an embarrassment. 'Well, not even yet, I think, so far as they'd like.'

'They'd "like" – heaven save the mark! – to marry?'

'I suspect them of it. What line, if it should come to that,' she asked, 'would you then take?'

He was perfectly prompt. 'The line that for Grace it's simply ignoble.'

The force of her deprecation of such language was qualified by tact. 'Ah, darling, as dreadful as *that*?'

He could but view the possibility with dark resentment. 'It lets us so down – from what we've always been and done; so dcwn, down, down that I'm amazed you don't feel it!'

'Oh, I feel there's still plenty to keep you up!' she soothingly laughed.

He seemed to consider this vague amount – which he apparently judged, however, not so vast as to provide for the whole yearning of his nature. 'Well, my dear,' he thus more blandly professed, 'I shall need all the extra *agrément*[10] that your affection can still supply.'

If nothing could have been, on this, richer than her response, nothing could at the same time have been more pleasing than her modesty. 'Ah, my affection, Theign, is, as I think you know, a fountain always at flood; but in any more worldly element than that I'm – as you've ever seen for yourself – a poor struggler with my own sad affairs, a broken reed; not a bit "great," as they used so finely to call it! You *are* great – with the natural sense of greatness and, for your supreme support, the instinctive grand manner of doing and taking things.'

He sighed, none the less, he groaned, with his frown of trouble, for the strain he foresaw on these resources. 'If you mean that I hold up my head, on proper grounds, I grant that

I always have. But how's that longer possible when my children commit such base vulgarities? Why in the name of goodness *have* I such children? What the devil has got into 'em? – and is it really the case that when Grace offers me for a proof of her license and a specimen of her taste such a son-in-law as you tell me I'm in danger of I've just helplessly to swallow the dose?'

'Do you find Mr Crimble,' Lady Sandgate asked as if there might really be something to say for him, 'so utterly out of the question?'

'I found him on the two occasions before I went away in the last degree offensive and outrageous; but even if he charged one and one's poor dear decent old defences with less rabid a fury everything about him would forbid *that* kind of relation.'

What kind of relation, if any, Hugh's deficiencies might still render thinkable Lord Theign was kept from going on to mention by the voice of Mr Gotch, who had thrown open the door to the not altogether assured sound of 'Mr Breckenridge Bender.' The guest in possession gave a cry of impatience, but Lady Sandgate said 'Coming up?'

'If his lordship will see him.'

'Oh, he's beyond his time,' his lordship pronounced – 'I can't see him now!'

'Ah, but *mustn't* you – and mayn't *I* then?' She waited, however, for no response to signify to her servant 'Let him come,' and her companion could but exhale a groan of reluctant accommodation as if he wondered at the point she made of it. It enlightened him indeed perhaps a little that she went on while Gotch did her bidding. 'Does the kind of relation you'd be condemned to with Mr Crimble let you down, down, down, as you say, more than the relation you've been having with Mr Bender?'

Lord Theign had for it the most uninforming of stares. 'Do you mean don't I hate 'em equally both?'

She cut his further reply short, however, by a 'Hush!' of warning – Mr Bender was there and his introducer had left them.

Lord Theign, full of his purpose of departure, sacrificed hereupon little to ceremony. 'I've but a moment, to my regret, to give you, Mr Bender, and if you've been unavoidably detained, as you great bustling people are so apt to be, it will perhaps still be soon enough for your comfort to hear from me that I've just given order to close our exhibition. From the present hour on, sir' – he put it with the firmness required to settle the futility of an appeal.

Mr Bender's large surprise lost itself, however, promptly enough, in Mr Bender's larger ease. 'Why, do you really mean it, Lord Theign? – removing already from view a work that gives innocent gratification to thousands?'

'Well,' said his lordship curtly, 'if thousands have seen it I've done what I wanted, and if they've been gratified I'm content – and invite *you* to be.'

Mr Bender showed more keenness for this richer implication. 'In other words it's I who may remove the picture?'

'Well – if you'll take it on my estimate.'

'But what, Lord Theign, all this time,' Mr Bender almost pathetically pleaded, 'is your estimate?'

The parting guest had another pause, which prolonged itself, after he had reached the door, in a deep solicitation of their hostess's conscious eyes. This brief passage apparently inspired his answer. 'Lady Sandgate will tell you.' The door closed behind him.

The charming woman smiled then at her other friend, whose comprehensive presence appeared now to demand of her some account of these strange proceedings. 'He means that your own valuation is much too shockingly high.'

'But how can I know *how* much unless I find out what he'll

take?' The great collector's spirit had, in spite of its volume, clearly not reached its limit of expansion. 'Is he crazily waiting for the thing to be proved *not* what Mr Crimble claims?'

'No, he's waiting for nothing – since he holds that claim demolished by Pappendick's tremendous negative, which you wrote to tell him of.'

Vast, undeveloped and suddenly grave, Mr Bender's countenance showed like a barren tract under a black cloud. 'I wrote to *report*, fair and square, on Pappendick, but to tell him I'd take the picture just the same, negative and all.'

'Ah, but take it in that way not for what it is but for what it isn't.'

'We know nothing about what it "isn't,"' said Mr Bender, 'after all that has happened – we've only learned a little better every day what it is.'

'You mean,' his companion asked, 'the biggest bone of artistic contention —?'

'Yes,' – he took it from her – 'the biggest that has been thrown into the arena for quite a while. I guess I can do with it for *that*.'

Lady Sandgate, on this, after a moment, renewed her personal advance; it was as if she had now made sure of the soundness of her main bridge. 'Well, if it's the biggest bone I won't touch it; I'll leave it to be mauled by my betters. But since his lordship has asked me to name a price, dear Mr Bender, I'll name one – and as you prefer big prices I'll try to make it suit you. Only it won't be for the portrait of a person nobody is agreed about. The whole world is agreed, you know, about my great-grandmother.'

'Oh, shucks, Lady Sandgate!' – and her visitor turned from her with the hunch of overcharged shoulders.

But she apparently felt that she held him, or at least that even if such a conviction might be fatuous she must now put it to the touch. 'You've been delivered into my hands – too charmingly; and you won't really pretend that you don't recognize that and in fact rather like it.'

He faced about to her again as to a case of coolness unparalleled – though indeed with a quick lapse of real interest in the question of whether he had been artfully practised upon; an indifference to bad debts or peculation[11] like that of some huge hotel or other business involving a margin for waste. He could afford, he could work waste too, clearly – and what was it, that term, you might have felt him ask, but a mean measure, anyway? quite as the 'artful,' opposed to his larger game, would be the hiding and pouncing of children at play. 'Do I gather that those uncanny words of his were just meant to put me off?' he inquired. And then as she but boldly and smilingly shrugged, repudiating responsibility, 'Look here, Lady Sandgate, ain't you honestly going to help me?' he pursued.

This engaged her sincerity without affecting her gaiety. 'Mr Bender, Mr Bender, I'll help you if you'll help *me!*'

'You'll really get me something from him to go on with?'

'I'll get you something from him to go on with.'

'That's all I ask – to get *that.* Then I can move the way I want. But without it I'm held up.'

'You shall have it,' she replied, 'if I in turn may look to *you* for a trifle on account.'

'Well,' he dryly gloomed at her, 'what do you call a trifle?'

'I mean' – she waited but an instant – 'what you would feel as one.'

'That won't do. You haven't the least idea, Lady Sandgate,' he earnestly said, '*how* I feel at these foolish times. I've never got used to them yet.'

'Ah, don't you understand,' she pressed, 'that if I give you an advantage I'm completely at your mercy?'

'Well, what mercy,' he groaned, 'do you deserve?'

She waited a little, brightly composed – then she indicated her inner shrine, the whereabouts of her precious picture. 'Go and look at her again and you'll see.'

His protest was large, but so, after a moment, was his compliance – his heavy advance upon the other room, from just within the doorway of which the great Lawrence was serenely visible. Mr Bender gave it his eyes once more – though after the fashion verily of a man for whom it had now no freshness of a glamour, no shade of a secret; then he came back to his hostess. 'Do you call giving me an advantage squeezing me by your sweet modesty for less than I may possibly bear?'

'How can I say fairer,' she returned, 'than that, with my backing about the other picture, which I've passed you my word for, thrown in, I'll resign myself to whatever you may be disposed – characteristically! – to give for this one.'

'If it's a question of resignation,' said Mr Bender, 'you mean of course what I may be disposed – characteristically! – *not* to give.'

She played on him for an instant all her radiance. 'Yes then, you dear sharp rich thing!'

'And you take in, I assume,' he pursued, 'that I'm just going to lean on you, for what I want, with the full weight of a determined man.'

'Well,' she laughed, 'I promise you I'll thoroughly obey the direction of your pressure.'

'All right then!' And he stopped before her, in his unrest, monumentally pledged, yet still more massively immeasurable. 'How'll you have it?'

She bristled as with all the possible beautiful choices; then she shed her selection as a heaving fruit-tree might have dropped some round ripeness. It was for her friend to pick up his plum and his privilege. 'Will you write a cheque?'

'Yes, if you want it right away.' To which, however, he added, clapping vainly a breast-pocket: 'But my cheque-book's down in my car.'

'At the door?' She scarce required his assent to touch a bell. 'I can easily send for it.' And she threw off while they waited: 'It's so sweet your "flying round" with your cheque-book!'

He put it with promptitude another way. 'It flies round pretty well with *me!*'

'Mr Bender's cheque-book – in his car,' she went on to Gotch, who had answered her summons.

The owner of the interesting object further instructed him: 'You'll find in the pocket a large red morocco case.'

'Very good, sir,' said Gotch – but with another word for his mistress. 'Lord John would like to know —'

'Lord John's there?' she interrupted.

Gotch turned to the open door. 'Here he is, my lady.'

She accommodated herself at once, under Mr Bender's eye, to the complication involved in his lordship's presence. 'It's he who went round to Bond Street.'

Mr Bender stared, but saw the connection. 'To stop the show?' And then as the young man was already there: 'You've stopped the show?'

'It's "on" more than ever!' Lord John responded while Gotch retired: a hurried, flurried, breathless Lord John, strikingly different from the backward messenger she had lately seen despatched. 'But Theign should be here!' – he addressed her excitedly. 'I announce you a call from the Prince.'

'The Prince?' – she gasped as for the burden of the honour. 'He follows you?'

Mr Bender, with an eagerness and a candour there was no mistaking, recognized on behalf of his ampler action a world of associational advantage and auspicious possibility. 'Is the Prince *after* the thing?'

Lord John remained, in spite of this challenge, conscious of nothing but his message. 'He was there with Mackintosh – to see and admire the picture; which he thinks, by the way, a Mantovano pure and simple! – and did me the honour to remember me. When he heard me report to Mackintosh in his presence the sentiments expressed to me here by our noble friend and of which, embarrassed though I doubtless was,' the young man pursued to Lady Sandgate, 'I gave as clear an account as I could, he was so delighted with it that he declared they mustn't think then of taking the thing off, but must on the contrary keep putting it forward for all it's worth, and he would come round and congratulate and thank Theign and explain him his reasons.'

Their hostess cast about for a sign. 'Why Theign is at Kitty's, worse luck! The Prince calls on him *here?*'

'He calls, you see, on *you*, my lady – at five-forty-five; and graciously desired me so to put it you.'

'He's very kind, but' – she took in her condition – 'I'm not even *dressed!*'

'You'll have time' – the young man was a comfort – 'while I rush to Berkeley Square. And pardon me, Bender – though it's so near – if I just bag your car.'

'That's, that's it, take his car!' – Lady Sandgate almost swept him away.

'You may use my car all right,' Mr Bender contributed – 'but what I want to know is what the man's *after.*'

'The man? what man?' his friend scarce paused to ask.

'The Prince then – if you allow he *is* a man! Is he after my picture?'

Lord John vividly disclaimed authority. 'If you'll wait, my dear fellow, you'll see.'

'Oh why should he "wait"?' burst from their cautious companion – only to be caught up, however, in the next breath,

so swift her gracious revolution. 'Wait, wait indeed, Mr Bender
– I won't give you up for any Prince!' With which she appealed
again to Lord John. 'He wants to "congratulate"?'

'On Theign's decision, as I've told you – which I announced
to Mackintosh, by Theign's extraordinary order, under his
Highness's nose, and which his Highness, by the same token,
took up like a shot.'

Her face, as she bethought herself, was convulsed as by
some quick perception of what her informant must have done
and what therefore the Prince's interest rested on; all, however,
to the effect, given their actual company, of her at once dodging
and covering that issue. 'The decision to remove the picture?'

Lord John also observed a discretion. 'He wouldn't hear of
such a thing – says it must stay stock still. So there you are!'

This determined in Mr Bender a not unnatural, in fact quite
a clamorous, series of questions. 'But *where* are we, and what
has the Prince to do with Lord Theign's decision when that's
all *I'm* here for? What in thunder *is* Lord Theign's decision –
what was his "extraordinary order"?'

Lord John, too long detained and his hand now on the door,
put off this solicitor as he had already been put off. 'Lady
Sandgate, *you* tell him! I rush!'

Mr Bender saw him vanish, but all to a greater bewilderment.
'What the h —[12] then (I beg your pardon!) is he talking about,
and what "sentiments" did he report round there that Lord
Theign had been expressing?'

His hostess faced it not otherwise than if she had resolved
not to recognize the subject of his curiosity – for fear of other
recognitions. 'They put everything on *me*, my dear man – but
I haven't the least idea.'

He looked at her askance. 'Then why does the fellow say
you have?'

Much at a loss for the moment, she yet found her way.

'Because the fellow's so agog that he doesn't know *what* he says!' In addition to which she was relieved by the reappearance of Gotch, who bore on a salver the object he had been sent for and to which he duly called attention.

'The large red morocco case.'

Lady Sandgate fairly jumped at it. 'Your blessed cheque-book. Lay it on my desk,' she said to Gotch, though waiting till he had departed again before she resumed to her visitor: 'Mightn't we conclude before he comes?'

'The Prince?' Mr Bender's imagination had strayed from the ground to which she sought to lead it back, and it but vaguely retraced its steps. 'Will *he* want your great-grandmother?'

'Well, he may when he sees her!' Lady Sandgate laughed. 'And Theign, when he comes, will give you on his own question, I feel sure, every information. Shall I fish it out for you?' she encouragingly asked, beside him by her secretary-desk, at which he had arrived under her persuasive guidance and where she sought solidly to establish him, opening out the gilded crimson case for his employ, so that he had but to help himself. 'What enormous cheques! *You* can never draw one for two-pound-ten!'

'That's exactly what you deserve I *should* do!' He remained after this solemnly still, however, like some high-priest circled with ceremonies; in consonance with which, the next moment, both her hands held out to him the open and immaculate page of the oblong series much as they might have presented a royal infant at the christening-font.

He failed, in his preoccupation, to receive it; so she placed it before him on the table, coming away with a brave gay 'Well, I leave it to you!' She had not, restlessly revolving, kept her discreet distance for many minutes before she found herself almost face to face with the recurrent Gotch, upright at the door with a fresh announcement.

'Mr Crimble, please – for Lady Grace.'

'Mr Crimble *again?*' – she took it discomposedly.

It reached Mr Bender at the secretary, but to a different effect. 'Mr Crimble? Why he's just the man I want to see!'

Gotch, turning to the lobby, had only to make way for him. 'Here he is, my lady.'

'Then tell her ladyship.'

'She has come down,' said Gotch while Hugh arrived and his companion withdrew, and while Lady Grace, reaching the scene from the other quarter, emerged in bright equipment – in her hat, scarf and gloves.

IV

These young persons were thus at once confronted across the room, and the girl explained her preparation. 'I was listening hard – for your knock and your voice.'

'Then know that, thank God, it's all right!' – Hugh was breathless, jubilant, radiant.

'A Mantovano?' she delightedly cried.

'A Mantovano!' he proudly gave back.

'A Mantovano!' – it carried even Lady Sandgate away.

'A Mantovano – a sure thing?' Mr Bender jumped up from his business, all gaping attention to Hugh.

'I've just left our blest Bardi,' said that young man – 'who hasn't the shadow of a doubt and is delighted to publish it everywhere.'

'Will he publish it right here to *me?*' Mr Bender hungrily asked.

'Well,' Hugh smiled, 'you can try him.'

'But try him how, where?' The great collector, straining to instant action, cast about for his hat. 'Where *is* he, hey?'

'Don't you wish I'd tell you?' Hugh, in his personal elation, almost cynically answered.

'Won't you wait for the Prince?' Lady Sandgate had meanwhile asked of her friend; but had turned more inspectingly to Lady Grace before he could reply. 'My dear child – though you're lovely! – are you sure you're ready for him?'

'For the Prince!' – the girl was vague. 'Is he coming?'

'At five-forty-five.' With which she consulted her bracelet watch, but only at once to wail for alarm. 'Ah, it *is* that, and I'm not dressed!' She hurried off through the other room.

Mr Bender, quite accepting her retreat, addressed himself again unabashed to Hugh: 'It's your blest Bardi I want first – I'll take the Prince after.'

The young man clearly could afford indulgence now. 'Then I left him at Long's Hotel.'[13]

'Why, right near! I'll come back.' And Mr Bender's flight was on the wings of optimism.

But it all gave Hugh a quick question for Lady Grace. 'Why does the Prince come, and what in the world's happening?'

'My father has suddenly returned – it may have to do with that.'

The shadow of his surprise darkened visibly to that of his fear. 'Mayn't it be more than anything else to give you and me his final curse?'

'I don't know – and I think I don't care. I don't care,' she said, 'so long as you're right and as the greatest light of all declares you are.'

'He *is* the greatest' – Hugh was vividly of that opinion now: 'I could see it as soon as I got there with him, the charming creature! There, *before* the holy thing, and with the place, by good luck, for those great moments, practically to ourselves – without Macintosh to take in what was happening or any one else at all to speak of – it was but a matter of ten minutes: he had come, he had seen, and *I* had conquered.'

'Naturally you had!' – the girl hung on him for it; 'and what was happening beyond everything else was that for your original dear divination, one of the divinations of genius – with every creature all these ages so stupid – you were being baptized on the spot a great man.'

'Well, he did let poor Pappendick have it at least – he doesn't think *he's* one: that that eminent judge couldn't, even with such a leg up, rise to my level or seize my point. And if you really want to know,' Hugh went on in his gladness, 'what for *us* has most particularly and preciously taken place, it is that in his opinion, for my career —'

'Your reputation,' she cried, 'blazes out and your fortune's made?'

He did a happy violence to his modesty. 'Well, Bardi adores intelligence and takes off his hat to me.'

'Then you need take off yours to nobody!' – such was Lady Grace's proud opinion. 'But I should like to take off mine to *him*,' she added; 'which I seem to have put on – to get out and away with you – expressly for that.'

Hugh, as he looked her over, took it up in bliss. 'Ah, we'll go forth together to him then – thanks to your happy, splendid impulse! – and you'll back him gorgeously up in the good he thinks of me.'

His friend yet had on this a sombre second thought. 'The only thing is that our awful American —!'

But he warned her with a raised hand. 'Not to speak of our awful Briton!'

For the door had opened from the lobby, admitting Lord Theign, unattended, who, at sight of his daughter and her companion, pulled up and held them a minute in reprehensive view – all at least till Hugh undauntedly, indeed quite cheerfully, greeted him.

'Since you find me again in your path, my lord, it's because I've a small, but precious document to deliver you, if you'll allow me to do so; which I feel it important myself to place in your hand.' He drew from his breast a pocket-book and extracted thence a small unsealed envelope; retaining the latter a trifle helplessly in his hand while Lord Theign only opposed to this demonstration an unmitigated blankness. He went none the less bravely on. 'I mentioned to you the last time we somewhat infelicitously met that I intended to appeal to another and probably more closely qualified artistic authority on the subject of your so-called Moretto; and I in fact saw the picture half an hour ago with Bardi of Milan, who, there in presence of it, did absolute, did ideal justice, as I had hoped, to the claim I've been making. I then went with him to his hotel, close at hand, where he dashed me off this brief and rapid, but quite conclusive, Declaration, which, if you'll be so good as to read it, will enable you perhaps to join us in regarding the vexed question as settled.'

His lordship, having faced this speech without a sign, rested on the speaker a somewhat more confessed intelligence, then looked hard at the offered note and hard at the floor – all to avert himself actively afterward and, with his head a good deal elevated, add to his distance, as it were, from every one and everything so indelicately thrust on his attention. This movement had an ambiguous makeshift air, yet his companions, under the impression of it, exchanged a hopeless look. His daughter none the less lifted her voice. 'If you won't take what he has for you from Mr Crimble, father, will you take it from me?' And then as after some apparent debate he appeared to decide to heed her, 'It may be so long again,' she said, 'before you've a chance to do a thing I ask.'

'The chance will depend on yourself!' he returned with high dry emphasis. But he held out his hand for the note Hugh had given her and with which she approached him; and though face to face they seemed more separated than brought near by this contact without commerce. She turned away on one side when he had taken the missive, as Hugh had turned away on the other; Lord Theign drew forth the contents of the envelope and broodingly and inexpressively read the few lines; after which, as having done justice to their sense, he thrust the paper forth again till his daughter became aware and received it. She restored it to her friend while her father dandled off anew, but coming round this time, almost as by a circuit of the room, and meeting Hugh, who took advantage of it to repeat by a frank gesture his offer of Bardi's attestation. Lord Theign passed with the young man on this a couple of mute minutes of the same order as those he had passed with Lady Grace in the same connection; their eyes dealt deeply with their eyes – but to the effect of his lordship's accepting the gift, which after another minute he had slipped into his breast-pocket. It was not till then that he brought out a curt but resonant 'Thank you!' While the others awaited his further pleasure he again bethought himself – then he addressed Lady Grace. 'I must let Mr Bender know —'

'Mr Bender,' Hugh interposed, 'does know. He's at the present moment with the author of that note at Long's Hotel.'

'Then I must now write him' – and his lordship, while he spoke and from where he stood, looked in refined disconnectedness out of the window.

'Will you write *there?*' – and his daughter indicated Lady Sandgate's desk, at which we have seen Mr Bender so importantly seated.

Lord Theign had a start at her again speaking to him; but he bent his view on the convenience awaiting him and then, as to have done with so tiresome a matter, took advantage of it. He went and placed himself, and had reached for paper and a pen when, struck apparently with the display of some incongruous object, he uttered a sharp 'Hallo!'

'You don't find things?' Lady Grace asked – as remote from him in one quarter of the room as Hugh was in another.

'On the contrary!' he oddly replied. But plainly suppressing any further surprise he committed a few words to paper and put them into an envelope, which he addressed and brought away.

'If you like,' said Hugh urbanely, 'I'll carry him that myself.'

'But how do you know what it consists of?'

'I don't know. But I risk it.'

His lordship weighed the proposition in a high impersonal manner – he even nervously weighed his letter, shaking it with one hand upon the finger-tips of the other; after which, as finally to acquit himself of any measurable obligation, he allowed Hugh, by a surrender of the interesting object, to redeem his offer of service. 'Then you'll learn,' he simply said.

'And may *I* learn?' asked Lady Grace.

'You?' The tone made so light of her that it was barely interrogative.

'May I go *with* him?'

Her father looked at the question as at some cup of supreme bitterness – a nasty and now quite regular dose with which his lips were familiar, but before which their first movement was always tightly to close. '*With* me, my lord,' said Hugh at last, thoroughly determined they should open and intensifying the emphasis.

He had his effect, and Lord Theign's answer, addressed to Lady Grace, made indifference very comprehensive. 'You may do what ever you dreadfully like!'

At this then the girl, with an air that seemed to present her choice as absolutely taken, reached the door which Hugh had come across to open for her. Here she paused as for another, a last look at her father, and her expression seemed to say to him unaidedly that, much as she would have preferred to proceed to her act without this gross disorder, she could yet find inspiration too in the very difficulty and the old faiths themselves that he left her to struggle with. All this made for depth and beauty in her serious young face – as it had indeed

193

a force that, not indistinguishably, after an instant, his lordship lost any wish for longer exposure to. His shift of his attitude before she went out was fairly an evasion; if the extent of the levity of one of his daughter's made him afraid, what might have been his present strange sense but a fear of the other from the extent of her gravity? Lady Grace passes from us at any rate in her laced and pearled and plumed slimness and her pale concentration – leaving her friend a moment, however, with his hand on the door.

'You thanked me just now for Bardi's opinion after all,' Hugh said with a smile; 'and it seems to me that – after all as well – I've grounds for thanking you!' On which he left his benefactor alone.

'Tit for tat!' There broke from Lord Theign, in his solitude, with the young man out of earshot, that vague ironic comment; which only served his turn, none the less, till, bethinking himself, he had gone back to the piece of furniture used for his late scribble and come away from it again the next minute delicately holding a fair slip that we naturally recognize as Mr Bender's forgotten cheque. This apparently surprising value he now studied at his ease and to the point of its even drawing from him an articulate 'What in damnation –?' His speculation dropped before the return of his hostess, whose approach through the other room fell upon his ear and whom he awaited after a quick thrust of the cheque into his waistcoat.

Lady Sandgate appeared now in due – that is in the most happily adjusted – splendour; she had changed her dress for something smarter and more appropriate to the entertainment of Princes. 'Tea will be downstairs,' she said. 'But you're alone?'

'I've just parted,' her friend replied, 'with Grace and Mr Crimble.'

' "Parted" with them?' – the ambiguity struck her.

'Well, they've gone out together to flaunt their monstrous connection!'

'You speak,' she laughed, 'as if it were too gross –! They're surely coming back?'

'Back to you, if you like – but not to me.'

'Ah, what are you and I,' she tenderly argued, 'but one and the same quantity? And though you may not as yet absolutely rejoice in – well, whatever they're doing,' she cheerfully added, 'you'll get beautifully used to it.'

'That's just what I'm afraid of – what such horrid matters make of one!'

'At the worst then, you see' – she maintained her optimism – 'the recipient of royal attentions!'

'Oh,' said her companion, whom his honour seemed to leave comparatively cold, 'it's simply as if the gracious Personage were coming to condole!'

Impatient of the lapse of time, in any case, she assured herself again of the hour. 'Well, if he only does come!'

'John – the wretch!' Lord Theign returned – 'will take care of that: he has nailed him and will bring him.'

'What was it then,' his friend found occasion in the particular tone of this reference to demand, 'what was it that, when you sent him off, John spoke of you in Bond Street as specifically intending?'

Oh he saw it now all lucidly – if not rather luridly – and thereby the more tragically. 'He described me in his nasty rage as consistently – well, heroic!'

'His rage' – she pieced it sympathetically out – 'at your destroying his cherished credit with Bender?'

Lord Theign was more and more possessed of this view of the manner of it. 'I had come between him and some profit that he doesn't confess to, but that made him viciously and vindictively serve me up there, as he caught the chance, to the Prince – and the People!'

She cast about, in her intimate interest, as for some closer conception of it. 'By saying that you had remarked here that you offered the People the picture —?'

'As a sacrifice – yes! – to morbid, though respectable scruples.' To which he sharply added, as if struck with her easy grasp of the scene: 'But I hope you've nothing to call a memory for any such extravagance?'

Lady Sandgate waited – then boldly took her line. 'None whatever! You had reacted against Bender – but you hadn't gone so far as *that!*'

He had it now all vividly before him. 'I had reacted – like a gentleman; but it didn't thereby follow that I acted – or spoke – like a demagogue; and my mind's a complete blank on the subject of my having done so.'

'So that there only flushes through your conscience,' she suggested, 'the fact that he has forced your hand?'

Fevered with the sore sense of it his lordship wiped his brow. 'He has played me, for spite, his damned impertinent trick!'

She found but after a minute – for it wasn't easy – the right word, or the least wrong, for the situation. 'Well, even if he did so diabolically commit you, you still don't want – do you? – to back out.'

Resenting the suggestion, which restored all his nobler form, Lord Theign fairly drew himself up. 'When did I ever in all my life back out?'

'Never, never in all your life of course!' – she dashed a bucketful at the flare. 'And the picture after all —!'

'The picture after all' – he took her up in cold grim gallant despair – 'has just been pronounced definitely priceless.' And then to meet her gaping ignorance: 'By Mr Crimble's latest and apparently greatest adviser, who strongly stamps it a Mantovano and whose practical affidavit I now possess.'

Poor Lady Sandgate gaped but the more – she wondered and yearned. 'Definitely priceless?'

'Definitely priceless.' After which he took from its place of lurking, considerately unfolding it, the goodly slip he had removed from her blotting-book. 'Worth even more therefore than what Bender so blatantly offers.'

Her attention fell with interest, from the distance at which she stood, on this confirmatory document, her recognition of which was not immediate. 'And is that the affidavit?'

'This is a cheque to your order, my lady, for ten thousand pounds.'

'Ten thousand?' – she echoed it with a shout.

'Drawn by some hand unknown,' he went on quietly.

'Unknown?' – again, in her muffled joy, she let it sound out.

'Which I found there at your desk a moment ago, and thought best, in your interest, to rescue from accident or neglect; even though it be, save for the single stroke of a name begun,' he wound up with his look like a playing searchlight, 'unhappily unsigned.'

'Unsigned?' – the exhibition of her design, of her defeat, kept shaking her. 'Then it isn't good —?'

'It's a Barmecide feast,[14] my dear!' – he had still, her kind friend, his note of grimness and also his penetration of eye. 'But who is it writes you colossal cheques?'

'And then leaves them lying about?' Her case was so bad that you would have seen how she felt she must *do* something – something quite splendid. She recovered herself, she faced the situation with all her bright bravery of expression and aspect; conscious, you might have guessed, that she had never more strikingly embodied, on such lines, the elegant, the beautiful and the true. 'Why, who can it have been but poor Breckenridge too?'

'"Breckenridge" –?' Lord Theign had *his* smart echoes. 'What in the world does he owe you money for?'

It took her but an instant more – she performed the great repudiation quite as she might be prepared to sweep, in the Presence impending, her grandest curtsey. '*Not*, you sweet suspicious thing, for my great-grandmother!' And then as his glare didn't fade: 'Bender makes my life a burden – for the love of my precious Lawrence.'

'Which you're weakly letting him grab?' – nothing could have been finer with this than Lord Theign's reprobation unless it had been his surprise.

She shook her head as in bland compassion for such an idea. 'It isn't a payment, you goose – it's a bribe! I've withstood him, these trying weeks, as a rock the tempest; but he wrote that and left it there, the fiend, to tempt me – to corrupt me!'

'Without putting his name?' – her companion again turned over the cheque.

She bethought herself, clearly with all her genius, as to this anomaly, and the light of reality broke. 'He must have been interrupted in the artful act – he sprang up with such a bound at Mr Crimble's news. At once then – for his interest in it – he hurried off, leaving the cheque forgotten and unfinished.' She smiled more intensely, her eyes attached, as from fascination, to the morsel of paper still handled by her friend. 'But of course on his next visit he'll *add* his great signature.'

'The devil he will!' – and Lord Theign, with the highest spirit, tore the crisp token into several pieces, which fluttered, as worthless now as pure snowflakes, to the floor.

'Ay, ay, ay!' – it drew from her a wail of which the character, for its sharp inconsequence, was yet comic.

This renewed his stare at her. 'Do *you* want to back out? I mean from your noble stand.'

As quickly, however, she had saved herself. 'I'd rather do even what you're doing – offer my treasure to the Thing-umbob!'

He was touched by this even to sympathy. 'Will you then *join* me in setting the example of a great donation —?'

'To the What-do-you-call-it?' she extravagantly smiled.

'I call it,' he said with dignity, 'the "National Gallery."'

She closed her eyes as with a failure of breath. 'Ah my dear friend —!'

'It would convince me,' he went on, insistent and persuasive.

'Of the sincerity of my affection?' – she drew nearer to him.

'It would comfort me' – he was satisfied with his own expression. Yet in a moment, when she had come all rustlingly and fragrantly close, 'It would captivate me,' he handsomely added.

'It would captivate you?' It was for *her*, we should have seen, to be satisfied with his expression; and, with our more informed observation of all it was a question of her giving up, she would have struck us as subtly bargaining.

He gallantly amplified. 'It would peculiarly – by which I mean it would so naturally – unite us!'

Well, that was all she wanted. 'Then for a complete union with you – of fact as well as of fond fancy!' she smiled – 'there's nothing, even to my one ewe lamb, I'm not ready to surrender.'

'Ah, we don't surrender,' he urged – 'we enjoy!'

'Yes,' she understood: 'with the glory of our grand gift thrown in.'

'We quite swagger,' he gravely observed – 'though even swaggering would after this be dull without you.'

'Oh, I'll *swagger* with you!' she cried as if it quite settled and made up for everything; and then impatiently, as she beheld

Lord John, whom the door had burst open to admit: 'The Prince?'

'The Prince!' – the young man launched it as a call to arms.

They had fallen apart on the irruption, the pair discovered, but she flashed straight at her lover: 'Then we can swagger now!'

Lord Theign had reached the open door. 'I meet him below.'

Demurring, debating, however, she stayed him a moment. 'But oughtn't I – in my own house?'

His lordship caught her meaning. 'You mean he may think –?' But he as easily pronounced: 'He shall think the Truth!' And with a kiss of his hand to her he was gone.

Lord John, who had gazed in some wonder at these demonstrations, was quickly about to follow, but she checked him with an authority she had never before used and which was clearly the next moment to prove irresistible. 'Lord John, be so good as to stop.' Looking about at the condition of a room on the point of receiving so august a character, she observed on the floor the fragments of the torn cheque, to which she sharply pointed. 'And please pick up that litter!'

THE END

Notes

1. *table d'hôte* – a meal at a hotel consisting of a set menu at a fixed price.

2. *à tantôt* – soon, presently, anon, in a mo.

3. *in terrorem* – (literally, into a state of terror). Done as a warning or to deter.

4. Salsomaggiore – the small town of Solcio on Lake Maggiore, one of the pre-Alpine Lakes of Northern Italy.

5. *rapport* – report, account, statement.

6. 'we few, we happy few' – Shakespeare, *Henry V*, Act 4, Scene 3, l. 60. Henry V rallies his troops for one final assault against the French. An appropriately jingoistic quote.

7. *feu de joie* – (literally, 'fire of joy'). A ceremonial or celebratory salute fired with rifles or other small arms. A joyful occasion; a celebration.

8. Mackintosh – a fictional art dealer.

9. damme – a seventeenth century euphemism for 'damn'.

10. *agrément* – pleasantness.

11. peculation – embezzlement or appropriation (from *peculium*, private property).

12. 'What the h— . . .' – Blasphemy, even in dashes, is, to say the least, a rarity in James. This line does not occur in the play.

13. Long's Hotel – a real hotel, at 16, New Bond Street, W.

14. a Barmecide feast – 'An imaginary feast where the dishes are empty; hence the reference to any appealing illusion. The allusion is to such a banquet given in jest for the poor Schacabac by a rich

Barmecide prince in the Arabian Nights' story, "The Barber's Sixth Brother"' (William Rose Benét, *The Readers' Encyclopedia*, 2nd edition, London, 1977).

Further Reading

Bailkin, Jordanna, 'Picturing Feminism, Selling Liberalism: The Case of the Disappearing Holbein', *Gender & History*, Oxford, 1999

The Earl of Crawford and Balcarres, *Art Treasures for the Nation: Fifty Years of the National Art-Collections Fund*, London, 1953

Edel, Leon, *Henry James: A Life*, New York, 1985

Edel, Leon, *Henry James and 'The Outcry'*, Toronto, 1949

Edel, Leon and Dan H. Laurence, *A Bibliography of Henry James*, London, 1961

Hart-Davis, Rupert C., *Hugh Walpole: A Biography*, London, 1985

James, Henry, *The Complete Notebooks*, edited by Leon Edel and Lyall H. Powers, Oxford, 1987

James, Henry, *The Complete Plays*, edited by Leon Edel, London, 1949

James, Henry, *Henry James: A Life in Letters*, edited by Philip Horne, London, 2000

James, Henry, *Henry James: Letters*, edited by Leon Edel, Cambridge, Mass., 1974–84

James, Henry, *The Outcry*, New York and London, 1909

James, Henry, *The Outcry*, California, 1995

Michael, Erika, *Hans Holbein the Younger: A Guide to Research*, New York, 1997

Spielmann, Isodore, 'The Acquisition of Holbein's "Duchess of Milan" for the Nation', *The Nineteenth Century and After*, London, October 1924

PENGUIN ⬤ CLASSICS

www.penguinclassics.com

- Details about every Penguin Classic

- Advanced information about forthcoming titles

- Hundreds of author biographies

- FREE resources including critical essays on the books and their historical background, reader's and teacher's guides.

- Links to other web resources for the Classics

- Discussion area

- Online review copy ordering for academics

- Competitions with prizes, and challenging Classics trivia quizzes

PENGUIN CLASSICS ONLINE

READ MORE IN PENGUIN

In every corner of the world, on every subject under the sun, Penguin represents quality and variety – the very best in publishing today.

For complete information about books available from Penguin – including Puffins, Penguin Classics and Arkana – and how to order them, write to us at the appropriate address below. Please note that for copyright reasons the selection of books varies from country to country.

In the United Kingdom: Please write to *Dept. EP, Penguin Books Ltd, Bath Road, Harmondsworth, West Drayton, Middlesex UB7 0DA*

In the United States: Please write to *Consumer Services, Penguin Putnam Inc., 405 Murray Hill Parkway, East Rutherford, New Jersey 07073-2136.* VISA and MasterCard holders call 1-800-631-8571 to order Penguin titles

In Canada: Please write to *Penguin Books Canada Ltd, 10 Alcorn Avenue, Suite 300, Toronto, Ontario M4V 3B2*

In Australia: Please write to *Penguin Books Australia Ltd, 487 Maroondah Highway, Ringwood, Victoria 3134*

In New Zealand: Please write to *Penguin Books (NZ) Ltd, Private Bag 102902, North Shore Mail Centre, Auckland 10*

In India: Please write to *Penguin Books India Pvt Ltd, 11 Community Centre, Panchsheel Park, New Delhi 110017*

In the Netherlands: Please write to *Penguin Books Netherlands bv, Postbus 3507, NL-1001 AH Amsterdam*

In Germany: Please write to *Penguin Books Deutschland GmbH, Metzlerstrasse 26, 60594 Frankfurt am Main*

In Spain: Please write to *Penguin Books S. A., Bravo Murillo 19, 1°B, 28015 Madrid*

In Italy: Please write to *Penguin Italia s.r.l., Via Vittorio Emanuele 45/a, 20094 Corsico, Milano*

In France: Please write to *Penguin France, 12, Rue Prosper Ferradou, 31700 Blagnac*

In Japan: Please write to *Penguin Books Japan Ltd, Iidabashi KM-Bldg, 2-23-9 Koraku, Bunkyo-Ku, Tokyo 112-0004*

In South Africa: Please write to *Penguin Books South Africa (Pty) Ltd, P.O. Box 751093, Gardenview, 2047 Johannesburg*

READ MORE IN PENGUIN

Published or forthcoming:

The Diary of a Young Girl   Anne Frank

This definitive edition of Anne Frank's diary restores substantial material omitted from the original edition, giving us a deeper insight into her world. 'One of the greatest books of the twentieth century ... If you have never read Anne Frank's diary, or haven't read it for years, this is the edition to buy' *Guardian*

Brideshead Revisited   Evelyn Waugh

The most nostalgic of Evelyn Waugh's novels, *Brideshead Revisited* looks back to the golden age before the Second World War. It tells the story of Charles Ryder's infatuation with the Marchmains and the rapidly disappearing world of privilege they inhabit. 'Lush and evocative ... expresses at once the profundity of change and the indomitable endurance of the human spirit' *The Times*

Oranges   John McPhee

From Thailand, where the sweetest oranges are as green as emeralds, to Florida oranges so juicy it is said they should be peeled in the bath, the orange exists in bounteous varieties. John McPhee has woven together history, anecdote and science to create a definitive guide to the world of oranges. 'A classic of American reportage. McPhee is quirky, original and intensely curious' Julian Barnes

Wide Sargasso Sea   Jean Rhys

Inspired by Charlotte Brontë's *Jane Eyre*, *Wide Sargasso Sea* is set in the lush landscape of Jamaica in the 1830s. Born into an oppressive colonialist society, Creole heiress Antoinette Cosway meets and marries a young Englishman. But as Antoinette becomes caught between his demands and her own precarious sense of belonging, she is eventually driven towards madness.

READ MORE IN PENGUIN

Published or forthcoming:

The Chrysalids John Wyndham

Genetic mutation has devastated the world. In the primitive society that has emerged from its ruins, any sign of deviation is ruthlessly hunted out and destroyed. David lives in fear of discovery, for he is part of a secret group who are able to communicate with each other through their thoughts. As they grow older they feel increasingly isolated. Then one of them marries a 'norm' with terrifying consequences.

The Waves Virginia Woolf

The Waves traces the lives of a group of friends from childhood to youth and middle age. While social events, individual achievements and disappointments form its narrative, the novel is most remarkable for the poetic language that conveys the inner life of its characters: their aspirations, their triumphs and regrets, their awareness of unity and isolation.

Heart of Darkness Joseph Conrad

In Conrad's haunting tale Marlow, a seaman and wanderer, recounts his journey to the heart of Africa in search of the enigmatic Kurtz. He discovers how Kurtz has gained his position of power over the local people, and radically questions not only his own nature and values, but those of his society. '*Heart of Darkness* seemed to reach into the heart of Conrad himself' Peter Ackroyd, *The Times*

The Garden Party and Other Stories Katherine Mansfield

Innovative, startlingly perceptive and aglow with colour, these fifteen stories were written towards the end of Katherine Mansfield's short life. Many are set in the author's native New Zealand, others in England and the French Riviera. All are revelations of the unspoken, half-understood emotions that make up everyday experience.

READ MORE IN PENGUIN

PENGUIN ILLUSTRATED LIVES

Penguin Illustrated Lives is a series of photographic biographies which offer a fresh, intimate portrait of some of our favourite writers. An incisive, lively text is accompanied by over one hundred evocative images, many in colour and some previously unpublished, which depict the author's world – family, friends, and artistic circle together with original book jackets, letters, and other ephemera.

Published in Penguin Illustrated Lives:

Samuel Beckett   by Gerry Dukes

Samuel Beckett was perhaps the most unconventional playwright of the twentieth century. In his work, he presents us with our own humanity; the hopelessness and the solitude, the bizarre tragicomedy of life itself.

F. Scott Fitzgerald   by Ruth Prigozy

Scott Fitzgerald's life reads like one of his own stories: a young man of great promise marries into wealth, but beneath the golden surface lie alcoholism, debt, insecurity and the mental instability of his wife, Zelda.

Franz Kafka   by Jeremy Adler

Born into a Jewish family in Prague in 1883, Kafka grew up amidst the social and political turmoil of the *fin de siècle*. His writing reflects these tensions as well as his own tortured emotional life.

Vladimir Nabokov   by Jane Grayson

In the Russian Revolution of 1917 Nabokov lost his homeland. In 1955 he published *Lolita*, which caused a sensation. Despite the shadow of exile, Nabokov's work exudes a tremendous vivacity and joy.

Virginia Woolf   by Mary Ann Caws

Virginia Woolf was one of the most significant novelists of the twentieth century. Her life and work reveal her feminist ideals, her modernism and her acute sensitivity to the minute details of human life.

READ MORE IN PENGUIN

HENRY JAMES

'He is as solitary in the history of the novel as Shakespeare in the history of poetry' Graham Greene

NOVELS

The Ambassadors
The American
The Aspern Papers *and*
  The Turn of the Screw
The Awkward Age
The Bostonians
Daisy Miller
The Europeans
The Golden Bowl

The Portrait of a Lady
The Princess Casamassima
Roderick Hudson
The Sacred Fount
The Spoils of Poynton
The Tragic Muse
Washington Square
What Maisie Knew
The Wings of the Dove

SHORT STORIES

The Figure in the Carpet
  and Other Stories

The Jolly Corner
  and Other Tales

TRAVEL AND OTHER WRITING

The American Scene
The Critical Muse: Selected Literary Criticism

BY THE SAME AUTHOR

The Ambassadors

The Ambassadors, Henry James's own personal favourite among his novels, begins with Lambert Strether being sent from Massachusetts by the formidable Mrs Newsome to rescue her son Chad from the decadence of Paris. Instead, Strether finds that Chad has not been corrupted but rather refined by his stay, and it is Strether who must alter his views on life. As winter moves into summer, the Old World and the New collide, and the American falls under the spell of Paris to find himself profoundly changed.

The Wings of the Dove

Kate Croy, beautiful, intelligent and desperate to escape her impoverished existence, is drawn into the rich, glossy London world of her formidable Aunt Maud. Maud is determined to launch her on a dazzling future, but Kate is in love with journalist Merton Densher. When Kate discovers the fabulously wealthy and ailing young American, Milly Theale, she invents an intricate scheme that will free her and Merton to marry, and give Milly a last chance for happiness. But the lovers' passionate desires lead them into a dangerous game of deceit and betrayal, whose climax, amid the melancholy beauty of Venice, is devastating and mysterious. *The Wings of the Dove* is a thrilling exploration of love tragically corrupted.

The Golden Bowl

The Golden Bowl, a highly-charged study of adultery, jealousy and possession, was the last novel that Henry James lived to complete, and along with *The Ambassadors* and *The Wings of the Dove* forms his trio of late, great works.

Maggie Verver, a young American heiress, and her widowed father Adam, a billionaire collector of *objets d'art*, lead a life of wealth and refinement in London. They are both getting married: Maggie to Prince Amerigo, an impoverished Italian aristocrat, and Adam to beautiful but penniless Charlotte Stant, a friend of his daughter. But both father and daughter are unaware that their new conquests share a secret – for Charlotte and the Prince are lovers. And it is an affair for which all concerned must pay the price.